THE VALIANT

STAR LEGEND BOOK ONE

J.J. GREEN

Cowards die many times before their deaths. The valiant never taste of death but once.

— SHAKESPEARE, JULIUS CAESAR

1

The distress signal was impossible, yet there it was: a flashing pinprick of red on the console screen, and steady beeps—three short, three long, three short— from the comm officer's headset. It was an ancient code, yet the ship's computer had recognized it and flagged it for immediate attention.

Major Wright gazed down at the enigmatic dot and passed the headset back to its owner.

"*Where* is it coming from?" he asked again, leaning closer to peer at the mountainous topography of the region.

"Nantgarw-y-garth," Corporal Singh repeated patiently. "West Britannic Isles."

"Nantgarw... Where the hell's that? It looks like the arse end of nowhere. Why would we have anyone there?"

The corporal didn't answer, no doubt guessing the question was rhetorical. "I didn't know if I should alert the brigadier, sir," he said. "Only..."

Singh didn't need to say any more. He hadn't wanted to wake Colbourn in the middle of the quiet shift. Smart choice.

Wright slammed one hand against the console and straightened up. A few of the officers on the *Valiant's* bridge looked his way. He remembered he was barefoot and wearing crumpled standard issue pajama bottoms. He began to fasten the uniform shirt he'd pulled on after Singh had commed him.

"Might be a covert mission," he murmured.

"Yes, but..." Singh ventured.

"What?"

"West BI? I thought the place was entirely EAC now, along with the rest of the country."

"It is," replied Wright. "Has been for a couple of years."

The European Democracy's epicenter, Berline, had fallen to Earth Awakening Crusade a decade previously, and the organization had pushed steadily westward, breaking down civilization as it went, eventually occupying the entire Britannic Isles. Wright had fought in some of the battles for his homeland, earning promotions, scars, and memories he would never forget.

"But," he added, "if they are covert operatives, why aren't they alerting SIS? Why send out a general distress?" He'd heard of resistance groups that were fighting on in some areas, but he couldn't see why any of them would broadcast a code that hadn't been used for centuries.

The two men regarded the puzzling blip.

Singh coughed. "If it *is* a genuine distress signal..."

"Yes, yes, all right," said the major testily, tiredness making him irritable. "I don't need you to inform me of the urgency of the situation, corporal." He loved his job, but a good night's sleep came a close second place in his heart. He rubbed his beard shadow, and then tried, absent-mindedly, to smooth down the tuft of hair that stuck up from the crown of his head. He was unsuccessful, as always.

"There's nothing for it," he said. "I'll have to tell the brigadier."

"Rather you than me, sir."

WRIGHT HAD FAILED to raise his superior officer via her ear comm, and she had refused an implant, so he had no choice except to wake her in person. By the time he reached Colbourn's quarters, he had finished fastening his shirt and had tucked it into his pajamas. He thumbed the door buzzer and leaned on the bulkhead, propped on his forearm, as he waited for a response. When none came, he pressed again, long and hard.

"*Goddammit!*" growled a voice over the intercom. "Someone had better be dying."

"It's Wright, ma'am. Something's come up that requires your immediate attention."

The intercom was silent, then, "Well, what kind of *something*?!"

"A distress call, only…"

Suddenly, the cabin door slid back, and an older woman's bony head thrust through the gap. Her eyes were narrowed, angry, and piercing.

"Only *what*?" Brigadier Colbourn asked, between clenched teeth.

Wright knew he wasn't receiving the full potential force of her ire, that she tolerated him better than others, yet he still took half a step backward before explaining about the incongruous signal.

"West BI?" asked Colbourn. "What the…?" Scowling, she said, "Hold on."

She withdrew into the darkness of her quarters. Seconds later she re-emerged, wrapping a gray bathrobe over her sleep suit.

As she marched down the passageway, he kept pace by her side and laid out the details of the situation.

Age and tiredness showed in the lines of the brigadier's

face, and her white hair was cropped close to her scalp, making her head look positively skeletal. He always thought of her as an old war horse who deserved to have been put out to pasture years ago. But she never spoke of retirement. Like him, service was in her blood, and she would probably die with her boots on.

When he finished updating her, the brigadier slipped in her ear comm and began barking orders. One of the *Valiant's* companion corvettes, HMSS *Daisy*, was to be prepped for a mission. The BA's corvettes were their only warships capable of space-to-surface travel.

Turning her head sharply toward the major, Colbourn said, "I want you to assemble a rescue task force."

After a beat, he asked, "We're going in?"

"Of course we're going in," the brigadier spat. "Do you think we should leave them there? It's our distress code they're sending. Those are our people. The only problem is, we don't have time to arrange a stealth op. We'll have to get in and out fast, before the EAC have time to respond."

"But what if they aren't our people? It could be an EAC trap."

"Then it's a damned good one," Colbourn replied. "They must know we'd never abandon our own."

The brigadier strode through the door to the bridge. Every back in the place became bolt upright, and all eyes became intent on their screens.

"Singh," Colbourn snapped as she sat down. "Report on the origin site of the distress signal."

"Yes, ma'am. It's called Nantgarw-y-garth—"

"I don't give a shit what it's called. Wright's already told me it's in the back of beyond. I want to know terrain, population, latest intel, if we have any. You *know* what I need. Do I have to spell it out to you in words of one syllable?"

"Yes, ma'am. S-sorry, ma'am. I do have some information..."

His voice petered out under the intensity of her glare, and his Adam's apple bobbed as he swallowed.

"Dammit, man. Speak!"

"It's mountainous," Singh blurted. "Highest elevation five hundred and fifty meters. Latest population estimate, er, zero point three people per hectare. No known military installations. Scan data doesn't indicate any evidence of armaments either." He rattled off the local temperature and weather conditions, which were wintry. "I still haven't established contact with the signal originator."

"Better. Wright, where are you with assembling the task force?"

"Nearly there. I've picked twenty of the best from the platoon aboard the *Daisy*."

"Good. You're leading the mission?"

"I was planning to."

The brigadier's stern expression grew pensive, and she didn't answer immediately.

The situation troubled Wright, too. No one in the Britannic Alliance would send a distress call from enemy territory unless they were in imminent peril. Even then, they might choose to fight it out rather than endanger the lives of their rescuers. This was going to be a high-risk expedition. They had almost no knowledge of what the rescue team might expect, and they would be under extreme time pressure.

He waited for Colbourn's decision.

Briefly making eye contact with him, she gave him a curt nod, adding, "I'll speak to SIS while you're en route and update you about anything pertinent."

Her words weren't particularly reassuring. If the individuals requesting rescue did have something to do with the Secret Intelligence Service, that didn't mean SIS would tell them anything relevant or helpful. In Wright's experience, the government department frequently operated as if it were independent, with interests and aims wholly distinct from those of the Britannic Alliance.

Yet, despite his many reservations, at the end of the day, Colbourn was right: if there was a chance it was the BA's people calling for help, they could not ignore them.

"I'll head over to the *Daisy*," he said.

Colbourn turned to speak to Singh again.

2

The game of xiangqi wasn't going well for Taylan Ellis. It was her turn, and she'd been trying to figure out her next move for the last five minutes, but she couldn't see a way to reverse the tide of battle. The enemy general was well beyond her reach, while her own was trapped in one quarter of the board, harried by soldiers, chariots, and cannon.

She looked up into the face of her friend, Emeka Abacha, knowing she would find no mercy there. He gazed back, amusement twinkling in his dark blue eyes.

"Take all the time you need, little chick," he said expansively, his voice not much more than a soft rumble among the snores of their fellow Royal Marines in the ten-rack cabin.

She'd never understood why he'd given her that nickname. She was far from little, and her days of being a 'chick' were long gone. Abacha was the only person Taylan would allow to call her that, and he knew it. At times like these, he took full advantage of the concession.

Strike that.

She *did* know why he used the nickname—it was to rile her, and he was doing a good job of it.

She screwed up her face in frustration.

Abacha's grin grew wider.

Wearing only undershirts and shorts, they crouched over a small table set against the bulkhead farthest from the cabin door. A single overhead lamp spilled its light over the table and aged board game. The lines of the game were nearly worn away, and the plastic pieces were barely identifiable anymore. But the game was the only thing the two insomniacs had to occupy them after lights out, when all electronics were banned.

Taylan reached toward one of her adviser tiles.

Abacha's eyebrows rose.

She hesitated, her hand suspended over the tile, before she dropped it to her side again and scowled.

Her friend leaned over the table and gave her shoulder a friendly slap, nearly knocking her from her seat. "Concede defeat! There's no shame in it. It's only a game. Besides..." he stretched his long arms wide "...it's late and I'm sleepy."

Taylan's scowl deepened, and she studied the positions of the tiles on the board more closely. There had to be a way out of her predicament, if only she could see it.

The figure of her friend suddenly stiffened, and Taylan, sensing the change in him, looked up. "What's wrong?"

"You don't hear it?" he asked.

She concentrated on the sounds around her. Aside from the noises of slumber from the other marines, all she could hear was the hum of the *Daisy's* engines.

Then she realized what Abacha meant: the engine noise had risen in pitch. They were no longer maintaining orbit, flanking the *Valiant*, they were on the move. Her stomach registered the new direction. The corvette was descending, which could only mean she was on her way to the surface.

A quiet excitement rose in Taylan.

"We're going down," she whispered.

"Uh huh," replied Abacha, but his look of delight as he'd anticipated beating her at xiangqi had faded. Now he looked sad.

She wondered what was bothering him, but then she felt the beads of her necklace under her fingertips. When she'd realized they were going to Earth, her hand had unconsciously strayed to the child's jewelry she always wore around her neck.

She snatched her fingers away and looked down, embarrassed.

Abacha was silent, and the cabin remained quiet, the sleeping marines unaware of the changing circumstances.

Taylan raised her gaze to her friend, and saw he touching the side of his head, listening to a comm. Every marine had an implant surgically installed just behind their left ears. When you were given an order, there was no avoiding it, whether you were asleep or awake. If the device sensed you were sleeping, it would break into your dreams with an alarm that wouldn't turn off until you were conscious. The comm would repeat until you gave the mental response you'd received it.

Abacha's eyes refocused as the message ended.

Grunts, groans, and the rustle of sheets came from the racks as marines began to stir.

Abacha got up and went to step away from the table, but then he halted. "You didn't hear it?"

"Nope," replied Taylan. "What's happening?"

"Rescue mission. Gotta attend a briefing."

"Hm. Looks like I'm not invited."

"Looks like it."

Abacha began to leave, but Taylan grabbed his wrist. "Rescue mission on the surface?"

"Wright didn't say, but I guess so. That's where we're headed."

"If they're sending a corvette down, it must be somewhere dangerous. Did he say where it is exactly?"

"No, he didn't."

Overhead lights came to life. Three or four grumbling marines dropped from upper racks to the floor and hastily pulled on their uniforms. The sleepers who hadn't been called to the briefing groaned and pulled their blankets over their heads.

Taylan hadn't released Abacha's wrist. She was thinking.

"Hey, I have to go," said her friend.

"How about..." She hesitated. "Wanna swap places with me?"

He sighed. "You know I can't do that. Wright ordered *me* on the mission, not you."

"I'll say you're sick and I'm taking your place."

"I haven't been to sick bay. If he checks out your story and finds out we both lied, I'll be in a world of trouble."

"I'll tell him...as soon as you woke, you threw up. Or something. C'mon, do this for me. How often do we go to the surface these days? This might be the last chance I get."

"You don't even know where we're going."

"I know we were above Europe."

"That doesn't mean anything. We're aboard a freaking starship. The rescue could be anywhere."

While they argued, the marines who had received the summons had dressed and run out of the cabin. Abacha looked toward the open door. "Tay, the briefing's in five minutes. I have to be there."

"*C'mon!*" she urged. "When do I ever ask you for a favor?"

"Well, there was that time you made me help you get the cook drunk so you could shave off his eyebrows."

"Okay. But he deserved payback for the slop he serves up."

"And I distracted that warrant officer for you while you hid her helmet in the freezer."

"She's a tool, and you know it."

"And let's not forget you persuading me to help you smuggle Boots aboard."

Boots was the ship's cat—a stray Taylan had rescued from the battle zone at their last engagement.

"Give me a break!" she protested. "Boots is the best thing that ever happened to this ship."

Abacha shot her a skeptical look. He might have been thinking about the cat's resistance to all attempts to house train him.

"You have to admit," Taylan went on, "he keeps the cockroaches down."

Abacha gently prised her fingers from his wrist. "I have to go."

She slumped against the bulkhead. "See ya later."

He put on his uniform in record time, and then strode quickly across the cabin, last to leave. Taylan felt bad. He would be reprimanded for being late. When he reached the doorway, however, he stopped and turned.

She'd been watching him, resigning herself to the fact she wouldn't be going to the surface. When Abacha halted, she sat up.

"How do you do it?" he asked.

"Do what?"

"Be so annoying yet so pitiful at the same time?"

She jumped to her feet. "You're gonna let me take your place?"

In answer, he swept his arm through the doorway, as if inviting her to go out.

She leapt up and yelled, "Yeah!"

A pillow thrown by a disgruntled marine hit her square in the middle, but she barely registered it. She was already running toward the door. On her way, she snatched her uniform from her rack with one hand and with her other she grabbed her boots. When she reached Abacha, she leapt up and grabbed him in a quick hug. "I owe you," she said, before racing out.

But as she reached the junction at the end of the passageway, she remembered something and pulled up abruptly. Abacha had remained in the doorway, watching her, his arms folded across his sizable chest.

She called out, "Which briefing room?"

"Two."

"Shit."

She ran back the way she'd come. As she reached her friend, he held up a hand for a high five. Taylan slapped his palm as she passed him.

She was going to Earth, perhaps even to the Britannic Isles, and who knew what she might find out while she was there?

3

As the marines who would take part in the rescue piled into the *Daisy's* Briefing Room 2, Wright was struck by how young they looked. They had to be at least eighteen—he didn't think recruitment had become so desperate the BA took on anyone younger—but some of them looked like kids.

The men and women quickly took seats.

How long had it been since he was as fresh-faced as them?

Before he knew it, Wright was rubbing the old wound in his knee. He'd received it at his first engagement, when he'd been no older than the marines in front of him, at the Battle of Queen Charlotte Bay, last stronghold of the BA on the Falkland Isles.

For more than sixteen years, he'd put off getting proper treatment for the injury. He needed the entire joint replaced, the doc had said. The lab could grow new bones and cartilage from his stem cells prior to the op, but afterward it would be two weeks before he was fit to return to duty. There had always been something happening that deterred him from taking so much sick leave; an upsurge in EAC attacks, new, illegal resource harvesting by the Antarctic Project, or influxes of new recruits, refugees fleeing lost homelands.

Time had slipped by so fast.

He took a head count. Only nineteen marines were present. Irritated, he decided to wait another minute for the latecomer.

All his life, he'd known nothing but war. When he'd joined up, the struggle had already lasted fifty-eight years. He'd been in primary school when he'd learned about its origins. The Antarctic Project had been the instigator. Intent on harvesting the remainder of Earth's depleted resources to build gigantic colony ships, the AP had been looting the planet, and it had been invading protected zones to stock up the finest genetic material from all species, including humankind.

As governments defied the Project, it had militarized. What it had once stolen by stealth or political machinations, it now took by force. Few had been able to withstand its march across the globe. Only the Britannic Alliance had managed to hold it back, safeguarding the homelands and historical territories. Elsewhere in the world, the AP had done as it wanted, and sovereign nations had been too cowed to stop it.

Then the Earth Awareness Crusade had appeared. When the organization first emerged, the EAC had seemed to be one of the BA's strongest supporters and allies, sharing the ideals of conservancy and preservation. But as the months and years wore on, the Crusade had shown its true colors. The BA's policy was to maintain the political status quo in the member states of its protectorate, never interfering in their governance. But the EAC would constantly try to subtly subvert this aim. Political leaders would die in mysterious circumstances, and their replacements would champion new and strange paradigms, ideas that happened to be central to the EAC.

After several repeats of these strange occurrences, the BA realized these events were not coincidences, that the EAC was secretly asserting control. What was more, it was turning the newly acquired country's populations toward bizarre, cultish belief systems at odds with concepts of personal autonomy and basic human rights.

And now the BA seemed to be fighting a rearguard action. No superior officer had ever described it that way within his hearing, but year after year they lost more ground either seized by the AP or taken over by the EAC, displacing entire populations.

He frowned. He didn't know the solution. Perhaps the higher ups had something up their sleeves.

Someone coughed, and Wright was mentally jerked back to the briefing. The latecomer still hadn't arrived. He was annoyed and surprised. He'd chosen the best from the platoon across the skills spectrum. He didn't have much of an idea what they would face so he'd wanted to cover all the bases. The last thing he'd expected was that one of the exemplary marines would be late.

He would find out who it was later. He didn't want to waste any more time.

He quickly opened the briefing, and then said, "We touch down in..." He looked up and left, activating a clock that superimposed on his vision. "Thirty-eight minutes. As I explained in the comm, this is a—"

The sound of a pair of rapidly running, booted feet echoed through the doorway. A woman burst into the room and stood to attention before noticing everyone except Wright was sitting down. She jumped into the nearest empty seat, keeping her eyes forward. One of her boots was unlaced.

Her arrival seemed to send a ripple through the room.

Clenching his jaw, Wright strode to the latecomer, coming to a halt a few centimeters from her.

"Name?" he demanded.

"Ellis, sir. Here to replace Abacha."

"Replace...?" He remembered he'd picked Abacha because the man was proficient at hand-to-hand combat. If they did meet any hostiles in the mountains of West BI, the fighting was likely to be up close and personal.

"He's sick, sir," continued the self-appointed replacement. "Threw up all over his rack as soon as—"

"Ellis," chided Sergeant Elphicke, sitting to her left.

Wright looked the woman up and down. He didn't recall seeing her before. She wasn't young like the others. She was closer to his own age. Her rank implied she'd joined up recently, unless her performance had been so appalling she hadn't been promoted once in fifteen years of service. She was average build, her hair mouse brown and cut just below her ears. Her cool gray eyes remained fixed forward.

The rest of the team didn't like her. That was what the non-verbal reaction had been about when she entered the room. He wondered what she'd done to earn the other marines' animosity.

Disappointed that he was down one of the platoon's best fighters, he hoped Abacha's mediocre replacement wouldn't prove too much of a liability.

Wright returned to the front, reminding himself to check Ellis's story later.

Addressing the room, he said, "We're going into BI—"

Had that annoying marine jumped a little?

"Currently EAC-held territory," he continued. "I'm going to be honest: It's a rescue mission, but I don't have a clue who we're rescuing. All we have are the distress signal coordinates. This area isn't well defended as far as we can tell, but the EAC is not going to miss the *Daisy's* arrival. Once we're on the ground, speed is going to make all the difference to our success or failure. We have to rescue this person or persons and get out of there before the EAC arrive. Flight time from the nearest military airport is thirty-five minutes, and we can expect them to detect us going in, so that leaves us with very little time."

He went on to share as many details of the mission as he could tell them, but they were precious few. Within a couple of minutes, he was finished.

He told the marines to suit up.

4

The *Daisy's* ramp split from the bulkhead and began to lower. Instantly, snowflakes whirled through the gap. As the outdoor air flooded in, Taylan watched the temperature displayed on her HUD drop to minus two degrees C. It was a cold night in West BI.

Along with the rest of the team, she lined up at the opening hatch. Ahead of her, a square of black night appeared, pierced by the corvette's lights.

In the few months since completing Basic, she hadn't got her space legs, and she was feeling like her stomach remained somewhere in the upper stratosphere. But she was jubilant. She was returning to her homeland. Despite the risks of persuading Abacha to allow her to take his place, she had no regrets. Anything she could find out while she was home could be useful.

The only downside was the short time they would be there.

So far, they'd been lucky. The *Daisy* hadn't been fired upon during the descent. The EAC must have had the surprise of its life when the BA warship swooped down from open skies, but even now it would be rushing to challenge the invasion.

The ramp hit the ground.

"Move out," came Elphicke's order.

Taylan jogged into the night, her rifle gripped across her chest, snowflakes melting on her visor. As she left the *Daisy,* the ship's lights cut out and her visor's night vision kicked in. A gray-green, rocky landscape appeared, cracks and hollows already filling with snow. The distress signal pulsed high on her display. According to the map overlay, it originated 634 meters north-north-west and 178 meters up.

The marines in front were already running up the rising ground, seeking paths between the boulders. Others were flanking out right and left, sweeping for hostiles. Her job was also to protect the core team, who would push forward and make the rescue.

As she looked from side to side, checking for movement or spots of heat that might signify enemy soldiers, she scanned for long range data too. The major hadn't been specific about the location, but her suit's computer soon began to extrapolate from the surrounding topography and narrow down the potential places. It quickly told her she was in West BI.

Yes!

It was more than she could have hoped for. The European mainland would have been good, the Britannic Isles even better, but the land of her fathers? It was as if it was meant to be.

Her computer identified a settlement in a valley to the east, naming it Trecenyyd. She turned her head sharply right, knowing what she would find. The name Efail Isaf popped up on her HUD.

She'd been there once, as a child. It was a tiny, old-fashioned village; a place out of time. She'd gone into its only shop and bought sweets with actual cash, not via a tele-trans, or even a card, but a paper note her grandpa had handed her before she set out. And then, as well as a bag of delicious chewy gums, the shopkeeper had given her round pieces of metal he called 'change'.

From the corner of her eye, she saw movement.

She jerked her head around.

The mountainous landscape spread out, gray-green, speckled with falling flakes, and still.

Nothing.

Had she imagined it?

She slowed to a stop and squatted behind a rock for cover. Leaning her back against the stone surface, she replayed her helmet recording of one minute prior.

There it was! She froze the recording. She *had* seen something.

She expanded the frozen image and brought up what looked like a shoulder and half a head poking out from behind a rock, among fuzzy motionless snowflakes.

The rest of her team was clearly marked on her HUD, the closest fellow marine seven or eight meters away. Whatever was out there, it wasn't one of her own.

They were being watched, and she'd caught one of the watchers just before he ducked out of sight.

"Sergeant," she commed to Elphicke, "we have a voyeur." She relayed the image and figure's coordinates.

"Good spot," Elphicke replied. "Blake, Chen, McEndry, assist Ellis in dispatching the gawper."

It seemed odd the EAC had operatives out here in this lonely place, assuming the watcher was EAC. He was suited up, so Taylan guessed he had to be.

How many more of them were out there on the hillside?

It was already too late to prevent him from sending a message to his command. If the arrival of the *Daisy* hadn't been enough to trigger an imminent attack, the marines were now on a rapid countdown before the soldier's buddies turned up.

Taylan rose and, keeping low, began to circle to the right,

round to the rear of the hostile's position. On her HUD, she saw Chen do the same in the other direction, while Blake and McEndry slowly approached him from the front. If the onlooker was alone, they would catch him easily as they closed in.

"Eyes open," said Blake. "Don't forget there might be more of them."

If the soldier wasn't by himself, Taylan might have to make and lose some new friends en route, but there was nothing of military interest in that remote place. She couldn't believe the EAC would have many troops on the ground.

She was five meters from the man, who didn't seem to have moved, when, as she stepped between two boulders, her right boot slid down into the gap.

She cursed and tried to pull it out, but it was jammed in.

After a couple of seconds of tugging, Chen asked, "What's up, Ellis?" He must have noticed she'd stopped.

"I'm stuck, but I'll be...*Shit!*" Her boot had slipped farther down. The narrow gap opened up at the bottom, and in her struggles she'd accidentally pushed when she'd meant to pull. Now, her foot was free below the opening, but she was trapped by her ankle.

She let her rifle swing free from her neck and shoulder and braced herself by her elbows against the rocks on each side of her. They were slippery with crystalline ice. With a great effort, she wrenched her leg upward. The hard stone ground into her ankle bones, but she couldn't free her foot.

Meanwhile, the other three marines had nearly reached their target.

"Going in without you, Ellis," McEndry said.

"No," she protested. "Wait." She groaned as she twisted her lower leg, feeling the bite of solid mineral and the tearing of her skin. Nothing seemed to help.

It was no good. She was well and truly trapped.

"We don't have time," came McEndry's impassive reply.

Taylan swore some more.

The friendly dots on her HUD showed McEndry and the others drawing closer to the watcher. There wasn't anything she could do to help her team now, but she guessed they would be okay. It was three against one, and they were all experienced marines.

She returned her attention to her foot and noticed that the gap between the boulders was uneven. If she could squeeze her ankle forward, she would reach a wider area where she might be able to lift her boot out.

A voice burst from her comm: "Chen, watch out!"

It was Blake.

Flashes exploded to her left.

Damn!

Her team was under attack. The EAC had closed in on them.

She desperately tried to force her lower leg forward.

More flashes erupted to her left. On her HUD she saw, with horror, the dot representing Chen wink from green to blue. He was gone. Dead in an instant.

Their sergeant had seen it too.

"Blake," barked Elphicke. "Sitrep."

"We've lost...Shit! I think, I think there's four of them."

Pulse rounds split the night.

Blake's comm remained open. Everyone connected heard his scream.

His dot changed color.

Taylan yelled, "No!"

She'd managed to push her ankle forward, but now it felt like it was cemented in. She couldn't move it a millimeter in any direction.

With a cry of frustration, she lifted her rifle above the boulder and pointed it upward. Squeezing the trigger, she let off round after round, frantically trying to draw attention away from McEndry, the remaining living marine of the three who had joined her to kill the watcher.

McEndry's dot turned blue.

Elphicke's curse came over her comm. "Ellis, what the hell are you doing? Why haven't you moved for the last two minutes?"

"I'm stuck, sir. I..."

She swallowed.

Three fellow marines had died, and there hadn't been anything she could do about it.

"Stuck? What do you mean?"

"My foot's trapped."

"Can you take off your boot?"

"Negative, sir." Even if she'd been able to reach through the gap, her ankle was now wedged so tightly, removing her boot wouldn't make any difference.

"Well, I can see you discharged your weapon," said Elphicke stonily, "and announced your location to the world. I can't send anyone to help. We're under fire here. You're on your own."

Taylan could see the flashes of pulse rifles firing higher up the mountain. The place was crawling with EAC, though even sheep would see no reason to be out on the mountain in the middle of winter.

In her peripheral vision, something moved.

They were coming for her.

"I understand, sir," she said.

Elphicke paused a beat.

"Good luck, Ellis. Over and out."

5

The distress signal blinked stubbornly on Wright's HUD. Glaring at it, he adjusted his scanners, short and long-range, for the second time, but the result was the same.

It was coming from *inside* the mountain.

He looked up the slope. The mountain face rose above him and disappeared from sight into darkness and falling snow. Nothing he saw indicated the presence of a passage into the hidden chamber.

Behind him, farther down the mountain, EAC troops were closing in. The organization had responded fast to the *Daisy's* arrival, he had to give them that. Unbelievably fast. Elphicke would keep the enemy back for a while, but not indefinitely. Wright estimated he had maybe ten minutes—fifteen, tops—to retrieve the person or people in distress.

But how was he supposed to do that when they were behind several tonnes of rock? He'd tried comming them on the same frequency as the distress signal but received no reply, and no other frequencies generated a response either.

Something else was bothering him deeply—how the hell was the signal penetrating solid stone?

None of it made any sense.

"Should I scout for an entrance, sir?" asked Marks, one of three marines accompanying him.

"Yes, do that."

He didn't hold out much hope the woman would find anything, but he didn't know what else to do. Maybe the people sending the signal had traveled through the mountain from another spot and then discovered there was no way out. Thinking about it, that was the only answer, but it didn't help him.

He climbed the final few meters up to the vertical mountain face. On a closer look, it appeared as though it might have formed from a rockfall eons ago. The surface was jagged and split, and tough, stunted shrubs sprouted from the nooks and crannies. Thin cracks divided the crammed rocks, but they were far too narrow for a human being to have slipped through. Even a child wouldn't have made it. Judging from the long, leathery roots that gripped the stone, it hadn't been disturbed for years.

Wright rested one hand on the impenetrable surface and, with the other, popped open his visor.

"Hello?!" he shouted. "This is Major Wright of the Britannic Alliance. Can you hear me? Please respond."

He awaited a reply, but all he heard was hiss of pulse fire coming from below and the sigh of the wind around the mountain. He tried to make contact a couple more times, with the same result.

He thumped the stone with a fist. Somewhere not far from where he stood, people were trapped, possibly injured or dying, and he had no way of reaching them.

Marks returned. "I couldn't find anything, sir," she reported breathlessly.

Should they stick around, trying to find a way in? The chances of a safe exit for his marines was growing slimmer. Or should he abandon the mission as hopeless? Could he justify continuing to risk the lives of his men and women?

"Can I make a suggestion, sir?" asked Marks.

"I'm all ears."

"Blow it open."

"Blow...the rock face?"

"We brought an XM57 along," Marks said. "We could try. What do we have to lose?"

"What we have to lose are the very people we are supposed to be rescuing, if they're anywhere near the outer wall."

Wright wondered what Colbourn would have to say if he returned to the *Valiant* bearing several rescued corpses.

"Sir," said Elphicke. "There's been a skirmish on the lower slopes. Blake, Chen, and McEndry have blued."

Wright closed his eyes.

Dammit!

"Okay," he said to Marks. "We'll give it one try." He gave the order for the XM57 to be brought up.

While he was waiting for the mortar to arrive, he yelled toward the rock face some more, telling anyone who was inside to move deep into the mountain.

He guessed there was a good chance they would cause a rock fall, but he was out of time and ideas.

Marks had been surveying the rock face. She inserted a hand into a gap. "I think here would be best."

In response to Wright's questioning look, she continued, "My family are miners. They all work for the AP." She grimaced. "I switched sides."

He nodded and moved away, down the slope. "You take the lead."

The XM57-bearer, Cole, appeared, scrambling over rocks, scattering scree as he climbed with the mortar on his shoulder.

Marks quickly directed him to a position to stand the weapon and indicated where he was to fire.

Wright gave the order for everyone else to stay well away.

The *whoomf* of the mortar was magnitudes louder than the soft hiss of a pulse round. Wright received the full force through his still-open visor. When the missile hit the mountainside, there was an ear-splitting explosion. Rock crumbled and fell. He ran up the slope, but when the dust cleared, the mountain face remained solid.

"One more try, sir!" said Marks. "If there is a cave there, I'm sure we'll break through next time."

"Just one, then we're out of here."

Marks gave more instructions, and the XM57 fired once more. After the second hit, the ground shook, and large stones tumbled down.

She ran up the slope. "We're in!"

The dust began to clear, and Wright saw what she meant: Among the shattered debris, a cleft had opened.

"Wait," he ordered, hurrying to catch up to the young marine, who was about to enter it.

Marks halted. Her helmeted head turned toward him.

"Get back," said Wright, conscious the opening could collapse any minute.

He passed her and leaned into the dark interior. His helmet light revealed a small space, only roughly four meters wide and deep, though the roof of the cave was higher. It rose to a central point about six meters above. It looked naturally formed with a dusty, sloping floor and a rugged ceiling and walls. More than half the space was taken up with rubble from the mortar fire.

He tensed. Were people buried under the broken rocks? He closed his visor. His enhanced view showed no signs of warm bodies as his gaze roved the rocks. He swept the rest of the place. No one seemed to be in the chamber at all. No people, no transmission equipment, and no exit. The rear wall was solid rock.

Except...

On the far side of the chamber, something glowed, very faintly.

The gap they'd blown open was narrow. He had to turn sideways to ease through it. A few steps across the chamber brought him to the scant heat source. At step three, he thought he might be able to save someone's life, but by the time he reached the figure, that hope was gone.

He stared down at it.

What lay upon the flat, raised, carved surface was barely recognizable as human. Fleshless skin stretched taut over the bones, the closed eyes were wells in their sockets, and the hair was wisp-thin, clinging to the scalp. The prone body might once have been a large man, but he had died years ago, probably due to a large wound that had torn open his stomach and chest.

The corpse wore strange ornaments. A thick torque encircled his neck, and another gripped his bicep, the pure gold gleaming richly, uncorrupted by the passage of years. The same could not be said of his clothes, which had rotted away to bare threads, exposing the man's skin in many places. Across his shoulders and upper chest, stylized tattoos of animals pranced, fixed in time.

Wright had heard of cadavers like these. In very dry conditions, the human body didn't rot but remained whole and preserved for millennia. He guessed the heat the body was giving off was caused by extremely slow decomposition. At another place and time, he might have found the mummy interesting, but right now it was only a distraction.

He scanned the rest of the cave again. There were definitely no exits other than the one the mortar fire had created. He concluded the body must have been placed there before the rockfall sealed off the place. Other than that, the place was entirely empty.

So where was the distress signal coming from?

He checked his HUD for it, and sucked in a breath.

The signal was gone.

Marks leaned in through the breech in the wall. "Find anyone, sir?"

"No. I thought I told you to get back."

It was time to leave. The fighting down slope had to be intensifying. Wright felt sick with disappointment and frustration. The BA had sent a warship into enemy territory and three men were dead, for nothing. The distress signal must have been...He had no idea what could have caused it.

"What's that?" asked Marks, focused on the mummy.

"Nothing important. We're pulling out, heading back to the *Daisy*."

The young marine took a final look at the dried-up cadaver, and then withdrew.

Wright told Elphicke the mission was over, but as he went to leave the chamber, he paused.

How remarkable it was that the mummy should be here, in the very place where the glitch in the system had placed the distress signal. An odd coincidence. If he had never come here, the body would have lain undiscovered for thousands of years, if not forever.

Now the chamber had been opened, the EAC would probably find it. It was just the kind of thing they liked. Maybe they would use it in one of their weird ceremonies.

Marks reappeared. "Are you coming, sir?"

"Yes, I'm on my way."

She hesitated.

"Go! I'll catch you up."

His attention had been drawn again to the stunningly beautiful torques around the dead man's neck and arm. It was a shame the EAC would get a hold of them, but he didn't have time to—

He started.

The thick curve of metal around the mummy's throat had moved. Or had it? He bent closer and opened his visor, shining his helmet light down to see the thing more clearly. The torque had only seemed to move a fraction, but it had caught his eye.

He exhaled a long breath.

It *was* moving.

Almost imperceptibly and very, very slowly, the torque was rising and falling, as if the mummy were breathing. He placed a trembling hand on the corpse's chest, but he didn't detect any movement through his thick gloves.

What am I thinking?

Incredulity gripping him, Wright activated his field medic scanner and requested the general health status.

Snapping his visor closed, he read the display.

He blinked, almost not believing what he was seeing, vaguely wondering if he'd taken a hit to the head.

His HUD displayed a health status of two percent and pulse and respiration rates that were impossibly low. He'd only ever seen such poor prognoses for survival in marines taking their last breaths. Yet this figure lying before him must have been here for years. The man was a living, breathing miracle.

How was it possible?

But he couldn't spare any more time to wonder at the phenomenon. He had to return to the *Daisy* with his team. He decided he couldn't leave the man there, not while he was still alive. Though he was certain to die soon, he felt obliged to do all he could to save him.

He scooped up the fragile figure in both arms, finding it hardly seemed to weigh anything. He carried it across the chamber and gently maneuvered it through the gap in the wall.

A strange feeling coursed through him, a sense of unreality, as if he were awake and aware while in the middle of a dream.

When he emerged into the night, the snow had stopped falling and the clouds had cleared. The mountainside was empty. Marks was gone, and so was Cole with the XM57. Way below, distant pulse shots flashed in the darkness, dancing like fireflies.

Above, a dark shield curved, bearing ten thousand stars.

6

Cradling the barely-alive man in his arms, Wright sped down the slope, sliding on scree and dodging rocks, trying to find the fastest route among the drifts of fallen snow. Soon, he was on the fringes of the firefight, and a few poorly aimed pulse rounds came his way.

He told his marines he was on his way, and they began to lay down covering fire. In a few minutes, he reached the base of the mountain, and in a few minutes more he was part of the retreat. Now that he was with them, the marines doubled their pace as they ran back to the *Daisy*.

While descending the mountain, he'd regularly checked the health status of the emaciated, dehydrated man he'd rescued. Every time he saw the stats, they'd improved. The 'mummy's' chances of survival had improved to nine percent, providing he received appropriate medical care. What the treatment would turn out to be, Wright was curious to find out. He didn't think any of the *Daisy's* docs had ever encountered a case quite like this one.

Despite his improving health, the man's appearance hadn't

discernibly altered. He looked just as ancient and very, very dead as when Wright had found him.

But that was a puzzle for later. Now, he had to get everyone safely back into space. The EAC troops hadn't fired on them for a while, and he had a suspicion why.

Elphicke commed him from somewhere ahead. "Sir, I think you should know, Ellis isn't returning to the ship."

"Why not? Where is she?" As he replied, Wright answered his own question, singling out the marine's location on his HUD.

She was still halfway up the mountain! And she wasn't moving. What the hell was the stupid marine doing?

"About 200 meters away, stuck in some rocks," said Elphicke. "She's immobilized, her foot's trapped. After Chen and the others bought it, I didn't expect her to survive. The EAC were on to her. But she's still there and still alive."

The sergeant didn't put the moral dilemma into words. They were tight on time. Should he send someone back to try to free her, risking everyone's lives with the delay, or should he abandon her?

Wright chewed over his decision. In the distance he could see the *Daisy*, resting at a slight angle on a field of stubble. Most of the team were nearly at the ship. If he did nothing, everyone except Ellis could be away within minutes, and, if his suspicion was correct, they didn't have much longer than that before they would have more problems to face than EAC infantry.

He also had no clue about how to get her out of her predicament. If she was trapped among the rocks and hadn't managed to free herself, was there any hope someone else could get her out in the scant minutes available?

The right thing to do was to sacrifice Ellis to save the team. On the other hand, Colbourn's words rang in his ears: *They must know we'd never abandon our own.*

He swore. *Damn the woman.* He'd known from the outset she was a liability.

Running to the nearest marine, he said, "You, take this man to the ship and carry him straight to sick bay." He passed the figure over. Next, he commed Marks and Cole and told them to follow him. Finally, he told Elphicke what he planned to do, and that the *Daisy* was to depart in ten minutes, or earlier if she came under fire, no matter what.

"That's an order, sergeant," he said. "You understand?"

"Understood, sir."

Turning, he set off in the opposite direction, back to the mountain, continuing to mentally curse Ellis.

What kind of dumb marine would get their damn foot stuck? If he did manage to save her, he was going to check out her story about Abacha being sick for sure. If she'd been lying, he'd put them both in the brig. He might even push for a dishonorable discharge for Ellis. Not Abacha, he was too valuable. The last thing the BA needed was idiots who put others in danger.

Now running uphill once more, he scanned the skies.

They were clear, for now.

On his HUD he saw two dots had broken free from the group near the *Daisy* and were moving in his direction. Marks and Cole were on their way. Another minute's running up the lower slopes brought him half the distance to the trapped marine. He slowed down as he drew nearer to Ellis.

It was possible he was walking into a trap. The EAC could be keeping her alive in order to lure in some BA marines. Now that the snow had stopped falling, the gray, icy rocks stood out sharp and distinct. There was no sign of life in the bare, desolate landscape.

"Ellis?"

"Yes, sir?"

Her voice had quivered, as if she were frightened. Was it

because she was alone and in danger of being left behind, or because an EAC soldier was holding a gun to her head?

"Sitrep."

"I-I, *shit!* I'm sorry, sir. My foot's stuck, and—"

"Yeah, Elphicke told me. What I need to know is..." How to phrase it so he didn't put her in danger. "Is there anything else I should know?" The question should give her a wide scope for a cryptic answer to warn him she was being held.

"I don't think so, but you should go back without me. I'll figure something out."

"Figure something out? You're trapped by your goddamned foot in the middle of nowhere. What the hell do you think you're going to *figure out*, marine?" Wright stopped himself from saying more. He didn't want to turn into another Colbourn, though at moments like these he could see her point of view.

Ellis was silent.

Her answer had seemed to indicate she wasn't being held by the EAC. She was just an idiot.

Marks and Cole had made it to fifty meters from his position. He waited as they climbed the final distance. When they'd reached him, he continued on with them.

This section of the slope was thick with rocks. He stepped down from a boulder, and only just redirected his foot in time to avoid stepping on a body.

The man was lying face down. Wright identified him from his ID dot, still blue on his HUD.

"McEndry," said Marks sorrowfully.

Wright passed by the corpse. He wanted to take McEndry and the others who had died back for a proper burial, but he didn't have that luxury. He was going to be lucky to save Ellis.

He made a 'down' gesture. Crouching as they continued, they slowly climbed the last thirty meters. He told Marks to flank out left and sent Cole to the right.

About five meters from her, he finally got a visual on Ellis in the shadow between two boulders. No EAC seemed to be around. One of her legs had sunk into the space between two rocks while the other was bent up, and she was holding herself up by propping her elbows on each rock.

"Holy shit," Marks blurted.

"What's up?" asked Wright.

"Ellis, how did you do it?"

"Do what?" replied Ellis. "Oh, you mean—"

"Marks," began Wright, but then he saw something that surprised him, too. Scattered in the spaces among the rocks between him and the trapped marine lay three EAC corpses. Two had been killed by pulse fire, direct, close-range hits to their chests. The third was on his back at Ellis's feet, his visor shattered and the handle of a knife sticking out of his right eye.

"You killed *three* of them?" Marks continued, "or did the others do it?"

Three of them? She had to mean three EAC soldiers, but she was on the other side of Ellis. She couldn't be referring to the bodies he could see.

"Uh, no, I did it," replied the trapped marine. "Look, I appreciate you coming back for me, but are you guys gonna be able to get me out? I don't see how, unless you cut off my leg, and I'd rather keep it and take my chances, if it's all the same with you."

"Did you kill these ones too?" asked Cole, setting down the XM57 at Wright's side.

"Marks, check out the rocks that are trapping Ellis," he said, stepping over the dead soldiers.

Had Ellis really taken out six hostiles by herself, all while her leg was stuck between two rocks?

But he had no time to dwell on the feat. He examined her trapped leg. The rocks to each side were gripping it like a vise. He pushed her calf, hard, and then tried pulling it toward him.

It didn't budge a millimeter. He grasped her lower leg and tugged it upward, with the same result.

It wasn't possible to see Ellis's face through her darkened visor, but from her hunched position Wright guessed she was exhausted. He was reminded of a fox he and his father had come across while out in the woods behind his home. The fox had been caught in an illegal trap for many hours and was lying on its side, its eyes closed, panting breaths shaking its rib cage. His dad had freed the fox, but its leg was broken, and as it staggered slowly away, barely able to move, he'd lifted his shotgun and killed it.

"Is there a way we can blast these rocks to get her out?" Wright asked Marks, who had watched his attempts.

She examined the two boulders from all sides.

When she replied, it was over one-to-one comm. "A hit from a mortar would definitely free her, and her suit will give her some protection, but whether she'll survive, I just don't know."

He grimaced and wondered if he'd made the right decision to come back. He checked the time. They had less than three minutes to get to the *Daisy*.

"Ellis," he said, "we can try to shift these rocks with mortar fire, but it might kill you. What do you say? I need your answer immediately."

For a moment, she didn't reply.

Then he heard her say softly, "Do it."

IN THE END, the explosion didn't kill her, but it hurt her badly and knocked her out. Blood seeped through the breaches in her armor, and her visor was blown out.

Wright scooped the unconscious woman from among the broken rock fragments and put her over his shoulder.

Now it would be a sprint to get back to the *Daisy* before she took off. He raced down the mountainside, struggling to keep his balance. He had the weight of Ellis plus her armor on one side and the slippery rocks to contend with, but somehow he managed to stay on his feet.

Marks quickly drew ahead of him, but Cole was by his side, burdened by the XM57. Wright told him to drop the weapon. He would answer to Colbourn for it later, but the man had risked his life for a fellow marine without question.

Suddenly, a whine ran through the atmosphere.

It was as Wright had feared. The EAC had told its troops to withdraw because its jets were on their way. It was planning an air strike.

His lungs heaving, he sped up, taking crazy risks as he leapt down the mountain. He reached level ground and hit it running. Cole was ahead of him now. He and Marks would make it to the ship, Wright was sure, but for him and Ellis, it was going to be close. He didn't even know if she was still alive.

The going was easier now the terrain was flat, but he felt as though his chest would burst. The open hatch of the *Daisy* and the ramp leading up to it seemed impossibly far away.

Wright felt Ellis move. She was coming around. He heard her groan, then...

"I can't feel my legs," she said.

7

The colony ship, *Bres*, stretched three hundred and eighty-five kilometers from tip to tip of her spiral structure, and the diameter of each turn of the corkscrew was exactly ninety-three kilometers. Her engine spread over one of the spiral tips like a colossal umbrella, and a cylinder that ran through the center of the ship held its fuel—enough for more than three thousand years of travel. Coupled with the engine spacetime compression capability, the ship could carry its passengers throughout the galaxy in their search for a new, habitable world.

For who knew how long it would take to find a planet suitable for colonization? The information on exoplanets gleaned by space telescopes over the centuries told of several potential candidates, but only visiting them would reveal for certain whether they could sustain human life. It was possible none were viable in that way, and the search would continue.

How long might the colonists spend in torpor, the processes of their bodies slowed to an almost-unmeasurable pace? How long before they could open their eyes upon their new, untouched world, rich in resources? These were questions

Lorcan Ua Talman had often pondered over the years, as the building of *Bres* and her sister ships, *Balor* and *Banba*, progressed.

He rose from his seat at the center of the *Bres's* central control room and picked up three soft balls—red, green, and blue—from a small, round-topped table at his side. As he began to stroll around, he tossed the balls in a simple, circular pattern. Juggling helped him think, and it helped keep his team on their toes.

Nervousness mounted in the men and women as he walked the open spaces between their workstations. Steadman, Head of Engineering, was casting glances his way; Kekoa, responsible for sustainable habitats, had become strangely still and rigid; and the suspended animation specialist, Jurrah, was clenching and unclenching his fists where they rested on his console. Less important team members echoed their disquiet.

Lorcan smiled.

He sauntered to the screen that occupied the entire wall of one end of the room. At the moment, the display featured a section of the Alciere Drive, where drones worked, hovering over its surfaces as they worked and arriving and departing, transporting new parts and tools.

He commanded views of other zones within the *Bres* to be displayed, both the completed and uncompleted areas. New scenes appeared on the screen: Agricultural regions, laboratories, life support hubs, banks of cryo chambers, storage cells for the vast stock of organisms to be taken along, and living quarters where the colonists—the cream of humanity's genetic heritage—would spend months of respite from the physical toll of deep hibernation.

All the while, as Lorcan assessed the progress of the ship building project, he juggled, meditative. *Bres* was to be the lead ship of the three colony vessels, *his* ship, where he would live for a few short years but sleep away hundreds, perhaps thousands, ensconced in a fluid-filled capsule.

Before he would entrust his life to his ship, she must be perfect.

One of the recreation habitats appeared on the display—an expanse of water surrounded by temperate forest. Young trees mounted the slopes to what appeared to be a blue, cloud-filled sky, though it was only an illusion created on the over-arching dome. Lorcan studied the habitat for a long moment, then he spun on his heel, took aim, and threw.

Kekoa ducked, but not fast enough.

The ball hit her forehead.

The small motions and noises within the control room abruptly halted.

There had been a time when Lorcan's behavior would have drawn sniggers and giggles from the people responsible for the *Bres's* construction, at least from those who weren't his target, but that time had passed long ago.

He marched to Kekoa, who sat cowering at her desk. She lifted her gaze to him, and then closed her eyes just before he launched the second and third balls at her head. They struck her and dropped with soft thunks to the floor between her feet.

"Dunderhead," he said between his teeth. Lowering himself until his head was level with hers, he added, his voice increasing in volume, "Fool. Buffoon. Idiot!"

Straightening up, he stabbed the index finger of his long right hand at the screen. "What is that?"

Kekoa leaned to one side to see around him.

"Uh, West Lake?"

"You sound like you're asking me a question. Is it West Lake or isn't it? I would have thought you might recognize it, considering you built it!"

"West Lake," Kekoa said, more firmly.

"And what is wrong with it?"

"*Wrong* with it?"

"That's funny, there seems to be an echo in here."

"Um..." Kekoa gave a short, tense cough. "Er..." She frowned and squinted at the image on the display.

When no answer appeared to come to her, she looked for help toward other members of the team, but everyone except herself and Lorcan was staring steadfastly at their consoles.

She swallowed. "I'm afraid I don't know."

"Of course you don't know. I'm surrounded by nitwits. Simpletons. Ignoramuses."

Lorcan slapped Kekoa's desk. Turning to address the room, he continued, "And to think you're the prime of your fields, the best I could find. If you represent Earth's elite scientists, the future of humankind is doomed. What will become of us?"

He snapped his head around to focus on Kekoa again. "Waves! Where are the waves? That stretch of water is still as a dew pond. Is there a waterfall? Are there feeder tributaries tumbling down from higher ground, through the forest?"

Kekoa quickly ran fingertips over her console as she sought the information.

"No!" said Lorcan, triumphant, yet angry that he knew the woman's work better than she knew it herself. "So where is the oxygen going to come from?"

"Yes, yes, I see." She covered her eyes with one hand. "I see now."

"Do you? Do you really? Or must I spell it out? Without oxygen, within a few years that water will become stagnant as a Mississippi swamp. All the precious fish and water creatures you've seeded it with will die. The entire lake will be one murky, stinking mess."

"Waves," said Kekoa. "I'll get on it right away."

"You need—"

"Wind generators, I know."

"Wind generators indeed. Without wind, that lake will die,

and, what's more, the trees surrounding it will eventually collapse, their roots too weak to support their weight."

Lorcan ambled toward his seat, leaving his juggling balls where they lay at Kekoa's feet. Eventually, someone would summon the courage to pick them up and return them to the small table.

Kekoa's fingers flew over her console as she tried to source wind generators from the *Bres's* stocks or, if none were to be found, to order some from the Antarctic Project's manufacturing plants on Earth.

Despite her tension and haste, she found time to monitor Lorcan's progress across the room, as if she were waiting for something.

The rest of the control room seemed in suspense, too.

When Lorcan reached his seat and lowered himself into it, he noticed, from the corners of his eyes, Kekoa's figure relax.

"I was forgetting," he said to her, "that'll be one month's salary for your mistake. Try not to make another, or you'll end up owing *me* money."

Kekoa hung her head.

Stretching out one of his long legs and placing his elbows on his arm rests, Lorcan rubbed a fingertip across his lips and smirked.

But his pleasure at punishing Kekoa soon faded. The woman shouldn't have made such a simple mistake, especially not one that he, an amateur, could pick up. What else had she missed? If the habitats aboard *Bres*, *Balor*, and *Banba* were not truly self-sustaining, the effect could be more dire than the colonists simply having no natural landscapes to enjoy during their respite periods. The flora and fauna the ships were sustaining could die, and when they settled a new planet, the humans would be forced to rely only upon the stored gametes to create Earth's organisms.

The Project was a unique, unprecedented venture. There

was no telling what species might be useful, or essential, to humanity's survival in its new home, or homes. He was not prepared to accept any unnecessary increase to the risk of failure.

It was humanity's destiny to travel beyond the Solar System and spread across the galaxy. It was *his* destiny, the explanation for his loss, and the whole reason for his existence.

He would not fail.

8

T he sick bay aboard the *Daisy* wasn't equipped to deal with Ellis's wounds, so Wright had her transferred directly to the *Valiant* as soon as the corvette returned from the surface. An extended debriefing session with Colbourn followed, during which he doubted she would have believed his account if it weren't for the undeniable evidence of the 'mummy'. When the brigadier finally dismissed him and he'd showered and changed, he decided to pay the injured marine a visit.

He discovered that the severely dehydrated man had been placed in the room set aside for cases that required intensive care. As he entered the main area, a medic in full protective gear and carrying a vial of blood emerged from the room and hurried off, paying the major no attention.

He'd been worried the duty doc might prevent him from seeing Ellis so soon after her surgery, but it seemed the medical staff were too preoccupied with their new patient to bother about a regular marine.

She was wearing a full torso cast, and one of her legs was held up by suspension wires. Her arms appeared unaffected by the mortar blast aside from reddening. She was resting an interface on her chest and watching it, her head raised on a pillow.

It was the quiet shift. Aside from the glow emanating from the window to the intensive care room, the ward was only in half light. Two other patients were there, but they were asleep.

Ellis's face was lit by the illumination from her interface. She was frowning slightly as she watched it, and also wearing a look of intense happiness that made him reluctant to interrupt. He was about to turn around and leave when she noticed him.

"Major Wright? Sorry, sir, I didn't..." She tried to sit up and salute simultaneously. In her position, neither was possible, and her efforts caused the interface to slip from her hands.

Wright dove for it and caught it just before it hit the floor.

"Shit!" Ellis exclaimed. "I mean..." She was still, for some unknown reason, trying to sit up.

"At ease, marine."

She relaxed. Her gaze traveled to the interface in his hand. "Sir, could I...?"

Curiosity overcame him and, though he felt bad about the invasion of privacy, he took a glance at the screen before passing it over. All he saw was a children's playground. Nothing special.

She turned the interface screen downward and put it on the table next to her bed.

"How are you doing?" Wright asked.

"Pretty good, thanks. They fixed up my spine. The doc said they did something to trigger the nerves to regrow and I shouldn't have any long-term effects. And they gave me some strong painkillers, so I'm high as a kite." As if suddenly realizing who she was talking to, Ellis's slightly unfocused eyes widened. "Um, what I meant to say was—"

Wright chuckled. "It's okay. Do you mind if I...?" He gestured toward a chair.

"Go ahead."

She watched as he slid the chair closer and sat down. Leaning forward, he rested his elbows on his knees. He wasn't sure how to broach the subject he wanted to discuss.

"You don't have to pussyfoot around," said Ellis. "I'm a big girl. Let's just get it over with."

He lifted his eyebrows. "Get what over with?"

"I have to be disciplined, right?"

"Disciplined for what?"

"Wasting time, putting other marines' lives in danger, being a dumbass. I don't know. Something."

"What...Are you telling me you deliberately got your foot stuck?"

"No. Why would I do that?"

"You said you might be a dumbass."

"I'm certainly a dumbass, but I'm not *that* dumb."

"Right. Did you ask to be rescued?"

"Uh..." Her eyes moved left as she appeared to try to remember.

"As I recall, you did not," said Wright. "I made the decision to go back for you. Therefore, if anyone was wasting time and putting lives in danger, it was I."

"It was? Then I guess you must be the d—"

Wright put on his major face.

Ellis gave a small cough. "Sorry, sir."

"I want to talk to you about the events that took place after you were trapped. There must have been a lot going on. What do you remember?"

"I remember we lost Chen, McEndry, and Blake," Ellis replied sadly.

"Yeah," said Wright, his expression grave. "All good men." He looked toward the separate room in the corner of the sick bay. Had the loss of life been worth it? The question was still open. Only time would tell if the marines' sacrifice had been in vain. He had no idea what he'd found within that mountain in West BI, and he couldn't imagine how the discovery might benefit the Britannic Alliance.

"After they were blued," continued Ellis, "I knew the EAC knew where I was, and they would try to take me out. Luckily, they didn't all get there at once. Whenever an EAC soldier got close enough, I killed them. Until, finally, they stopped coming. I thought they must have been recalled for some reason. All I could do then was carry on trying to get my leg free. Then you and Marks and Cole showed up. So here I am, alive, and very grateful."

"About the EAC soldiers." The officer knit his fingers. "We found six of them. You said you'd killed them all yourself. Are you sure that's right?" He wanted to give her the chance to change her story. When he'd reached her she'd been on her own for some time and she was in a lot of pain. She didn't seem the type to exaggerate, but it was possible she'd been confused.

"Huh?" She tried to sit up again, sending her suspended leg swinging. "You think I'm lying?!"

"Hey, it's just a question."

"Just a question? Why would I lie about something like that?" When Wright didn't answer, she continued, "You think I made it up so I'd look good? That I stole kills from the men who died? What the hell?"

"Ellis," he said sternly, "remember who you're talking to."

High or not, he wasn't going to put up with her insubordination.

She slumped onto her bed and stared at the ceiling, her lips set and her jaw muscles twitching.

"You have to admit it's...unusual," he said.

Ellis didn't reply.

"Isn't it?" he probed.

"Is that a question, *sir*?" she asked.

"Yes."

"I don't know, sir."

"You don't?" He wasn't sure if her answer was genuine or she was only being difficult now he'd offended her.

"I'd never been trapped on a mountainside while under attack from EAC soldiers before." Her gaze remained glued to the ceiling. "Sir."

Wright unknitted his fingers and sat upright, all the while studying her. He found he couldn't read her. He'd looked up her file prior to coming to the sick bay. She'd enlisted only a few months previously and had taken part in only two engagements since passing Basic. There was no way she could have learned to handle herself so well during her short term of service. The information on her past had been minimal and vague. All he knew was she was from the Britannic Isles, a refugee from the EAC invasion.

Conflict conditions on the surface meant for many all their documents were lost, entire life histories vanishing as data centers were destroyed and internet lines severed. If she wasn't exaggerating the truth, he wondered what had happened in Ellis's past that had made her such an effective killer.

But he doubted she would tell him now, not in her current outraged, insulted state.

He stood up. "Let me know when the docs say you're fit to return to duty. We'll talk again."

Nothing but silence came from the woman, who seemed on the verge of exploding.

Wright turned to leave.

"Sir."

"Yes?"

Ellis was deigning to look at him again.

"Who's in there?" she asked, nodding toward the intensive room. "I tried asking one of the medics but they wouldn't tell me a thing. Who did we rescue?"

"Honestly? Your guess is as good as mine."

9

A s Lorcan relaxed in his private suite at the end of the working day, a familiar starscape filled the viewing portal. His rooms were one of the few places aboard the *Bres* that included an actual window looking out into space. Nearly everywhere else, the travelers would rely on screens if they wanted to see outside their ships.

He spread an arm over the sofa and gazed out at the stars. Hanging in the void at Earth-Moon Lagrange 4, the slowly whirling constellations didn't alter, and the planets wandered into and out of view. Over the years of his ships' construction, the sight had become almost a comfort to him, a reassurance that one day, he would look upon a different sight.

He wondered what he might see once the ship was underway, during the months or years of relief from life suspension. What new stars, nebulae, comets, and galaxies might hove into view?

Returning to a more practical state of mind, he reached for one of two glasses of champagne standing on the low table at his knees. As he moved, he checked his ocular display for the time. He tutted before taking a drink and returning the tall flute to the table.

His visitor was late.

Just as he was about to comm the *Bres's* landing bay to confirm the shuttle's arrival, his door chime sounded.

"Ah."

Rising to his feet, and feeling unexpectedly nervous, he instructed the door to open.

A woman stood in the doorway, but she didn't immediately enter, apparently allowing time for her appearance to have its full effect.

Lorcan didn't blame her. She created quite the impact.

Two forward-facing, curved, single horns rose thirty centimeters above her head, forming the structure of her head-dress. A gray, iridescent cloth hung between the horns and cascaded down her back to the floor, forming a cloak over her shoulders. Her white, inner robe also fell to the floor. Not a strand of her hair was visible. All was wrapped inside a white cloth that encircled her face and head and disappeared beneath her cloak.

Sufficient time had passed. She stepped into the room. Silently, she descended the few steps that led to the lowered, circular space at the center of the lounge. Her cloak caught the low light and glimmered.

Lorcan admired her showmanship, though he also found it amusing. He wondered how Kekoa, Steadman, and Jurrah would react if he turned up to work in a similar get up.

"Thank you for agreeing to speak with me in private, Ua Talman," said the woman.

"Call me Lorcan, please. Shall we sit?" He gestured to an armchair opposite the sofa.

"Do you mind if I sit...here?" She pointed at the spot next to Lorcan.

"Um, not at all."

As he sat down, he moved closer to the sofa's corner.

"It's so difficult to communicate securely these days," said the woman. "We encrypt, create sealed networks, even send physical messages, yet something always gets out." She lifted her cloak to spread it out as she sat. "Speaking to you face to face seemed the only way of keeping our conversation private," she went on. "You *are* confident we won't be spied upon here?"

"Thoroughly confident, Dwyr Orr."

He was, naturally, recording every moment of their encounter.

But she knew that.

His hand rested on the sofa between them, and when she spoke next, she laid hers on top of his.

"You may call me Kala, Lorcan."

He stiffened at the touch and slowly slid his hand out before placing it on the back of the sofa, trying to behave casually, as if he'd intended the movement all along.

Her lips turned up slightly at the corners, though Lorcan thought he also detected a hint of offense taken. He'd never seen the head of the Earth Awareness Crusade in person. Now that he was close to her, he noted her features were regular, and her irises so dark they were almost black. Though her eyebrows were not plucked, they framed her eyes perfectly.

As a young man, he would have found her attractive.

From the way her gaze roved his face, she appeared to be sizing him up, too.

He was used to it. Most people he met were momentarily distracted by his red hair, a rare color in any human population, though he guessed it was more than a third gray now.

"I confess I was surprised to receive your request," he said.

"You were? I suppose it is unusual in the circumstances."

She turned her attention to the two glasses on the table and picked up the one that was entirely full.

"Is this champagne?" she asked sweetly before sipping the liquid.

Realizing the faux pas, Lorcan was ashamed to feel a flush spread up from his neck and over his face. The EAC were famously covetous of their rare, local specialty products, never exporting them. The only way the Antarctic Project could have come into possession of champagne would be via an assault on an EAC province.

Still, what was the matter with him? There was something about the woman that unnerved him—he, who hadn't been unnerved by anyone or anything in a very long time.

"It is," he admitted. "You have me."

"Genuine champagne, from my region in Old France? The choice would make you very daring or exceptionally rude. Which is it, I wonder?"

She reached out and trailed a fingernail up his blushing cheek.

He resisted the temptation to snatch the digit away.

"Perhaps it is a very old vintage," she said, "from before the days of the Crusade."

"Perhaps so," he replied, grabbing the out. "I had to provide something fitting for the occasion. I have to confess, I never thought we two would ever meet face to face. Though we aren't strictly enemies anymore, neither are we exactly friends. I'm gratified that the EAC has turned its attention to grabbing BA territory, and not mine. Shall we get down to business? It's a delight to have the pleasure of your company, Kala, but I'm sure you're here to discuss something important."

She put down her glass and shifted in her seat to face him full on. She was perched on the edge of the sofa.

"You're very direct. I like that." Placing her hands in her lap, she said, "I think it's fair to say we have different and oppositional goals. My organization seeks to celebrate and enshrine the spirit of Mother Earth, while yours wishes to..." her face twisted in an effort to suppress a strong emotion "...shall we say, exploit her resources?"

"I think that accurately summarizes the essence of our aims."

"Yet, one day..." she cast her gaze around his suite and to the starscape beyond the window "...one day, this starship and the others you're building will be finished. You'll depart the Solar System forever and have no further interest in Earth."

"That's the plan."

"But until that time, you'll have a thorn in your side—a thorn that also pricks the EAC."

Finally, she was coming to the point. He'd guessed this might be the reason for the clandestine visit.

"The Britannic Alliance."

"Exactly,' said Dwyr Orr. "There was a period when the EAC thought we could work with them, that our philosophies were similar, but, sadly, that proved not to be the case. They don't understand our ideals and motivations, and theirs.... Well, theirs are only too apparent: Keep everything exactly as it has been for centuries, for millennia. They have no vision, no spirit, and lately they've been frustrating our efforts at every turn."

"Is that so? I thought you were winning against the BA. The latest reports I've received stated you've gained considerable ground."

"We've had several successful encounters lately and added land to our stock, but recently, they acquired something that has a deep significance to us. After long years of research and months of scouring the countryside, just as we were on the verge of achieving our goal, they snatched it from beneath our noses. I...we want it back, very badly. But the BA's military capability remains strong on land, despite the losses we've inflicted. And, as I'm sure you're aware, they control most of near-Earth space. We need help penetrating their defenses if we're to retrieve it."

Lorcan looked into the woman's dark eyes, his interest piqued. "What is this thing you want so badly?"

She gave a sigh of exasperation. "It isn't anything that would interest you, Lorcan. I know what you seek—raw resources, new technology, and uncommon or exceptional organisms. Your thirst for materials and diverse genetic code is legendary, but this isn't anything like that. It's something that only threatens the EAC."

Lorcan leaned back and studied her. "So you want us to join forces."

"It makes sense, if only on a temporary basis. I know the BA is blocking your prospecting and mining efforts, and they're fighting us at every turn. If we work together, share our intel and military resources, we can increase concentrated assaults on the Alliance and wipe them from the map."

"And, as a byproduct, you'll get this object."

"Get it and destroy it. More importantly, the BA won't bother either of us anymore. How much longer will it be until you're ready to leave?"

"We're on track to complete all three ships in another four and a half years."

"I think Mother Earth can withstand another four and a half years of resource gathering. You'll stick to non-EAC land?"

"I'd like some time to assess exactly what we need going forward. But I'm interested in your proposition. I suppose your idea is that, when we go, you'll have the planet to yourselves."

Kala's features glowed. "Yes. Our temple will belong to us alone."

Lorcan was not one for any kind of religious fervor. The look on Dwyr Orr's face made him uncomfortable, but he hadn't been lying when he'd said her offer tempted him. A reduction in the BA's efforts to thwart his operations would speed up the Project immensely. He'd been building the *Bres*, *Balor*, and *Banba* for eighteen years, and he hadn't been a young man when he'd started. Any time he saved would be time he could spend living out the rest of his life on a new planet.

"You don't have to decide immediately," said Kala. "I understand I'm asking you to trust me and take my word. We should relax a little, get to know each other better."

With an enigmatic look, she suddenly shrugged off her cloak, allowing it to spill onto the sofa.

Lorcan's gaze became fixed on her. What was she up to?

Next, she lifted her headdress from her head and placed it behind her on top of the cloak. Putting a hand to each side of her head, she pushed back the white covering to well below her shoulders, revealing smooth, pale skin and long, thick, dark brown hair, which she pulled from her dress and spread out.

Now she was no longer an imposing figurehead of a powerful, cultish sect, but a woman in her prime, confident and sensual. When she raised her face to Lorcan again, he found himself moved by the sight of her, despite his years of self-imposed celibacy.

Yet he was confident that, if her intent was to persuade him by seduction, she was going to be disappointed.

10

Taylan lifted the back of her gym shirt.

Abacha whistled as he saw the scar from her operation. "Impressive. Looks like they cut you bow to stern."

She dropped her shirt and faced him. "They inserted titanium vertebrae and silicon discs, and then they regrew my spinal cord through them."

Her friend wrinkled his nose. "Gnarly."

"More like lucky. If I'd been home in West BI, I might never have walked again."

"If you'd been home, you might not have been blasted from between two boulders."

"You've got a point. The doc said they could grow replacements for the parts of my spine that were damaged from my stem cells, but Colbourn wanted me back on duty ASAP. Something for the future, maybe. Let's start, okay? I really want to get back in shape."

They were in the *Daisy's* gym. Taylan had been discharged from sick bay the previous day, and she'd taken the first transport from the *Valiant* to the corvette, 'forgetting' Wright's request to go and see him. She still hadn't forgiven him for accusing her of lying about the EAC troops she'd killed.

What a jerk.

She'd thought the major was okay, or at least a better alternative to that hard-nosed bitch, Colbourn, but she'd been wrong.

"Sure," said Abacha. "What do you want to do? Knife fight? Or straight hand-to-hand?"

"Uh..." Taylan rolled her shoulders and winced as pain jabbed her spine. Another one of those painkillers wouldn't go amiss, but then she pushed the thought aside. She'd cut down her dosage even before the doc began to wean her off them. The thought of her friend slamming her onto her back on the mat didn't appeal. "Knives. We can do hand-to-hand another time."

As Abacha walked to the equipment store to get the blunt training knives, Taylan heard a door open above in the observation gallery.

Major Wright appeared at the railing, and her stomach sank. He rested his arms on it and leaned over, peering down and looking her right in the eyes. She was in deep doo-doo for sure.

Why wouldn't he leave her alone? Going to see him after she'd been discharged from the sick bay couldn't be *that* important. What was he going to do to her? She had a feeling that her excuse of a poor memory wouldn't wash, even though she'd been flying when he gave her the order.

Then a second figure arrived and stood next to Wright.

Colbourn.

Taylan's stomach sank to her feet. What in all hell was the brigadier doing here? It didn't require two of them to discipline her, surely?

Abacha returned, carrying a knife in each hand as well as two sparring helmets and protective vests. He registered her expression and then followed her gaze upward.

The two officers looked down impassively.

Giving Taylan a *What are they doing here?* look, he passed her a helmet and vest.

She returned a *Damned if I know* expression, and put on the safety equipment. Neither Wright nor Colbourn said anything. They seemed to be there just to watch.

Abacha was ready too. He tossed her a knife, and she snatched it from the air by its handle.

She crouched, shifting her feet apart, and bending her knees.

Abacha did the same.

They began to circle.

Taylan enjoyed sparring with Abacha. He was skilled, but never held back because she was a woman. He was also never embarrassed or pissed when she beat him, which, so far, she had every time.

It hadn't been like that in Basic. At first, the other recruits had complimented her, impressed as she won fight after fight. Then the dark looks and muttered conversations started. Being good was fine, being too good wasn't acceptable. Soon, there seemed to be some kind of competition going on as her opponents came at her harder and harder. And the trainers didn't intervene, as if they also thought she was too big for her boots.

No one ever said anything to her face, but she felt the others' resentment and guessed she'd acquired a rep of being stuck up and arrogant. She didn't think she was either of those things. She was just a good fighter, and she was damned if she was going to hold back in order to be popular.

Fighting had always been easy for her. It was her dad's doing. From as far back as she could remember until he died, he'd trained her every day. One of her earliest memories was of him teaching her blocking moves. She recalled, at the age of three or four, running through a set in order and after that, randomly. She knew if she got them all correct he would give her a piece of chocolate. Even back then the confection had been rare and expensive, making it a powerful incentive to learn.

As time had gone on, he'd taught her more techniques and schooled her in the use of a range of hand weapons as well as the old pulse rifle he'd kept from his days in the military. Sometimes, the sessions were grueling, but Dad wouldn't let her rest until she'd met whatever goal he'd set for the day. She never complained, no matter how much her muscles ached or how sore she was from blows she hadn't managed to deflect. The truth was, despite the pain, she loved it. It hurt, but it felt like learning how to breathe.

Mum had despaired at the two of them, always fighting or training, but she had grudgingly admitted that Taylan had a talent for it, a genetic trait that she must have inherited from her father.

Once, when she'd grown to be a teenager, Dad had told her that, though she was female, she had the ability and stamina of the ancient knights who had fought to repel the Saxon invaders. Her mother said he was daft.

With the benefit of hindsight, she'd later realized her father's motive hadn't only been to nurture a special ability in his daughter. At times when they rested, panting and sweating after a tough session, she would sometimes see a certain look in his eyes—a sad, fearful look that chilled her blood. Looking back, she'd guessed that, even then, he'd known the days of peace in the Britannic Isles wouldn't last forever, that one day the EAC would push across the Channel and seize the homeland.

He knew his family would not be among those who would

accept the new regime and their strange religion. For them, it would be fight or die. Or both.

Abacha lunged.

Taylan stepped a little to the side, but not far, seeing at the last moment it was a feint, lacking a full commitment. As the man made his true move, an attempt to punch her in the side of her head, she ducked. She launched herself at him, long and low, thudding her shoulder into his chest and driving him upward, lifting him momentarily off his feet.

Pain lanced from her spine and she grimaced, trying to ignore it.

Abacha's feet hit the ground. Off balance, he staggered and toppled backward. Before he'd entirely fallen, Taylan leapt at him, raising her knife.

But Abacha already had a knee up, ready to deflect her.

She landed stomach-first on his knee and grunted at the impact, which forced her diaphragm up and expelled the air from her lungs. He forced her off and over.

Now she was the underdog.

Her friend grabbed her right bicep to keep her knife down as he followed her rolling motion, jabbing his knife at her. With her free hand she knocked his arm away. Reaching out, she grabbed his wrist and gripped it, immediately twisting it.

Abacha grimaced but didn't drop his knife.

Though his other hand remained wrapped around her upper arm, she could still bend her elbow. She jabbed his thigh with the blunt knife.

He gasped. They struggled. Her grip on his knife arm was solid. She continued to turn it to an unnatural angle. Abacha thrust his forehead down, trying to headbutt her, but she turned her face away and he only hit her above her ear. Her helmet protected her from the full effect of his blow. All the while, she was jabbing his unprotected thigh.

With a grunt of pain, he dropped his knife.

In another second, Taylan had rolled him over and was on top of him, her blade at his throat.

Abacha smiled. "Again! If only you played xiangqi as well as you fight, little chick."

Taylan grinned and climbed to her feet. Holding out a hand to her friend to pull him up, she replied, "With your understanding of strategy, you'll be an officer one day, while I'll remain a grunt, butting heads with the other numskulls."

"I'm not too sure about that. Another round?"

She nodded and stepped a couple of paces backward.

They fought again. And again. By their fourth bout, she was sweating and breathing heavily, and it was getting very hard to ignore the pain from her healing back.

It was also taking her longer and longer to gain the upper hand. At the fifth fight, she was seriously worried she might lose.

But she won again.

They moved apart and paused, each catching their breaths.

Abacha shook his head, flinging droplets of sweat from his nose. He waggled a finger at her. "You need a license."

"A license for what?"

"You're a deadly weapon."

A snort of laughter came from above.

Taylan had forgotten about their audience. When she looked up, she saw it was Wright who must have laughed. He was smiling, while Colbourn's stony face hadn't cracked.

Ignoring the onlookers, Taylan said, "Call it a day?"

"Yeah. I wanna get out of here alive."

As she walked past her friend on her way to the equipment store, she shouldered him. "Don't be stupid. I would never hurt actually you."

"Is that so? Tell that to my thigh. It's gonna be black and blue tomorrow. I'd hate to fight you if you *did* want to hurt me."

Taylan returned her knife to its slot and dropped her training equipment in the sanitizer before walking through the changing room and into the shower room, where she stripped off. She let the hot water sluice the sticky sweat from her skin and then washed her hair, all the while wondering why the two officers had been watching her and Abacha sparring. She hoped they would be gone by the time she left the gym.

She re-entered the empty changing room and put on clean clothes before slinging her bag over her shoulder and walking to the exit. The door opened, and she found her wish hadn't come true. Wright and Colbourn were waiting right outside the door in the passageway.

"Back up, marine," said the brigadier.

Inwardly groaning, Taylan reversed direction. She was tired and her back hurt like a bitch. Why were they intent on harassing her, a nobody of the lowest rank?

The two officers followed her in.

"From what I saw today, you have some skill at close combat, Ellis," said Colbourn, "and from what Major Wright has told me, you're handy with a rifle too. I'd like to put you to better use than your current rank allows."

Not invited to answer, Taylan kept silent.

"I'm promoting you to corporal and reassigning you to the *Valiant*. You're to assist in training. 'Assist' is the operative word. You don't have the rank to supervise the sessions. But you may get there, depending on your performance." She paused, as if waiting for something. "You may speak."

"Thank you, ma'am. Could I ask…"

"*Yes?*"

"Could Abacha come with me to the *Valiant*? He's my sparring partner. He could help me…demonstrate moves."

"I'll consider your request. Supporting training sessions is one thing I have in mind for you. I'm sure I'll find more for you to do. Perhaps some covert missions." Colbourn leaned in, focusing on Taylan's eyes, which stared ahead. "You might receive invitations to work for other branches of the BA's military, or from SIS. You're to ignore them. That's an order. You're a Royal Marine. You're mine. Do you understand?"

"Yes, ma'am."

"Good. Remember it."

Taylan was struggling to figure out what this new development could mean. When she'd joined up, her intention had been to help free her homeland from EAC control. She'd had other, more personal, motives, but a free West BI would help her achieve them. She wasn't sure this new direction Colbourn was pushing her in would allow her to do what was important to her.

"What's *that*?" the brigadier suddenly asked.

She was glaring at Taylan's necklace.

Her heart rate began to speed up. "It's...uhh."

"*Uhh* what?" Colbourn pressed sarcastically.

"It's my, my..." The words wouldn't come out. Taylan was exhausted from the sparring session, in pain, and under pressure from this nasty woman. To her shame, tears pricked her eyes.

The brigadier reached for her neck and, before she knew what was happening, the woman had fastened her fingers around the necklace and ripped it away from her, breaking the thread.

Taylan sucked in a horrified breath.

"This is *not* regulation," Colbourn spat, the necklace dangling from her fingers. "You are only to wear the items you've been issued."

Without another word, the brigadier pivoted and strode away.

Taylan's knees turned weak. She wanted to protest, to

demand the evil bitch return her property, but she was too shocked.

Before she knew it, both Wright and Colbourn were at the changing room door.

The major gave her an apologetic look as he stepped through the opening, and then the two officers were gone.

11

Colbourn had left the *Valiant* to attend General Council and military meetings at a secret location on the surface. With her departure, tension among everyone aboard had dropped a notch and morale had risen. The reprieve was only going to last a week or so until the brigadier returned. For the time being, however, Wright was in charge, which meant he had to carry out his superior's duties as well as his own.

He didn't mind too much. He never had much use for free time anyway. The Royal Marines was his life—his soul, even. He'd never wanted anything more and couldn't imagine living any other way.

The only thing that came close to his love of serving was sleeping.

So devotion to duty wasn't at the forefront of his mind when, after a long day carrying out Colbourn's work and his own, he was woken by a message alert just after he'd fallen asleep. Groggy and confused, he slapped behind his ear, trying to silence his comm implant like it was an old-fashioned alarm clock.

Then he woke up properly and turned off the alert with his mind.

His cabin was pitch black and cool air from the fan wafted over him, just how he liked it for a good night's sleep. Sighing as he remembered this was the second time he'd been woken from a deep slumber recently, he opened the message.

It was from the duty doc in the sick bay.

"The man you rescued from West BI is coming around, major. I'm not sure how to proceed. I'd appreciate it if you paid us a visit."

Coming around?

How could that shadow of a human being he'd carried in his arms down the mountainside still be alive, let alone approaching consciousness?

He hadn't given the man much thought since completing the mission. As far as he was concerned, his part in what happened to the mystery figure he'd taken from the cave was over, and now it was up to Colbourn or other higher-ups to decide what was to be done with him.

Only now he *was* the highest-up, on the *Valiant* anyway.

Puffing out a breath of sleepiness and frustration, he sat up and smoothed down the annoying tuft of hair that always appeared after he'd slept. After getting out of bed and quickly pulling on his pants, shirt, and shoes, he was out the door and on his way.

THE MAIN SICK bay was empty. Wright stopped outside the intensive care room, unsure if he could go in, and commed the doc to tell her he'd arrived.

"It's okay," she replied. "Come and see him."

As he entered the room, she explained, "We're thinking of

moving him into the main room tomorrow. We're confident he isn't harboring anything infectious, and he's doing really well."

Wright couldn't equate his memory of the dried-up mummy in the mountain cave with the idea of someone doing 'really well'.

The doc moved to the side to give him a view of the patient.

His mouth fell open.

"I know, right?" said the doc. "He's made amazing progress."

Self-consciously snapping his jaw shut, Wright walked to the unconscious man's side and stared down at him. The patient remained asleep, but his eyes beneath their lids were moving, and his lips moved, too, as if he were having a conversation in his sleep. If it weren't for the blue-black animal tattoos on his upper body, the major would never have believed this was the same person he'd rescued.

He was looking at a tall, well-built man in his thirties. The skin that had been pale, dry and leathery as parchment was now plump and fleshy, and the wound on the man's stomach had disappeared, as if it had never existed. The sunken eyelids had filled, and the wisps of hair had been replaced by a thick fuzz on his face, scalp, and lower arms, promising to grow out red-gold. His muscular chest rose and fell in a deep, steady rhythm.

An electrode at each temple and a drip inserted into the back of his hand were the only signs that the man had hovered once between life and death for untold years.

On a table next to the bed sat the man's thick, ornate torques.

Wright turned to the doc.

"Can he hear us?"

"It's hard to say. Possibly."

"Then let's talk outside."

Outside intensive care, in the quiet, dimly lit sick bay ward, the doc said, "His brain activity is increasing. That was why I messaged you. I expect he'll wake up in an hour or so."

"Look, I'm out of the loop on this. What's been happening with him?"

"Yeah, sorry. I forgot we've been reporting to Brigadier Colbourn. Let me show you his chart."

She began to move away, but Wright said, "A summary would be fine."

"Oh, okay, well, it's been remarkable. I've been the one doing obs on him every day since you brought him in, and even *I* can't quite believe it. We started him on intravenous fluids immediately, of course, though it was nearly impossible to find a vein, and when we did find one we weren't sure anything would go in. He was hypothermic, too, so we used warm water to irrigate...you probably don't want to know about that part."

The doc paused and gave her head a small shake. "The fact that he still had a heartbeat while in that condition is a medical impossibility. And there's no way his brain could have recovered from the degree of dehydration it suffered, yet here we are. His brain, liver, kidneys... everything's functioning normally. To try to understand what was happening, I gave the lab some of his inner cheek cells to culture. They found they were reproducing at a phenomenal rate *and* growing healthier at each new division.

"I still don't understand it," the doc went on. "I've never seen anything like it or read anything comparable in case studies. The lack of precedent means I have zero idea what to expect when he regains consciousness. By all rights, he should have severe brain damage and remain in a vegetative state, but, honestly, right now all bets are off. I can't guess what his ongoing health status might be."

If the doctor didn't know what to make of her patient, Wright certainly didn't. If the miracle mystery man's history so far was anything to go by, he would probably wake up, invent an intergalactic space drive, and disappear to explore the universe.

The major knit his brows. Colbourn hadn't left any instructions regarding their surprise visitor. She might even have forgotten about him. She'd seemed preoccupied before leaving for the General Council meeting. He didn't want to bother her with non-urgent comms.

Should the man be allowed to return to full consciousness? Should he be questioned about what he'd been doing in the cave, and where on Earth the distress signal had come from? Or should he remain under sedation until Colbourn returned and decided what to do with him?

A sudden roar of anger came from the intensive care room, followed by yelling in a language Wright didn't recognize.

The man from the cave had woken up.

The door to the room jerked open, and the man stood there, stark naked, blood dripping from his hand where he'd ripped out the cannula. His eyes were round and staring and his body was rigid, his fingers splayed at his sides.

"Hey," said the doc, "you need to—"

Giving another roar, the man raised a fist and ran at her.

Wright dove between them just in time. He grabbed the big guy around his chest and tried to heave him upward, planning to unbalance him and push him to the floor, where he might be able to subdue him.

But the patient was having none of it.

He punched Wright in the head.

Sparks flew into his vision, and darkness closed in, but he clung on to the man and concentrated on staying upright.

As the threat of unconsciousness cleared, he became aware of someone grabbing his arms trying to force them apart. He realized his captive was trying to free himself. The major gripped tighter. Another great roar of anger came from the big man's mouth. Wright tensed, expecting to be punched again. A second hit would put him out of the game for sure, but there wasn't anything he could do to defend himself. If he let go of the patient, he would go for the doctor.

The punch didn't come. Instead, he heard a hiss, and the struggling, fighting figure in his arms went limp and very heavy. He found himself trying to hold onto him as the man slipped from his grasp.

"Put him down gently, if you can," said the doc. She was holding up a discharged pressure hypodermic. "It's always good to have some knockout juice on hand."

Wright squatted and tried to ease the man's fall, but he slumped ungracefully to the floor and knocked his head on the tile.

Wright stood up. The man was entirely out of it, his mouth open and his eyes closed. The doc was silently mouthing something, probably sending a comm, requesting assistance to get her patient back into bed.

Taking a second look at the prone figure, Wright said, "That decides it. I want him sedated until Colbourn gets back. And in restraints."

12

In the Caribbean Kingdom, on the island of Barbados, Hans Jonte, head of the Secret Intelligence Service, was taking a final look in his hotel suite mirror, appraising his tailored suit, polished shoes, and groomed beard. His suit fitted like a glove, accentuating his broad chest and narrow hips; his shoes were real leather, including the soles, and they showed it; and his beard had been freshly styled that morning.

He couldn't fault his appearance.

He smiled, nodding approvingly at his reflection. His large, white, even teeth shone.

Appearances counted for a lot when you wanted to look the part among the people who count, and the meeting of the General Council was the perfect occasion for that purpose.

He went into the bathroom, where he'd placed the unique cologne he'd brought along. The scents had been perfectly matched to his pheromones, designed to create an attractive and alluring scent. Visual input was important to humans, but smells were even more important. Aromas triggered emotions and remained embedded in memories, so that the whiff of a long-forgotten perfume could conjure up an event from decades ago.

And he wanted to be remembered.

He puffed the cologne over his neck and face before massaging the fine droplets into his beard and skin. After washing and drying his hands, he left the suite.

A few minutes later, he was downstairs and outside the assembly room, which hummed with conversation and anticipation of the momentous discussions about to take place. The BA had suffered a serious blow in the loss of its historic homeland, and something had to be done to win it back. Also, the AP was attacking Australia, sovereign state of Oceania, probably hungry for the uranium mines. Though the mines had been shut down decades ago due to falling interest in nuclear energy, they remained full of the precious ore. Meanwhile, after finding itself blocked by the boundary of the Great Atlantic to the west, the EAC was creeping steadily southward, threatening to take Gibraltar and with it control of the Strait.

But more than the discussions on how to reverse the tide of the BA's fortunes, everyone was waiting for something else to happen, something even more significant than the debate on the future of the Britannic Alliance.

Queen Alice hadn't been seen in public for two years and three months, one week, and five days—Hans had been counting. Rumors of her illness, senility, and even undisclosed death had run rife. He knew the detail of many of the rumors because he'd been responsible for many of them. People loved to gossip, and he loved to give them things to gossip about, especially when it came to Her Majesty.

She was scheduled to attend the council in her usual nonparticipatory capacity. Hans had no doubt she would read out the speech Parliament had written for her, and then she would affect polite interest in the proceedings until she could gracefully retire. But her presence would achieve the sense of unity and common purpose intended.

Hans wondered how much the Prime Minister and the Queen's advisers had implored her to attend the event. The old woman had obviously lost interest and enthusiasm for public life many years ago, but somehow she'd been persuaded to hang on and not abdicate, giving her successor time to grow to manhood. A man made a much better figurehead to a failing monarchy than a young boy.

Pausing at the entrance to the assembly room, Hans surveyed the tiered seating around the walls of the oval chamber. The sections designated to the attending groups stood out, even without the benefit of signage.

The armed forces occupied a quarter of the available space, the admirals, generals, air marshals, and lower ranking officers, dignified in their dress uniforms. A few generations previously, it would have been unthinkable to invite such a large number of military personnel to a general meeting, but now all and sundry seemed to have influence in political affairs.

Ministers of Parliament, including the Cabinet and the Prime Minister himself, were all dressed formally, similar to Hans. Their somber suits took up another significant chunk of the room. Media reps in more fashionable gear ranged around the upper gallery, captains of industry had been allotted a portion of the seats, and non-governmental organizations a smaller portion. Out of SIS, only he and his immediate subordinates were attending.

Had his officers desired to be present—he had no doubt they did *not*—the idea was out of the question. Their anonymity was paramount, superseding their right to participate in debates or decision making.

Hans walked sedately across the floor of the chamber and climbed the steps that led to his organization's section.

The meeting was about to begin.

"Mr. Jonte, you barely made it," said his secretary as he took the seat beside her.

"And yet...I did!" he replied pleasantly.

He liked Josephine. She wasn't the sharpest tool in the box, and that suited him perfectly. She never bothered him with awkward questions about his activities, only doing exactly as she was told.

Soft chimes began to echo through the chattering, growing gradually louder. The voices quietened down, and after five more resounding chimes, they stopped.

The chamber was silent.

Parliament's Speaker was acting as chairperson. She stood up, alone in her box, wearing her traditional black gown.

"Ministers, ladies, and gentlemen, welcome to this seven hundred and eighth meeting of the Britannic General Council." She continued with some more platitudes, and then said, "We have a long afternoon ahead of us with many urgent matters to address. Therefore, without any further ado, I would like to welcome to our assembly, Her Majesty Alice the Second, Queen of the Britannic Isles and her Realms and Territories, Head of the Commonwealth, Commander-in-Chief of the Armed Forces, and Mother of her Nations."

Hans fidgeted in his seat and suppressed a yawn.

Next to the Speaker's box, a larger one protruded from the wall. It was empty, but as soon as the introduction was over, the curtains at the rear of the box drew apart, and an old lady in a jewel-encrusted ceremonial dress and wearing a small tiara stepped into the space.

All the attendees, including Hans, rose to their feet and bowed.

As he lifted his head, Queen Alice raised a frail hand to give her usual wave, cleared her throat, and began to speak. Hans sat down.

The woman's quiet, tremulous tone meant that, despite

electronic amplification, he could barely make out what she was saying. He didn't think he was alone in that either, yet all the attendees sat motionless, as if hanging on to her every word.

Hans's attention wandered.

Tall, slim windows divided the seating sections, giving views of a beach and crashing ocean waves on one side of the hotel, and deep green vegetation on the other. He watched the waves, his mind traveling along the hidden, twisted paths of his machinations, as he waited for the Queen to finish.

It didn't matter what the elderly lady said. The words had been placed in her mouth by the people who wanted the Establishment, an entity whose primary purpose was to maintain its ancient grip on executive power. Its members wanted everything to go on as it had for thousands of years. They *wanted* an impotent figurehead; someone who would stand in front of the shadowy elite who controlled everything and viewed that control as an ancestral right, merited, deserved, and inviolable.

But things were about to change.

The Queen had no direct heir, and though the line of succession to her late nephew's son was clear, the distance of the relationship would introduce doubt and fragility to the entire question of monarchy, in Hans's estimation. He was banking on it, in fact. Now that Alice II's life was drawing to a close, it was the perfect time to bring all his efforts of the previous few years to bear fruit.

It was time for the Britannic Alliance to become a Republic.

It would take back the lands it had lost, defeat the EAC, and banish that madman, Ua Talman, before he drained the Earth of her remaining precious resources. The BA was about to be born again, in a different and better form.

If blood had to be shed for that to happen, so be it. It was only through pain, labor, and strife that new life came into the world, and the same was true of new systems of government.

Josephine tapped his elbow, retrieving Hans from his reverie. He saw that the Queen had departed, and the meeting was about to begin.

The Prime Minister rose. "Firstly, may I say what a delight it is to see Her Majesty here today, and in such good health."

Hans rolled his eyes.

The Prime Minister fired off a few more platitudes, and then handed over to an under-secretary to give a report on the state of the Alliance.

All the woman said was common knowledge. The Britannic Isles remained under EAC control, along with much of Europe and Asia, excepting India and Pakistan, and the Antarctic Project continued to steadily strip the resources of many countries. Much of Brazil was infiltrated by the AP's mining companies, which were ransacking the Amazon Forest for bauxite. Non-BA countries, including the Middle East and the States, were maintaining their independent, neutral positions. Hans attention wandered again. He had a far better understanding of the state of things than the overview the under-secretary was giving.

She finished speaking and sat down.

At the same time, the Prime Minister gave a small cough and took the podium. He gripped the sides of the lectern and glanced downward at his prompt screen, preparing to begin his speech.

Hans expected the PM to express solidarity with BA nations that had fallen, followed by assurances that everything possible was being done to free them. The man would probably then go on to praise the efforts of the military and auxiliary services, and state his confidence that the future of the BA was rosy, her foes would be vanquished, and she would eventually return to her former days of glory.

That was what Hans was expecting.

But just as the PM opened his mouth to speak, a distinct,

piercing whine came from overhead. Along with the rest of the attendees, Hans looked upward, puzzled. He saw the chamber's elegantly decorated, wooden ceiling, but the noise was coming from outside the building, and it was getting louder.

Suddenly, someone among the military ranks screamed, "Get down!"

Then the ceiling exploded.

Hans's eardrums burst.

He had a brief impression of shattered, fiery splinters raining down and thick smoke blooming, and that was all.

13

W right unfastened the buttons on his shirt, took it off, and pushed it into the laundry chute. Then he took off his pants, folded them neatly, and placed them on the single chair in his cabin. He yawned and stretched his arms and back. He'd just finished a double shift, covering for Colbourn as well as doing his own work, and he was looking forward to at least six solid hours of blissful slumber. The brigadier was due back in a couple of days, and he thought he was doing a reasonable job of keeping the *Valiant* shipshape and ticking along while she was away.

He padded into his tiny shower room and completed his bedtime routine before returning to the main area of his cabin and getting into bed. He thumped his pillow to fluff it up, and then buried his head in the soft cushion. After exhaling heavily, he said, "Lights, off."

The room instantly plunged into darkness. He closed his eyes, gave a soft smile, and his body entirely relaxed. As he banished the cares of the day from his mind, sweet sleep overtook him.

"Major."

"Ughhh..." Wright opened his eyes.

"I'm sorry to disturb you, but..."

"Yes, corporal?"

"There's fighting in the quarters, sir, and Captain Tyler's having trouble getting it under control. I thought maybe you'd—"

"I'm on my way." He threw off his covers and got up. Cursing to himself, he quickly put on a fresh shirt, his pants and boots, and then stomped out into the passageway.

Whoever was responsible for waking him up was going to pay.

The marines' quarters occupied only one section of the *Valiant*. As he neared the place, he didn't need to check with Singh which of the cabins was the scene of the fight. When he was still a couple of minutes away, he could hear it. Thuds and bumps, shouts and cheers as watchers egged the fighters on, and over everything, Tyler's impotent shouts, imploring the marines to cut it out and for everyone to calm down.

Wright slammed into the cabin with such fury everyone near the door instantly fell silent, and then the effect rippled through the room. Most of the onlookers were clustered in the far corner of the room, where bunks had been knocked away from the bulkhead. Men and women in their underwear looked over their shoulders, saw the major, and began to draw away, slipping into their racks, or quickly finding other occupations. All of them tried to look as though they had nothing to do with what was going on.

All except Captain Tyler and the fighters. The captain had a split lip, probably from an accidental elbow to the face as he'd tried to pull the small, tussling group apart.

"Major," said the captain, approaching him, "I..."

Wright shook his head. Tyler fell silent.

One marine lay on the floor, unconscious. Four others were

fighting, crushed into the corner, but they were not fighting in pairs.

It was three against one.

Just as Wright registered the target, crouched with her back to the bulkhead, she punched one of her attackers in the gut, and then kneed him in the jaw as he went down. The man's eyes rolled back and he collapsed like a puppet with its strings cut.

Wright filled his lungs, and then bellowed, "Atten-*shun!*"

Perhaps because they recognized his voice, or perhaps out of reflexive habit, the two remaining assailants snapped upright, clapping their legs together, putting their arms to their sides, and thrusting their shoulders back.

Ellis maintained her crouched position, swaying and panting, blood running from her nose and a cut above her eye. Her knuckles were bloodied, too, but Wright guessed from the state of the bullies' faces, the blood might not be her own.

"Corporal Ellis, stand to attention!" yelled Wright.

She slowly straightened up, her eyes hard and her jaw set. Her chest heaving, she followed his order.

Aside from the heavy breathing of the fighters, the cabin was silent.

"Captain Tyler, remove these brawlers to the brig. Not you, Ellis. You're to come with me."

Their gazes averted, the marines in the cabin parted wordlessly to allow him and the corporal through.

Wright didn't speak to Ellis until they'd reached his office.

Lights blinked on in the dark room as they went inside. He sat behind his desk as Ellis followed him in. He rubbed an eye and gave a small sigh. As they'd traversed the ship, his annoyance at being woken and anger about the fighting had worked themselves out of his system, and now he was only tired and irritated.

"At ease," he muttered.

Ellis's upper lip, nose, and one of her eyes had puffed up and were turning purple. She hadn't bothered to wipe away the blood from her injuries, it was beginning to crust and turn brown. She looked a sorry sight, but he knew better than to immediately take her side.

"I need an explanation, corporal," he said. "What the hell was—"

"I want to resign," Ellis interrupted, her voice muffled somewhat by her swollen lip and nose.

"What?" Her answer had been the last thing he'd expected her to say. It took him a second to redirect his thinking. "Pull up that chair."

She scraped the chair's legs across the floor to his desk before plonking herself down on it.

When she'd taken a seat, he went on, "*Resign*?! You can't resign. Is this because of what was happening back there? You should know the Royal Marines doesn't tolerate bullying. I'll put a stop to it one way or another. But you can't just walk out. You still have...Uh..." He pulled up her file on his interface. "Four and a half years to serve yet. Ellis, serving as a marine isn't like working in a factory or bartending. You can't just leave whenever you feel like it. Didn't you understand that when you enlisted?"

"I want to return to the Britannic Isles," she said stubbornly. With a slight tremor in her voice, she added, "I want to go home."

He inwardly groaned. A homesick marine. That was all he needed. Especially one Colbourn had plans for. The brigadier would not be slow to forget or forgive if, when she got back, Ellis was no longer around.

"How did the fight start?" he asked, in an effort to change the subject.

Ellis's mouth remained shut.

"You were clearly being picked on," he said. "Are your cabin mates jealous about your recent promotion? It can piss people off if they think a newcomer is getting preferential treatment."

She gave no sign she'd even heard him, let alone that she was going to reply.

"How are the training sessions going?"

Silence.

"Corporal Ellis, I order you to answer."

"I don't remember how the fight started."

Wright thumped his desk. Her insubordination was infuriating. "What was going on in your quarters?" he asked, raising his voice. "Why were those marines attacking you?"

The woman's gaze flicked to him and away again. "All I know is, the one who was knocked out when you arrived—Abacha—he didn't have anything to do with it. They took him out when they first attacked me, because they knew he'd defend me. He shouldn't get into trouble for anything."

"Abacha?" The name rang a bell. He'd heard it recently. Wright found the man's file, and as he brought it up he remembered where he'd heard the name. Ellis had requested that the man be transferred along with her from the *Daisy* to the *Valiant*.

Wright scanned the file. Abacha had signed up three years prior to Ellis. He had a clean record and had been singled out for a mention in several reports. Then Wright realized another reason why the man's name was familiar. He'd picked him for the rescue mission to West BI. "You took his place on the rescue assignment. You told me he was sick."

The oddities surrounding that mission had made him forget the mental note he'd made to check her story.

"He *was* sick, sir."

She was a bad liar.

He reached into his desk drawer, grabbed a packet of wipes, and tossed it to her. She took one out and began to gingerly clean the blood from her face.

"Sounds like Abacha is a good friend."

Ellis winced as she pressed the wipe to the cut over her eye, but she didn't answer.

"Why are you making this so hard?" When she still didn't speak, he said, "Maybe I should throw you in the brig with the others. How long do you think you'd last in there with them now?"

She gave him a hurt look, and he immediately regretted his threat.

"I'd be okay," she said. "If I'd had more time, I would have wiped the floor with them."

He paused, taking in the enigma who sat before him. How had she learned to fight so well? Her short time in the Royal Marines couldn't have taught her that.

"I bet you would." He put his elbows on his desk and leaned forward. "Ellis, help me out here. The last thing I want to do is punish a victim of an unprovoked attack, but I need to know for sure you and Abacha really are innocent. Fighting is strictly prohibited. If you refuse to give your—"

"I...don't...care!" she enunciated loudly. "Don't you understand? I want to leave. I've had enough. I thought if I joined up I might make a difference, but it's been a waste of time. I don't want to be a corporal. I don't want to train other marines. I want to fight. The EAC are everywhere in the BI, and the Alliance has done *nothing* against them. They're in every town, every village. They were even in Nantgarw-y-garth, for god's sake. The only thing that lives there is sheep!"

A pause followed as he tried to figure out how to reach her. It would be a crime to let such a valuable person go, and, though she might not understand it, she would be more helpful to her cause working within the BA than outside it.

"Are you from that area?" he asked. Her file only stated BI as her address, probably because her town or village didn't exist anymore, having been destroyed in the EAC invasion.

"Yes, I'm from around there," she replied. "And I want to go back."

"Sheep weren't the only thing living on that mountain, though, were they?"

"What do you...Oh, the man you rescued. Yes, I suppose he was there, too."

"Did you see him? As we brought him back, I mean."

"No, I didn't. The medics put me under for the trip. I didn't wake up until after the operation on my back, and then he was in intensive care."

"Hm, well, he was in a terrible state. He shouldn't have been alive. I wouldn't call his survival a miracle, I'd call it impossible."

"That's strange. No one in their right mind would be out on the mountain in that kind of weather. Do we know why he was there?"

Wright shook his head. "Not a clue, though he wasn't in the open, he was inside a cave. We had to use the mortar to get to him, the same as we used it to free you. He began to regain consciousness the other day and I went to see him. He's entirely recovered, fit and healthy, without any lasting effects, as if nothing had happened to him. But he seems dangerous, so I'm keeping him under sedation until Colbourn returns."

"So, you're wondering if *I* might have an idea about who he is, or what he was doing, as I'm from that area."

"Right. Do you?"

"No, I can't help you. After the EAC moved in, all my family and friends scattered. I've lost contact..." She swallowed. "It's been so long."

"You might still know something. If I had to take a guess, I would say the man was alone in that cave without food or water for a very long time, quite possibly years."

"*Years*?"

"I know. It sounds impossible, right? Come over here. I want to show you something." Relieved that he seemed to have broken through the barrier the corporal had been putting up, he found his cam recording from the day. With Ellis leaning over his shoulder, he played it.

Once more, he saw the pitch black cave interior, his helmet's light slicing through the darkness. The picture shifted and bobbed as he moved in, reaching the stone platform in a few steps. On a second viewing, the dusty figure looked even more skeletal and long dead in the vid than it had appeared the first time around.

He heard the corporal suck in a breath. When he saw his own arms reaching out to pick up the man, he turned off the recording.

"*That* was what you rescued?" breathed Ellis.

"It was. And now *that* is now one hundred and eighty-five centimeters and about ninety kilos of living, breathing muscle."

"No, how can that be true?"

"Do you want me to show you? I could look up his medical file."

She returned to her chair and sat down. "I'm sorry, I can't explain it. I lived not far from there all my life, but I've never heard of anything like that. I mean, tourists would sometimes get lost and someone would have to go and help them, but... that's as much of a mystery to me as it is to you."

Her brow was furrowed, but, nevertheless, Wright had a feeling she was holding something back.

He decided not to push her. The patient in the sick bay wasn't a big concern, and he'd achieved his intention of softening the atmosphere between them. "Ellis, I'm going to be frank with you. If you're gone when Colbourn gets back, my life won't be worth living. And please believe me when I tell you you're going to help free the BI better up here than down there. I tell you what, you don't have to tell me anything about the fight. I'll speak to Abacha, and if he says you weren't the instigator, we'll leave it there."

She went to say something, but he continued, "Wait here a minute."

He left his office and went into the brigadier's, which was next door. Colbourn had given him access to everything in there while she was gone. After a brief search, he found what he was looking for.

He returned to his room and handed the broken necklace to the corporal. "I think this is yours."

The look of elation and gratitude she gave him as she took it told him he'd done the right thing. She teared up, and then ducked her head in embarrassment.

"Are you going to stay a Royal Marine?" Wright asked.

"Uh..." she replied, her voice thick. "I'll think about it."

14

Aloud ringing, underlain by a dull roar, throbbed in Hans's ears, and hot smoke filled his nostrils and throat, searing and choking him. He tried to get up but found he could not. A heavy weight was pressing against his back, pinning him down.

He quickly gave up trying to move. Each effort brought a feeling like knives stabbing his lungs. He guessed his ribs were broken. As he lay, face downward, in the remains of the meeting chamber, he began to assess his situation.

There had been an attack.

The dreadful whine of the approach of the first bomb remained vivid in his mind. Then the ceiling had exploded. Everyone who hadn't immediately reacted to the warning shout from the military section—most of those present—had dived to the floor. But little could be done to protect oneself from the rain of dagger-like, burning shards of wood.

How many had died there and then from the falling debris? Hans didn't know. There had been no time to take stock, no time to take action to protect the still-living. Then a second bomb had hit, this time blasting open the wall on the far side of the chamber, where the Queen, Speaker, and Prime Minister had stood to speak.

A cacophony of screams of fear and agony followed. Those who were still alive and uninjured had run for the exits. It had been a stampede, a rout. The weakest and unluckiest had fallen underfoot and been trampled. Some of the military officers had tried to take control, but it had been hopeless. Terror had driven the Council members mad. They obeyed no order or instruction, heard nothing, in their primal instinct to save their lives.

Except Josephine. His secretary had been one of the few to keep her head.

Hans's section hadn't been devastated by the first or second explosion, but the aisles between the seats were soon thickly jammed by those trying to escape. His staff also tried to exit that way. The people already on the steps became crushed by others trying to join them. He hadn't known what to do. He stood no chance of leaving via that route until the crowding eased, and meanwhile a third bomb seemed likely.

"Over the seats, Mr Jonte," Josephine had shouted over the noise. "We have to climb over the seats. This way." Lifting her skirt, she stepped neatly across the seat back in front of her. "Come on!" She held out her hand to encourage him.

Of course. In their panic, nearly everyone had reverted to habitual behavior. The usual way to leave tiered seating was via the stairs, so that's what they were trying to do. Only a handful like Josephine had realized there was a much better way to get out.

He joined his secretary, and together they began to climb down.

Fire was taking hold in the wooden building. The panic in the room grew even more intense. People were in a frenzy as they tried to retreat from the encroaching flames. The place was going up like tinder.

Smoke and ash were obscuring Hans's view of the rest of the chamber. All he could see were shadows of fleeing attendees, and the far side of the room was entirely obscured. He wondered if the Prime Minister and Speaker had been hurt. It seemed impossible they hadn't when their area had taken a direct hit. And what had happened to the Queen? Had she left after she'd given her speech and avoided the bombing?

"Please hurry, Mr Jonte," said Josephine. "We might be hit again."

The fact hadn't escaped him, but others had seen what she and he were doing and had begun to copy them, causing the seating to become crowded with slow-moving seat hoppers.

Who was attacking them? It had to be either the AP or EAC. Why had his officers uncovered no intel about the strike? How had the bombers infiltrated BA airspace? Barbados was in the heart of BA territory. The assault was an insult, an outrage!

"Mr Jonte!"

Josephine had nearly reached the bottom of the seating, but she'd stopped and was waiting for him. Paradoxically, the area at the base of the seating wasn't overwhelmed with people yet. Most were still fighting their way down the aisles, and if they now understood their mistake, it was impossible for many to leave their chosen escape route. They were trapped on the stairs, the fallen clogging the bases of the steps.

The fires crept closer.

A third bomb must have hit, but Hans didn't remember it. One moment he'd been about to reach Josephine, and the next he'd woken up within roaring, choking chaos. He guessed the ringing in his ears was from the explosion of the bomb. He was relieved the flames hadn't reached him yet, but he knew he didn't have much time.

With a great effort and agonizing stabs from his ribs, he managed to turn his head.

Immediately, he came face to face with Josephine's staring

eyes. His secretary was lying mere centimeters away. The force from the bomb must have thrown them together as it simultaneously buried them under the destroyed seating. Josephine hadn't survived the blast.

A twinge of sadness and regret hit him as he felt her loss. The woman had been more resourceful than he'd given her credit for.

That couldn't be helped now. He had only himself to rely on to get out of here.

Though something was pinning his torso, his arms were free. Hans dug his elbows into the debris that littered the floor and tried to pull himself forward. It took a great effort, but he succeeded in dragging himself a centimeter or two. Whatever was lying across his back had moved with him, however. He wasn't pulling himself out from under it.

He reached back with his right hand and touched warm metal. Feeling around, he discovered some kind of strut had landed on him. The chamber wasn't entirely made from wood after all. A skeleton of metal had supported it. The warmth of the steel told him fire wasn't far away.

Beyond the ringing of his ears and the roar of flames, he heard running footsteps. He listened, and they grew louder. He had no time to turn his head in their direction, but intuitively he shot out a hand, grabbing blindly. His fingers brushed fabric, and he gripped, hard.

A man crashed down, giving a shout of pain as he hit the shattered, smoking detritus from the explosions on the floor.

"Help me," moaned Hans, not loosening his hold on the man's pants leg. Through the smoke, he recognized a sooty, blood-splattered, military dress uniform.

The man kicked his leg, trying to make Hans let go, but his fingers were like iron, certain this officer was all that stood between him and death.

"All right," the man growled, and reached over Hans. His face and hair were black with ash.

He felt the strut lying on his back begin to move, causing fresh waves of pain. He gasped, but he didn't relax his grip on his savior. Grunting with effort, the officer inched the metal farther. Hans felt it slide onto his waist, and then lower, moving diagonally. When it reached his hips, he found he could wriggle forward, but in doing so, his hand released the pants leg.

"You're fine now," said the officer. "You can do the rest yourself."

The next second, he'd disappeared into the haze and drifting ashes.

Hans swore, but in his heart he didn't blame his reluctant helper. He would have done the same in the circumstances.

But perhaps the officer was right. Perhaps he *could* rescue himself now.

Pressing his palms against the floor, he tensed his stomach muscles and, grimacing at the shouts of protest from his broken ribs, levered himself upward. The strut slipped off him and clattered somewhere behind.

He was free.

He staggered upright. Instantly, a wave of coughing overcame him, sending him to his knees. The air was unbreathable. He began to feel faint and nauseated.

He started crawling.

Where was the way out?

He had no idea in which direction he now faced, and nothing he saw was recognizable any longer. Dead bodies lay in his path. He could hear cries for help, but he ignored them. He was only able to save himself, and even that was looking uncertain.

If only he knew where the nearest exit was. He had to find it before he suffocated or the fire reached him.

Suddenly, his arms and legs gave way, and he sprawled on his face.

As blackness edged in, narrowing his vision, he understood it was all over for him. He was going to die, and all his schemes and intrigues would come to nothing. The Britannic Alliance was going to remain a monarchy, and there wasn't anything he could do about it.

Then, like manna from heaven, a powerful jet of ice-cold water hit him. He shuddered at the sudden icy wetness, but he was jubilant. He might be saved yet. The fire service had finally arrived.

But he was too exhausted and too stifled by smoke to halt his slide into unconsciousness.

Just before darkness closed around him, he heard someone call out, "The Queen! The Queen is dead!"

15

The stairs to the top of Dwyr Orr's private tower curled in a spiral around its outer wall. She had no idea why the stone steps hadn't been built on the inside, sheltering the climber from the elements. The castle's origins were unknown, though she surmised it had to be at least three thousand years old, built during the age when stone edifices were the only protection from attack. Long, tedious wars had ravaged nations in those ancient times, a constant vying for land, wealth, and power.

As the Dwyr lifted the hem of her heavy gown and mounted the steps, she wondered if things had really changed that much in the intervening millennia. Perhaps it was only that fewer players participated in the great game now. The Britannic Alliance, the Antarctic Project, and the Earth Awareness Crusade were the only major powers anymore, and they all wanted the same thing: Control.

She turned the first curve of the spiral, which brought her to the ocean-facing side of the tower. A dark sea churned before her, and the wind swept her river of black hair away from her face. At the horizon, the sky was lightening, fading out the stars in the east and gilding distant waves in the busy water.

Touching the stone rail, she paused to take in the view, assessing the strength of light from the as-yet invisible sun. She still had plenty of time.

She continued to climb.

No doubt each point of the triangle of powers that fought for Earth believed their cause to be just, she reflected, but at the same time she was confident the EAC was the only righteous one. Her order was the only organization that held the planet herself in the heart of its doctrine. The living Earth was a sacred being, and she, with the help of her followers, intended to ensure its proper treatment in perpetuity.

What cause could be more pure and noble?

Unfortunately, along the way, sacrifices had to be made. Joining forces with Ua Talman meant temporarily allowing the AP's violation of the Earth's sanctity to continue. But if it meant that, together, they could put an end to the BA, it would be worth it. As long as she did penance, the imbalance would be redressed, and when Talman and his deluded disciples departed, the world would be whole once more and for eternity.

When she'd nearly reached the door at the top of the tower, she halted her climb for a second time. Now she faced inland, where the castle's ramparts rose tall, wide, and strong, surrounding the inner courtyard far below. Beyond the fortification, the green mountains of West BI spread out as far as she could see, gaining color at the approach of the sun.

It was a beautiful land, and she was glad she had wrested it from the BA's hands. Had the country remained under their government, they would have continued to exploit it, prioritizing the needs of their citizens over everything else. Now she was its guardian, she would reassert the natural order.

She climbed the final steps.

The door to her sanctum at the top of the tower was never locked. Everyone who lived and worked in the castle knew that entry to anyone except herself was strictly forbidden.

She grasped the iron ring at the door's edge, turned it, pushed open the heavy wooden door, and stepped inside.

The side of the tower wall that faced inland was solid stone; the other half, facing the ocean, consisted of stone struts between empty squares. The cold sea breeze blew strongly at the top of the tower. Kala's skin rose into goosebumps, despite the thickness of her robe.

Propped against a wall was a short staff that had long, lithe silver birch twigs tied around one end. The young shoots had lost their fresh, green shine and were coated brown.

Kala unfastened the lacing at the front of her robe, loosening the tightness around her waist and hips, and allowed the gown to drop to the floor. She stepped out from it, naked. Reaching down, she undid the laces of her shoes and pulled them off. The brown-stained, granite-tiled floor was icy beneath her bare feet. She began to shiver, and her teeth chattered.

She stepped to the birch switch and picked it up.

After returning to the center of the circular room, she moved her discarded clothing and knelt down on the cold floor, facing the sea. She pulled all her hair forward so that it spilled over her knees, leaving her back bare.

From below came the sound of waves smashing into rocks, rhythmic and relentless.

Clenching her teeth, she gripped the switch stoically and waited patiently for the edge of the sun to appear above the watery horizon.

Earth slowly spun in space, bearing her toward the light of its star. Her body trembled and shook. Finally, she was rewarded with a sunbeam striking out over the ocean.

A new day had begun.

She raised the rod over her right shoulder and, with practiced skill, struck her back with the whip-like twigs. This first strike made little impression against the tough, ridged scars.

She would need to strike herself many times to break her skin, but break her skin she must. Earth required a blood sacrifice. The resources the AP ripped from it while allied with the EAC must be paid for in order to maintain the balance between humanity and its home.

Kala struck her back again, harder this time. She moved the staff to her other shoulder, and hit herself again.

As she continued to work and the sun rose, she warmed up. The chilliness of her position didn't affect her anymore. Sweat broke out on her face and neck and soddened her armpits. Her animal smell rose around her. She breathed it in, relishing her musk, which mixed with the smell of the sea.

After ten or fifteen minutes, she was gratified to feel a trickle run down her back and over her buttocks. She was bleeding freely at last. When she knelt in a puddle of her own blood, she would stop.

Then a scraping sound came from behind her, the sound of metal against metal.

Someone was opening the door!

She put down her flail and looked over her shoulder, ready to snap a reproof at the newcomer. Whoever it was would receive a severe punishment for disturbing her.

The door opened, and a boy peered around it.

"*Perran!*"

The adolescent's eyes stretched wide and his pupils darkened as he took in the sight of her naked, bloody back.

"What are you doing, Mummy?"

"Get out!" she snapped. "Who gave you permission to climb my tower? Get away from here!"

But he didn't move. His eyes only widened further and his mouth hung open.

"Leave, now! Or I'll have you flogged."

Perran did begin to withdraw, but his gaze lingered on her, an inscrutable expression on his face.

"Out!"

He left, and the door closed.

The iron catch swung shut.

Vexed and irked that her son had witnessed her act of sacrifice, she continued with her task, but it was hard to fight the distraction. Instead of focusing on the rising sun and devotional thoughts as she should have, she found herself thinking of Perran's conception and childhood.

She didn't know who his earthly father was. Many men had come to her in the guise of the Horned God that night in the oak grove, and Perran's appearance gave no clue about his sire —he looked like a male version of herself. Not that his physical father mattered. He was hers and hers alone to raise in the ways of the Crusade. When he matured to a man, a great role awaited him.

Later, when her arms and back throbbed painfully and her blood sat sticky around her knees, Kala stopped. Her penance completed, she rose from the floor and returned the dripping switch to its position next to the wall.

She almost cried out as she put on her gown and the cloth contacted her open, dripping flesh, but she bit her lip. Complaining when she was the person who had the honor to make the sacrifice would be churlish.

She slipped on her shoes and walked to the door. Turning the iron ring, she pulled it open and stepped out onto the stone stairway. Before she began to descend, she noticed something odd. Far below, within the castle's inner courtyard, the level of activity was far greater than usual. People were running about or congregating in the open space, as if to discuss an important event. She lifted her skirts and began to walk down the steps.

When she'd nearly reached the bottom of the tower, the

castle's bell began to toll, and faintly, between the chimes, she heard the cry, "Queen Alice is dead!"

She halted.

They'd done it. The EAC and AP's air fleet had broken through the Britannic Alliance's defenses and sent the queen to her grave. The blow to the BA's morale would be devastating. They had ripped the heart from their mutual enemy.

Only one thing now stood in their way, one final achievement that would be the coup de grace: They had to find the man who had been taken from the mountain at Nantgarw-y-garth, just as her soldiers had been closing in on him. Did the BA know who he was? Did they even believe his existence was possible? She barely believed it herself.

If the Crusade were to succeed, he had to die.

16

C olbourn was back. She'd arrived during the quiet shift and—for once—she hadn't summoned Wright to her office immediately. Instead, her comm requesting his presence had popped into his mind as soon as he woke. He wondered if she was becoming more considerate of others, but it turned out he was wrong.

After the brigadier's summons came an urgent news report: the General Council had been bombed, and, along with other important figures, the Queen had been killed.

He sat up in bed and rubbed his head. It was quite the news to wake up to. How on Earth had it been possible to attack the General Council? Even if the time and location had been leaked, the army and navy would have set up heavy defenses of the area.

He checked the rest of the news report.

It was believed the AP and the EAC had mounted a joint attack. So the two had joined forces? That spelled serious trouble for the BA.

He got up and walked to his shower room.

Poor Queen Alice. The old lady hadn't deserved to die in

such a violent fashion. She'd been on the throne all his life, and, as far as he knew, she'd never been anything but kind and gentle. He guessed Prince Frederick was now king and preparations for his coronation would be underway. Where would they hold it? If a bombing raid against the General Council in the heart of the BA's domain could succeed, was anywhere on Earth safe anymore?

So much had changed within just a few hours.

A second summons arrived from Colbourn:

You've been awake five minutes already, Wright. Where are you?

HE STOOD outside Colbourn's office, awaiting admittance. For all her impatience in demanding his attendance, she was being awfully slow at actually letting him in. He straightened his uniform jacket and shifted his weight to his other foot.

After another full minute, the door finally slid open.

Wright almost swore in surprise, but stopped himself just in time. He gawped at the scene inside as a medic pushed past him on her way out.

The brigadier had been burned, quite severely. One side of her face was red and blistered and half her hair had been singed away. Her skin glistened, wet with ointment. She was only partially dressed. Her shirt covered the right-hand side of her torso, but her left arm and chest were swathed in dressings, which the medic must have been applying or renewing while he waited.

"Close your mouth, man, and sit down."

Wright snapped his jaw shut, unaware it had fallen open.

"Ma'am, I had no idea...I'm very sorry..."

The withering look Colbourn made his words dry up. She didn't need or want his pity.

He took a seat.

"I'm sure it's obvious we're in a serious situation," she said. "The *Valiant* and her corvettes are to mobilize, battle ready, within the next three hours. I haven't received the coordinates yet, but we must go as soon as they arrive."

"Understood, ma'am."

"You don't need to do anything right now. I've already given the orders. I wanted to talk to you about something else."

He waited, but she didn't speak immediately. Some emotion seemed to come over her. Sorrow? Regret? He couldn't tell. She lost her usual steely look and suddenly appeared tired and older, as if the inner strength and resolve that had kept her going for years was weakening. She passed a hand over her forehead and gasped in pain as she accidentally touched her seared skin.

Finally, she seemed to decide what she wanted to say. "Wright, I'll speak plainly. As things stand at the moment... we're screwed."

It was not the kind of thing he expected to hear from the brigadier.

In the years she'd been his CO, she'd never been anything except positive and determined. The woman was the exact opposite of a quitter. At times, he'd suspected she would fight off Death himself when he finally came calling.

"I-I'm sorry, ma'am?"

"That's twice you've apologized to me for no reason. If you do it once more, I'll have you thrown in the brig."

"Sorr—" He sealed his lips.

Colbourn gingerly rearranged herself slightly in her chair, as if to try to get more comfortable, wincing as she moved. "You're too young to remember how things used to be, major. When I first entered the Royal Marines as an officer cadet, the BA was at the peak of its power. We'd been successfully rooting out and putting a stop to AP activities for years, preventing damage to ecosystems and helping to preserve Earth's resources. Other nations lived in security because of us, and, for the most part, the planet was a safe and pleasant place. The EAC was only a fledgling organization, one that, at the time, was believed to be a force for good. We welcomed it with open arms."

"I learned about it at school," said Wright, wondering where the brigadier was going. This was history. He wasn't sure what it had to do with what was happening now. "Then the EAC's true agenda was revealed, after it had begun to weaken the BA. Then we threw them out, and..."

Colbourn was shaking her head. "That's the story the politicians love to tell, and that's what they demand goes down in the history books, but the truth is, the rise of the EAC isn't to blame for the BA's changing fortunes. The rot had already begun from within, and the EAC only exploited the opportunity. If the BA had been a solid, ethical, incorruptible entity, the EAC would never have been able to get a foothold. But they saw the infighting, the petty jealousies, the machinations and intrigues, and they found it easy to pit us against each other. Military branch against military branch, politician against politician, business sector against business sector. When the army and the navy don't work together, battles are lost. When politicians refuse to agree on anything, economies and the citizens' well-being suffer. When business sectors undermine each other, corporations collapse."

She paused and turned to the motto framed on the wall behind her. She read it out quietly, as if talking to herself: "Per Mare, Per Terram, Per Astra."

By sea, by land, by the stars.

Returning her attention to Wright, she said, "It was even true within the ranks of the Royal Marines, and it still is. I may be a bad-tempered, crotchety old bitch, but if you knew the decades of bullshit I've endured, you would understand why."

She spared him an almost-indiscernible smile.

He didn't bother to deny her description of herself. The brigadier was certainly not fishing for compliments.

"The attack on the General Council has probably come as a shock to you, but I've been expecting it for years. Every few months there's a new defeat, another small territory lost. The assault at the heart of BA territory and the murder of Queen Alice are just more nails in the coffin. I don't know what the answer is. It seems things have gone too far, and there's nothing anyone can do to stop it. I've been trying not to dwell on the truth, but my injury has brought my mortality into painful relief. I thought, while I still can, I should let you know the true state of things."

She was silent, but, for once, she didn't seem intent on kicking him out of her office and off to work as soon as humanly possible. He took advantage of her unusual frame of mind to properly digest what she'd said. The more he thought about it, the more he understood the severity of the situation. The brigadier was the last person who would openly state the BA's total defeat was likely. If *she* was telling him this, was there any hope at all?

"What you do about it is up to you," Colbourn said finally. "I've decided I'm going to stick it out to the end, but you're still young, and none of this is your fault. I don't see why people like you should become cannon fodder for the incompetents above you."

"What do you think the future holds?" he asked, in reflex. She seemed to be suggesting that he got out before everything fell apart, but what would he do? Where would he go? He couldn't imagine a life outside of military service. The brigadier had thrown him a spin ball and he didn't know what to do with it.

"Honestly? I think, with the help of the AP, the EAC will wipe us off the map. It will seize every last scrap of BA soil and water on Earth and all our space territories. Then, if the AP's colony ships aren't completed in time for them to escape, the Crusade will turn on them and destroy them, too. After that, all humanity will be forced to live under the odious cult, gradually devolving into barbarism, cannibalism, and who knows what else, until we're back to grunting at each other while we hunt with spears. Within a single lifespan, thousands of years of human civilization will be gone."

"You don't paint a very pretty picture."

"There's no point in sugar-coating it, major."

"There has to be something we can do."

"I used to believe so, but now I'm not sure there is. Perhaps what's happening is inevitable. Perhaps there's something about the human species that prevents it from ever truly over-coming its instinct to destroy and kill. Perhaps we have always been, and will ever be, doomed."

17

A bacha snoring in his rack above her, the ship's cat, Boots, transplanted from the *Daisy*, curling at her feet, and the farting, heavy, rhythmic breathing, and mumbled words of marines talking in their sleep told Taylan she was the only one awake in the cabin.

She pushed her hand between her mattress and bed frame and took out her interface. Electronics after lights out were strictly forbidden, but she didn't give a shit anymore. The *Valiant* was mobilizing, and her already slim chances of returning to West BI were gone. She would have to remain in military service and fight, when she could have been...

She opened her device, turned down the brightness, and navigated the familiar, well-trodden digital path to the vids buried in her files.

After escaping to Ireland, she'd only managed to retrieve a small amount of her personal data from the lifetime's worth she had in her cloud before the EAC blew the banks on BI, thus destroying most records of her life along with quadrillions more items of private, governmental, and corporate information.

She usually viewed the few vids she had remaining in chronological order. It had always seemed the best way to try to make sense of everything that had happened, but in truth it never really worked.

This time, instead of going automatically to her earliest recording, made when she was a child, she picked the last one, created just before she'd fled the BI and enlisted with the Royal Marines.

She tapped the screen, connecting the vid to her implanted comm so only she would hear the audio, rested her head on her pillow, and watched.

She'd begun recording just before the attack, clipping her small interface to the front of her jacket. Why exactly she'd decided to capture that moment, she didn't know. Maybe, somehow, she'd foreseen what would happen.

A brilliant green hillside. It was raining, the raindrops on the screen distorting the picture. The scene jerked up and down as she ran, but then her pace had slowed. She'd turned, looking back. Behind her ran the slower of her neighbors: the old, the young, the sick, the disabled.

Beyond them, over the rise, came EAC troops, firing.

Pivoting forward again, she'd raced on.

Her emotions from the time swept over her, as if she were there again: fear she and her family would die, guilt that she couldn't do anything to help the others, her friends, her neighbors. She had no weapon, and even if she had, stopping to fight off the invaders would put her children in more danger.

Through the rain, the object of their flight appeared. At the base of the hill an old farmhouse huddled, and a narrow ribbon of gray road wound away from it across the landscape. If they could reach the building, they had a chance of escaping.

Suddenly, a chubby, pink knee blocked the camera's view.

Kayla.

Taylan gripped her interface tighter.

A scream!

One of the villagers had been hit. The EAC were within firing range.

They would pick them off, shooting the slowest runners first, gradually catching up to them and shooting more and more until no one was left. The EAC took no prisoners. They were not interested in the natives of any area they stole. Anyone who wasn't in their cult was impure and beyond redemption. They wanted only the land for their own people.

It had become a race to the death.

A second scream. This one went on for long seconds until it abruptly cut off.

The knee blocking the view moved as Taylan shifted her daughter to her other hip. As she did so, her jacket swung and her interface caught a glimpse of Patrin, running ahead. He'd always been fast, beating all the other boys his age at school.

The farmhouse had moved closer.

She recalled her terror, wondering if they would make it.

The bumping, lurching recording picked up movement at the door to the farmhouse. It had opened, and figures were emerging.

For a few terrifying heartbeats she'd thought they were EAC troops, the house already in enemy hands, and they were coming out to attack from the opposite side. She, her children, and the rest of her village would be slaughtered.

But they were not. The men and women now running toward them were West BI resistance. They were coming to their rescue.

For some, it was already too late. As the resistance fighters were speeding up the hill toward them, more shouts of pain and agony came from the rear. Taylan thought she recognized the voices, but she didn't dare take the time to look around and see who had fallen.

She only had to make it to the farmhouse, or, failing that, if she was hit, she could cover Kayla with her body. Maybe the resistance fighters would find her later. Patrin would make it on his own. He was nearly in the lead, despite his young years. He would make it. He had to make it.

The resistance was forking into groups and swinging out, probably intending to attack the EAC from each side to avoid catching the villagers in crossfire. A handful continued to run directly ahead.

The recording continued another half a minute as she'd run on, dashing through the long, wet grass, fearful of tripping—a misstep could be the death of her and her daughter.

One of the fighters had reached Patrin! The woman spurred the exhausted boy on and called out to the other villagers to run, that there were transports at the farmhouse ready to take them somewhere safe.

Then the heavens seemed to open and what had been an annoying drizzle became a downpour. The recording at this point was nothing more than a blur of moving colors, the sound of the pelting rain mixed with the shouting and yells of pain. She remembered the water blinding her and turning the hillside into a river.

Though she'd barely been able to see, she hadn't slackened her pace. She knew where the house sat. All she had to do was get there. So it was that she blindly ran directly into a fighter coming from the other direction. They bounced off each other, then both hit the ground and tumbled down the slope. Clutching her screaming daughter, she protected Kayla's head with one hand until she came to a stop.

When she stood up, she was nearly at the refuge. The low stone wall marking the boundary of the farmyard was only meters away. When she couldn't see Patrin, she assumed he was already inside and hopefully being loaded onto one of the trucks to make an escape. Behind, up on the hill, the villagers were streaming down like the rain pelting from the heavens, and the fighters were engaging with the EAC troops.

The man she'd collided with was rising to his feet, but as he did so, he cried out and collapsed.

Taylan ran over to him. "I'm so sorry. Are you okay?"

The fighter couldn't answer. He only gripped his knee and gasped and grimaced in pain.

He must have dislocated his knee or broken a bone.

"Can you get up? Let me help you inside."

The man still didn't answer, but he lifted his arm, and she helped him to his feet. Her child on one hip, and the resistance member's arm over her shoulder, she slowly walked to the farmhouse entrance.

An old woman was waiting there. The minute she saw Kayla, she beckoned. "We have a transport ready to go. We're taking all the mothers and children first."

"Is that where my son has gone?" asked Taylan, helping the fighter hobble through the doorway.

"The little boy, about seven years old?"

"He's six, but, yes."

"He's already on board. Hurry, there isn't much time."

The resistance fighter slid onto a nearby chair. He was pale and sweaty, and blood was seeping through his pants leg. Her neighbors were arriving at the farmhouse and flooding into it. Out on the hillside, the fighting had begun in earnest.

Taylan looked at the man she'd accidentally injured. The West BI Resistance was one person down, and it was her fault.

"Do you know where the children are going?" she asked the woman.

"A safe house. From there, they'll travel to Anglesey and then sail to Dublin."

She clenched her jaw, indecision hounding her.

"Mummy," said Kayla, patting her face.

Suddenly, Taylan held out her daughter to the old woman. "Take her to the truck. You go with her."

Kayla cried and struggled, trying to get back onto Taylan's hip.

"What?" the woman said. "No, I can't do that. You must go with your child."

"Please. I'm able-bodied and fit. I should fight. I want to help stop the EAC reaching the transports. I can make a difference. I know I can. Please take her."

With a look of reluctance, the woman took Kayla into her arms.

The little girl screamed.

Taylan stooped down and slid the injured man's weapon from his shoulder. He was in too much pain to protest. The old woman hadn't moved.

"Please, go," Taylan repeated loudly over the sound of her daughter's wailing. "Look after my kids. Their names are Kayla and Patrin. I'll follow later."

The woman nodded and carried Kayla away, only holding on to the yelling, struggling child with some difficulty.

Taylan forced her way against the tide of incoming people and out into the rain.

"Little chick."

The screen blacked out. The recording ended. Her interface had been hit by a stray pulse round, saving her life. The device had been a total loss, but its automatic upload to her cloud meant the recording had survived.

"Little chick."

Taylan looked up, dragged away from the farmhouse in West BI and the green hillside and the pouring rain, and returned to the *Valiant*, her new life, and the silent, dark cabin.

"You shouldn't watch those vids," said Abacha. "They only make you sad."

He was leaning down from his bunk, though she could only

just make him out. She wiped the wetness from her face. Without replying to her friend, she turned off the interface and slid it between her mattress and bed frame.

"And no more picking fights with the knuckle-draggers, okay?" he said. "I don't like lying for you, especially not to a good guy like Wright. And my head's not so hard that it can take all the punishment it gets trying to defend you."

"I don't need your help."

Abacha sighed and lay down, making the bed springs creak.

18

The Caribbean island of Antigua was an emerald in a sapphire sea, hoving into view as the shuttle banked. According to Dwyr Orr, while fighting on Barbados continued, Antigua was safely in the hands of the combined EAC and AP forces. The island had been the first to fall, succumbing to EAC landing forces in an operation that incurred little damage.

Lorcan was glad. With its infrastructure intact, harvesting Antigua's resources would be all the easier. But he doubted he would have time to pay the place a visit. He had more important business to attend to, and he didn't like spending more than twenty-four hours away from his shipbuilding sites. He simply couldn't trust the nincompoops working for him not to cock something up in his absence.

The shuttle evened out as it dipped lower. White caps on the waves below became visible under the brilliant blue sky. Lorcan lowered the arm rests on each side of his seat. His private space/air vessel held four passenger seats, but, as usual, the rest were empty. He couldn't recall the last time he'd had company on a trip, for business or the rare recreational jaunt he allowed himself. He'd preferred things that way for a long time, though he couldn't deny that a woman like Dwyr Orr might be a pleasant occasional ornament.

"Prepare to submerge, sir," said the pilot over the intercom.

He fastened his seat belt.

The shuttle slowed and its nose dipped. The moment of passing from air to water was a critical one. The speed and angle had to be such that the vessel's buoyancy was counteracted, allowing it to plunge into the ocean without damaging its structural integrity. The ship's computer would do the hard work, but the pilot was trained to perform the maneuver manually if necessary. The man was one of the very few people Lorcan trusted with his life, and he was well compensated for it. Additionally, when the day of departure came, the pilot and his family's sleep capsules on the *Bres* would be guaranteed.

It was the main motivator of every one of his vast team, he guessed. Each had their own motivation, but they all wanted to come along.

The stomach-lurching impact hit, forcing him sharply forward. Outside his window, water appeared to boil. The cabin darkened, and echoes of churning sea infiltrated it. Internal and external lights came on simultaneously.

The shuttle straightened up, and he relaxed and unclipped his seat belt. The journey to the seabed would take another half an hour.

Boredom was already nagging at him. He opened a slot on his arm rest and pulled out an ear bud, which he popped into his right ear before selecting a report from Kekoa on the screen in the opposite arm rest.

Closing his eyes, he relaxed in his seat and listened. The report began with a summary of Kekoa's latest work on *Bres's* habitats, specifically mentioning the installation of wind machines at West Lake. He smiled. She was trying to find favor, but she still wouldn't receive her docked credits. He couldn't afford to allow any of them to get sloppy.

As Kekoa's voice droned on, drowsiness crept up on him. The monotonous rendition of the report seemed to fade while the drone of the shuttle's engine grew louder, and he felt himself slipping away into slumber. He didn't fight it. A nap would pass the time.

He was in his private suite, sipping champagne with Dwyr Orr. She didn't speak as she sat facing him, her glass in her hand, only watching him with her dark eyes, an amused expression on her face. He wasn't sure what she found amusing, but he was not offended.

She put down her glass, and, without a word, began to untie the laced cords at her bosom.

He choked in surprise.

Then he tried to speak, to protest, but his tongue and lips would not obey him. He tried to stand and move away, but he couldn't. It was as if an invisible, heavy blanket was weighing his body down.

The Dwyr slipped her gown from her shoulders, exposing her naked flesh. Lorcan didn't want to look, but he couldn't help himself. Animal desire welled up in him, mixed with outrage and shame. His lungs labored as he desperately sought an exit from the situation.

She moved closer.

He caught her scent—it was a strange odor, reminding him of wood smoke mixed with roses. The odd perfume only increased his hunger for her.

She leaned in, turning her head so their lips—

Lorcan jerked awake, panting and wet with sweat.

His dream receded, and the audio of Kekoa's report surged louder. Somehow, the cabin looked unfamiliar and otherworldly though it was identical to how it had been before he'd fallen asleep. He roughly pulled out the ear bud and sat up. Uncomfortable prickles ran across his skin.

Was someone watching him?

It was impossible. Apart from the pilot in his separate cabin, he was alone. Outside, the water was empty and, beyond the range of the shuttle's beams, dark.

Why did he feel he was being observed?

"Five minutes to arrival, sir," said the pilot.

Lorcan wiped his face, and then pressed the button to retract the ear bud into its slot. He needed to compose himself. He drew in a deep breath and exhaled, focusing his mind on his visit.

Why had he dreamed that scenario? It had felt so real.

The shuttle's speed had slowed almost to a stop. Beyond the window sat the opening to an underwater bay. The pilot eased the vessel another few meters forward, into the bay, before shutting off the engines.

Lorcan waited for the small impact as the shuttle hit the buffer. After the bounce, the bay's pumps started up, and the water drained out. Gradually, the vessel dropped lower until it rested on the bay floor. He got out of his seat and went to the hatch. The pilot was there before him and already opening it.

Outside, the site's chief engineer and coordinator, Khanh, was already waiting, standing at the other end of the ramp that led out of the bay. "It's good to see you, sir."

He nodded and stepped onto ridged metal plate. Small sea creatures flopped and crawled on the floor as he walked up the ramp to the exit. The scent of the ocean was strong.

"All operations are ready for your inspection," said Khanh. "The workers are keen to show you the results of their hard work."

Lorcan grunted a non-committal reply. He didn't want to waste time touring the station itself—he'd seen enough living quarters and admin departments to last a lifetime, so he told her he wanted to go to the mine site, directly and immediately.

"Oh, yes, of course," she replied, looking surprised. "Well, we're in the right place. We can take a submersible from the next bay over."

She led him to the adjacent hatch and thumbed a security code into the panel. There was the sound of metal locks releasing, and Khanh turned the wheel. Swinging the hatch open, she stooped and stepped through onto a second ramp before walking down to a small submersible.

The walls and floor in here were dry and the ocean wildlife that had made its way inside was long dead. A horrible, rotting smell pervaded the place. Lorcan lifted his upper lip.

"How often is the site visually inspected?" he asked.

"Twice-daily. We don't usually use this submersible. It's a reserve as it's only a two-seater."

Lorcan acknowledged her explanation with a second grunt.

THE BARRACUDA RIDGE MINE spanned fifteen kilometers of seabed, and it was the Antarctic Project's most productive source of gold, copper, and cobalt. Up until the successful EAC/AP attack on the Britannic Alliance's Caribbean Territory, the site had been forced to perform its operations in secrecy, and Lorcan had resented the additional expense this entailed. Now, there was no need for subterfuge. The BA had its hands full defending the islands it continued to hold—for the time being.

As Khanh piloted the narrow craft through the dark water, she didn't speak, apparently quick to catch onto his dislike of unnecessary chatter. He liked that the woman was a fast learner. The hum of the engine was the only sound.

Above the transparent submersible's hull, the black ocean

passed by. At this depth, no light penetrated from the surface. Below, a sandy seabed was dimly revealed by the vessel's lights. Lorcan saw crabs and a dead fish being devoured by worms. Many-fronded plants or animals sprouted in patches, colorless and gently moving in the current.

He stole a sidelong glance at Khanh. For her level of seniority, she seemed young. She was attractive, mahogany-skinned, and black-haired. His mind began traveling along a certain line of thought, but he caught himself, sickened. He deliberately diverted his attention to the view ahead.

It was Dwyr Orr's fault. Firstly, her overly flirtatious behavior when she'd come to see him, and, secondly, the dream he'd had. Though it seemed unfair to blame her for the wanderings of his subconscious, he couldn't help but feel she was somehow responsible.

"We're getting close," said Khanh. "Can you see? Just over there." She indicated with her gaze, keeping her hands on the submersible's controls.

He picked out the lights in the darkness, fuzzy and shifting, as if beyond the heat shimmer above a road on a hot day.

"Why do the extractors' lights look like that?" he asked. "Is it the ocean currents?"

"No, some hydrothermal vents stand between us and the main operation."

"Ah, I see." He'd known about the vents. Seawater, superheated through contact with tectonic subduction zones, spurted from them but didn't boil due to the pressure at that depth. They were rich with minerals and the entire reason for the mining operation, but he'd never set eyes on them before.

The submersible drew closer to the natural undersea structures, and he began to make out their tall, columnar forms, the funnels for the intensely hot water. The submersible's lights brought out their vivid colors, garish and artificial-looking in the seascape.

"They're quite spectacular, aren't they?" commented Khanh. "I would take us in to give you a better look, but it's dangerous to get too close."

"No, this is close enough." Lorcan gazed at the strange phenomena. They looked like something he might expect to see on an alien planet one day, yet here they were on Earth.

"In a way," Khanh said, "it's a pity we have to destroy them to extract the ore."

"A pity?" He turned to her in annoyance. "It isn't a pity at all. I concede they may be rather pretty, but they're a resource, and resources are there to be exploited. What's the point of them sitting there for hundreds of thousands of years, no use to anyone? Eventually, at the encroachment of our bloated sun, even these vents will crumble and disperse to dust. What'll be the point of them then? Much better to put them to a practical purpose for the furtherment of humanity, and move on. The galaxy is there for us, and us alone, Khanh. Remember that. I don't like my staff getting sentimental."

Looking suitably abashed at his admonishment, the chief engineer piloted their machine onward in silence, taking a route that avoided the vents.

Throughout his inspection of the mining site and the rest of his visit, her mood remained subdued, but Lorcan didn't pay her any mind.

Overall, he was pleased with what he saw, and before he left to return to the *Bres*, he asked Khanh to formulate plans to double the Barracuda's production, and to liaise with his prospecting team to seek out new potential deep sea mining sites. His regular mines in China were costing him more and more to run each year, yet producing less and less ore. If he could recreate Barracuda's success elsewhere, he might be able to bring forward the completion of the Project by several months.

19

"He has to come off sedation immediately," said Colbourn. "He must be ambulatory in case we're attacked. I can't have my medics wasting their time moving a perfectly fit and healthy man."

"But—"

"Are you questioning my order, major?"

"Of course not." Wright inwardly sighed. Colbourn hadn't been around when the man he'd rescued had woken up; she hadn't seen him go berserk or the effort it had taken to subdue him. Knowing the brigadier, she would also most likely refuse to view the security vid. She was the kind of officer who knew no middle ground, which made her very good and very bad at her job.

"Medic," Colbourn barked.

"Er, doctor, actually," corrected the duty doc, the same person who had told Wright about the patient waking up.

"Cease sedation on this patient," Colbourn continued, without acknowledging her mistake.

"Gladly," said the doctor. "I think it's for the best," she added, to Wright. "We can't keep him under forever." She leaned over the miraculous mummy-turned-living-human-being and closed the valve on the drip that was running into his hand. Next, she gently pulled out the cannula and puffed a spray on the insertion point, instantly drying up the blood leaking out. "He should be awake in an hour or so."

"That's that," Colbourn said with an air of finality. "I'll be in my office," she said, exiting the sick bay.

Wright grimaced. That was not *that*, not by a long shot, if his previous experience of the wakened patient was anything to go by.

"I guess I'd better leave the restraints on," said the doc.

The man was now dressed in a hospital gown and lying under a sheet. He continued to look remarkably healthy, and his hair and beard had been growing incredibly fast, now a couple of centimeters longer than when the major had seen him a few days ago.

"Yes, leave them on," he said, "and let me know as soon as he begins to come around."

With a sense of foreboding, he walked out of the bay and headed toward one of the *Valiant's* gyms. Ellis was due to provide support for the first time at a training session, and he wanted to observe her. The corporal was another problem pressing on his mind. She was clearly troubled, and while he usually avoided getting too involved in the day to day lives of the marines, she was a special case. She was an exceptional combatant, and in the coming war against the joined EAC and AP forces, they would need every edge they had.

He took the elevator outside the gym to the second level and walked out onto the gallery. Resting his elbows on the railing, he looked down. The session had already begun. The instructor was explaining a move that could be deployed when attacked from behind. The man asked Ellis to step forward and take part in a demonstration.

She got up from her spot on the mat with the trainees, and

as she walked over to the instructor, she happened to glance up. She registered Wright watching. She gave him a sullen look— what was the woman's problem? After halting at the instructor's side, she turned to face the watching men and women, her legs standing apart and her hands held loosely together behind her back.

Another participant was called: a burly male marine who stood a head taller than Ellis, who was above average height herself, and about twice as wide. He swaggered toward her, grinning. She remained stony-faced, not even looking at him.

Wright's sense of foreboding over the waking patient transferred to the young corporal. She was excellent at combat, but the man the training sergeant had set her up against was a giant. If the marine didn't hold back, Ellis was in danger of getting seriously hurt. What was the trainer doing? Was he trying to prove a point? Did he resent being told to use Ellis as support for his sessions? Wright recalled the first time he'd seen her, at the briefing session for the rescue mission. He'd sensed the other marines didn't like her then. And there had been that fight in the cabin. The corporal had never stated she didn't start it. Was Ellis universally disliked, except for that other marine, Abacha, who she'd requested be transferred with her to the *Valiant*?

The instructor told her to stand with her back to the large marine. She swiveled around and let her arms hang loose at her sides. The instructor stepped backward, and then nodded at her would-be attacker.

The marine immediately ran at her, but before he reached her, she dropped like a stone into a squat, causing him to overbalance as his hands swiped empty air. Reaching above and behind her, she grabbed his hips and tugged him the rest of the way over her, so he ended up sprawling on the mat. She was on him in a split second, driving her fist into his stomach.

Wright heard the thud of impact and the explosive groan from the victim even away up in the gallery.

Ellis was pulling back her arm for a second punch when the instructor reached her and grabbed it.

She wrenched her arm from him and leapt up, furious. The marine she'd felled rolled onto his side, clutching his stomach.

"That was *not* the move I'm teaching, corporal!" The instructor's angry voice echoed around the gym.

"It was the best move in the circumstances! I used his weight against him. That's what you should—"

"How the hell are you supposed to guess the weight of an attacker you can't see?"

"But I did see him!" She got up in the sergeant's face and poked his chest.

Anger and outrage drained the color from the man's face, but that didn't stop her. "If you want—"

"Ellis, stand down!" Wright yelled from the gallery.

Everyone's gazes turned to him, many looking surprised as if they were noticing him for the first time.

"Wait for me outside, corporal," he ordered.

In the privacy of the elevator as it descended to the first level of the gym, he cursed, all concern for Ellis's well being gone. He had enough on his plate without dealing with undisciplined, hot-headed non-coms.

She was leaning against the bulkhead in the passageway, her arms folded. As he approached, she stood to half-hearted attention.

"My office," he said and set off, not checking if she was following.

He felt like he'd finally seen the real Ellis. *This* was why no one liked her. She was arrogant and refused to follow orders. Maybe it would have been better to allow her to resign. It didn't matter how proficient she was, if she wouldn't work with the others, she would be a burden and a risk, especially now things were hotting up.

But when they'd nearly reached his room, a comm arrived from the sick bay duty doc.

"Could you come over here, major?" she asked. "We have a bit of a situation."

"Don't tell me. The mummy's awake?"

"Yes, the sedation wore off faster than I thought it would, and—" The comm cut off. "Shit, that was close," the doc continued a second later. "Please come as fast as you can. Security can't hold him."

"I'm on my way," Wright replied. But what to do with Ellis? "Come with me," he said.

He ran in the direction of the sick bay, the corporal at his side.

It sounded like the doc had removed the bed restraints for some reason. That seemed odd, considering she'd been a first-hand witness to the patient's violence.

The noise of the disturbance reverberated down the passageway. Crashing, clanging, shouting, and the roaring of the patient was coming from the sick bay. Wright pushed open the door on a scene of chaos. Medical equipment was scattered over the floor, beds were askew, and in the middle of it all was the wakened man.

The doc hadn't removed his restraints. *He was still strapped to his bed.*

One restraint—the one holding an ankle—had broken and, somehow, the man had managed to get to his feet. His bed held firm to his back by the remaining restraints, he was swinging it around, smashing into anything and everything nearby. His face was contorted and red, and his eyes were wild.

Two security officers and the doc stood in a corner, having given up on trying to approach him. One of the officers was holding his hand to a gash on his face.

"Hey! Hey!" Wright yelled and clapped his hands to attract the man's attention.

He turned crazed eyes to the major and paused momentarily, but then continued to struggle and rage. Wright realized he wasn't actually trying to hurt anyone this time, he was trying to free himself.

"Should I sedate him again?" called the doctor from her corner.

Colbourn would be furious if her orders were countermanded.

"No, not yet." But what else could they do? The man had already caused a huge amount of damage to the sick bay. If they didn't get him under control, the place and equipment would be wrecked, and the patient could hurt himself.

Suddenly, the patient lunged at him, possibly aiming for the exit. Wright darted out of the way.

He looked around for something he could use to force him away from the door. He doubted the man would get through it with a bed on his back, but he couldn't take the risk of a crazed sick bay escapee roaming the passageways.

"Get away from there!" shouted Wright.

But if the man heard him, he took no notice. He ran at the door. The top of the bed caught on the frame, and he bounced back, staggering and yelling.

Then, as if the situation wasn't insane enough, Wright heard the sound of *singing* coming from his right.

It was Ellis.

The corporal was standing nearby, her chin tilted up, singing in a language Wright didn't recognize. He stared, his mouth agape. What on Earth was she doing? As he watched, she briefly paused, filled her chest, and sang louder.

He realized the commotion from the patient had stopped.

Ellis was looking at the man as she sang, holding his gaze with her own.

He seemed entranced. His expression softened, his breathing slowed, and the knotted muscles of his neck and arms relaxed.

Ellis stopped singing. She walked to the calmer patient, who swayed slightly. Touching his cheek, she spoke softly, again using the foreign language.

The man replied. It was the first time Wright had heard him utter something other than a roar of rage and confusion. Ellis shook her head, and then continued speaking to him.

The doctor and security guards ventured from their corner. One of the guards marched toward the patient, holding a set of handcuffs, but Wright frowned at him and shook his head. He figured trying to lock the man up now would only send him into another episode of rage.

The doctor began straightening the beds that had been knocked askew.

Meanwhile, Ellis kept on talking to the patient, who watched her steadily. After a little while, she turned to Wright and said, "I think he's calmed down now. We can take off the restraints."

20

Try as he might, Hans could remember nothing of his rescue from the bombing of the General Council meeting or the evacuation flight out of Barbados. He hadn't been able to glean much information from vidnews channels either. The government was undoubtedly limiting media coverage of what had happened, hoping to avoid panic. All he knew was that the Alliance was fighting to hold onto the Outer Caribbean Islands, and if it failed, then he would have to be evacuated again, out of the Kingston Hospital in Jamaica to a safer BA-held territory. As time went on, such places were becoming fewer.

He reached for the interface screen on its extendable arm and turned it off before pushing the device away from his bed. He pressed a button to request assistance.

"When will I be discharged?" he asked the nurse who appeared a few moments later.

"You're doing well, Mr Jonte," the man replied. "Your blood oxygen is almost back to normal." He stepped to Hans's bedside and peered at the display screen on the wall. "Still, it won't hurt to have another puff of this." He removed Hans's nasal cannula and replaced it with a mask that covered his mouth and nose. The mask was attached to a nebulizer, and as the moist, medicated air filtered through, Hans's breathing became easier and less painful.

"I said," he repeated, "when can I expect to be discharged?"

The nurse pulled the mask away from his face. "What was that?"

"How much longer am I to stay here? I have important work to do, especially now we have this crisis."

"I'm sorry, I don't know. Not for a few days, I expect. Your wounds still require twice-daily dressing. If you're discharged too early, they could become infected, and then we would have to admit you again."

He released the mask over Hans's face, but Hans caught it and held it. "I can't wait a few days. I have to...Never mind." There was no point in arguing with the nurse. He would have to discharge himself, regardless of medical advice. He loathed lying impotently in a hospital bed while others turned the gears of the Britannic Alliance.

"Whatever you say." The nurse fiddled with the display over the bed head. "Can I get you anything?"

"No."

The nurse waited another five minutes, fiddling with the bed and the display, before removing the nebulizer. "Dinner's in half an hour," he said, on his way out. "Someone will be in to dress your wounds this evening."

As he opened the door, he halted. "Oh, hello."

Someone on the other side spoke, but Hans couldn't make out the words.

"Yes, until seven-thirty," replied the nurse. "Then visiting hours are over."

He held open the door.

When Hans saw who entered, he sat bolt upright. "Josephine! I thought you were...I mean...I thought..."

The woman smiled sadly and shook her head as she crossed the room to his bed. She waited until the nurse left before saying, "My name isn't Josephine. Josie was my twin. I'm Mariya."

"I see." He realized he sounded disappointed. He *was* disappointed. His deceased assistant's resourcefulness had only been revealed just before she died. "I'm very sorry for your loss," he added, hoping to turn his tone of regret into sadness.

"Thank you," said Mariya, pulling over a chair and sitting down. She was dressed in the colorful clothes of the islands, including a banana-yellow wrap around her hair.

Her resemblance to her sister was remarkable, even for a twin. Usually, adult twins could be told apart, but this woman was Josephine's mirror image.

Hans wondered why she'd come to see him. "Someone will have cleared out Josephine's office. Her personal items should have been shipped to—"

"I'm not here about Josie's things," said Mariya softly.

"Ah." He was at a loss. Much as he enjoyed manipulating other people, their emotions always made him uncomfortable.

"No, I have another reason for visiting you, Mr Jonte." She regarded him steadily. "I've given it a lot of thought. Josie was very happy in her job. She felt she was doing something worthwhile, something to be proud of. And...I would like to take her place."

"You want to be my assistant? I'm afraid—"

"We attended the same university, took the same courses. I'm equally qualified."

"I'm sure your qualifications are excellent. However, there are many more examinations and assessments to pass in order to join SIS. And these all take time. I can refer you to our applications section. I understand things must be difficult for your family right now, but stepping directly into your sister's shoes is out of the question."

"Mr Jonte, I know how bureaucracy works. Do you have *anyone* ready to take Josie's place today, tomorrow? Or will you have to wait for a suitable person to be appointed? Do you really want to wait two or three weeks for someone to assist you in doing your job?"

"I doubt I would have to wait two or three weeks."

But she did have a point. He was feeling the lack of a personal assistant already, and he'd heard nothing from his department about his new one.

"All our lives," Mariya said, "everyone who knew my sister and I commented on how alike we were, not only in appearance, but also in personality and capabilities. I'm sure you found Josie more than capable, didn't you?"

"I can't deny it. In fact, I think I underestimated her."

"Most people did. Would it hurt to give me a chance? We could have a trial period of, say, a month. If, after that, you aren't satisfied with my work, then I'll leave. No hard feelings."

"May I ask why you're so determined to step into your twin's shoes?"

Mariya looked down. "I miss her. I don't know if you have any siblings you're close to, but it was like she was part of me. I feel as though I've had an amputation. I think if I were to do her job, it would help me feel closer to her, to ease the pain. Not only that, we're at war, and though the vidnews doesn't say it in so many words, we seem to be losing. I want to do what I can to help. I feel it's my duty."

Her reasoning made perfect sense, and it was fortuitous that, just as he was ruing the loss of his assistant, another, seemingly nearly identical, person had stepped into the gap. He didn't believe in airy fairy mumbo jumbo of the type the EAC loved, but he found the serendipity of Mariya's unexpected arrival hard to resist.

Though he'd had no idea his deceased assistant had a twin —he'd never inquired about her family—there was no denying

Mariya was Josephine's sister. He had the evidence of his eyes to attest to it. And the background and security checks *could* be carried out while she was in position. He only had to be careful not to allow her access to highly sensitive information.

"Very well. You've persuaded me. We'll do a month's trial and then look toward a permanent position providing you pass the security checks."

"Thank you, Mr Jonte," Mariya said, looking up at him with shining eyes. "You won't regret it."

"There's no need to thank me." He had a burst of inspiration about what would be just the right thing to say: "It'll be a nice way to honor Josephine's memory. After the first month's trial there will be a standard six month's probation."

"I know. Josie told me about it. She loved her job, loved working for you. And I'm sure I will too."

"We'll have to see about that. I may be harder to work for than you imagine."

"I don't mind hard work, and I've always been interested in working in intelligence."

"Good. The first thing you can do for me is help me to get out of here. I'll need some clothes, and—" His interface buzzed. He swung the screen around and opened the comm.

A contact he had working within Parliament had sent it. When he scanned the message, he was outraged. Did the ministers think they could slip this past him just because he happened to be recovering from the bombing? Why hadn't he been invited?

"I need those clothes right away, Mariya," he said, "and have an autocab waiting for me outside the hospital. The government's calling an emergency meeting I cannot miss."

"I'm on it, Mr Jonte."

21

Absent-mindedly juggling, Lorcan paced up and down his suite aboard the *Bres*. Coordinating the Project single-handed took considerable concentration, and his hobby helped him to think. It always took him a few minutes of deep thought to bring all the many important details to mind and mentally slot each part into place in the massive scheme.

But just as he achieved the required depth of focus, his door chimed. The carefully held pieces of the gigantic puzzle of the Project slipped from his hands and scattered into the ether.

Dammit.

"Open," he said through clenched teeth.

Kekoa was the person who had the misfortune to interrupt him.

"I'm sorry, sir," she blurted as soon as she saw him.

"There's a reason my comm is turned off. I said no interruptions!"

"We're aware of that, but—" She gave a soft whimper as the ball Lorcan threw at her hit the middle of her forehead. "We've

received a message we thought you would want to hear immediately."

He guessed the others had coerced her into the role of
disturbing him since she was already in his bad books.

"*And*?"

"Um..." Kekoa swallowed.

"What is it?!"

"It's from Dwyr Orr, sir. She's requesting to meet with you
urgently. In person."

"Is that all? In that case, show her in."

"She-she isn't here, sir. She wants you to see her at her
residence."

"In BI? But I've only just got back from...Hell, all right.
You've told me. Now go before I dock your wages again."

Kekoa retreated.

Damn the Dwyr. His trip to the Barracuda Mine had taken
days of precious time. Yet could he refuse the request? The
campaign against the Britannic Alliance was going well, but
they needed to discuss their next move. Also, previously, she'd
come to see him on the *Bres*, so it only seemed fair that for their
next meeting he should be the one making the journey.

The thought of entering the EAC's regressive, barbarous
realm made his stomach churn, but he set off for the shuttle
launch bay.

BY THE TIME his pilot set the shuttle down outside a castle
within the middle lands of BI, he was feeling no better about
the visit. If anything, his distaste for the EAC's mode of living
had grown.

He stepped down from the shuttle hatch onto a landing pad
made from stone. He rolled his eyes. Stone flags were clearly
preferable to plain concrete, according to EAC mentality.

Lorcan looked around. The pad had been constructed in the grounds of an ancient castle, set on the high ground in the surrounding landscape. A fresh breeze was blowing in from the ocean, and the midday sun stood overhead. A road passed near the edge of the grounds in the distance, but, as to be expected, it was empty of traffic. He knew that, if he inspected it more closely, he would find potholes and cracks filled with grass and weeds.

Such were the ways of the EAC.

In certain parts of the Dwyr's realm were the usual manufacturing plants and offices. While she waged her wars, they were unavoidable, but all knew these were stopgap measures until she achieved her aims.

He would be glad to leave Earth to the cult. He would certainly not want to live in the world it was intent on creating.

"Ua Talman," said a man as he appeared at the castle gate, "welcome. If you would come with me, I will take you to the Dwyr."

Wordlessly, Lorcan followed him. The man looked and behaved like a servant.

I think of the EAC as a group of individuals, but really, it is one person, Dwyr Kala Orr. She is the driving force. She would never accept the title, but she's actually a Queen.

He was led through the gate and into the open, arched castle doorway. They climbed stone stairs, each tread worn at the center edge by the passage of feet over thousands of years.

Tapestries hung on every wall of the large chamber they entered, and Kala Orr sat in the middle on a seat of carved wood, dark with age. The floor was wooden also and heavily varnished and polished. Furniture made hundreds of years ago lined the edges of the room: sofas padded with hand-embroidered upholstery, cabinets, display cases holding hideous, moth-eaten stuffed animals and ancient books. Even the smell of the place was old. It smelled musty and dank, as if the castle hadn't encountered sunlight or fresh air in centuries.

Lorcan felt like he was inside a history docuvid.

The woman herself completed the picture. Whereas aboard the *Bres* the Dwyr had appeared entirely out of place, here she was the perfect complement to the scene. Her deep blue, velvet gown hung to the floor, where embroidered cloth slippers peeked from beneath the hem. The sleeves also hung low, though the upper sections were cut to just below her wrists, revealing her small, pale hands. She wasn't wearing her headdress, and her hair had been elaborately plaited and coiled, with jewel-tipped pins holding it in place.

He was pleased to see that this time she didn't appear intent on revealing excessive flesh.

"Ua Talman, thank you for agreeing to my request."

"It's my pleasure, but call me Lorcan, if it isn't too presumptuous of me to assume we remain on first-name terms?"

The Dwyr waved the servant away. When the man had left, she said, "Not presumptuous at all."

Despite her words, Lorcan got the impression she thought she was allowing him a large, potentially unwarranted, concession. Dwyr Orr on her home turf was a different animal from the woman who had come to his colony ship to seek an alliance.

"Please be seated, Lorcan. Can I offer you some refreshment? Champagne, perhaps?"

Had he seen the shadow of a wink? He took the gilded stool that was the only other single seat in the room and moved it close to her before sitting down.

"Refreshment won't be necessary, thank you. While it's delightful to visit you at home, Kala, I'm afraid I can only stay a short time. I'm a very busy man. Starships to build and all that. Shall we get down to business?"

"We must decide our next maneuver regarding the BA, yes.

The battle for the Caribbean Islands is going well. But I have another purpose in asking you here, which I would like to discuss first, before we move onto more important matters."

"Hm. What is it? By all means, let's get it out of the way."

"Well, he should be along any minute."

He?

Lorcan was not prepared to accept a third party into the AP/EAC pact, if that was her intention. And definitely not someone Kala had unilaterally enlisted. He was about to say so when the door handle squeaked as it turned and the door opened.

A boy aged around nine or ten walked in. He was dark haired and pale skinned, like his mother. His large, dark eyes were like pools of black water.

"Perran, come here. Come and meet Ua Talman."

The boy ran to Kala's side and rested a hand on the arm of her chair, regarding Lorcan shyly—or was it slyly?

"I would like to introduce my son."

Though he was careful not to show it, Lorcan was speechless with outrage. What was the woman thinking? Why would she think he was remotely interested in her family? Did she believe he was paying a social call?

"Perran is fascinated by your project," said Kala, then, turning to her boy, she added, "aren't you? He's been reading all about it."

"Yes, but one thing I don't understand," piped Perran. "Could you tell me why it's called the *Antarctic* Project, when it's in space?"

"It's, er..." Lorcan's mind was working overtime. His rage at being subjected to this domestic nonsense was proving hard to overcome, yet he didn't want to say anything that would jeopardize the delicate alliance between him and the Dwyr. He purposefully unclenched his jaw. "The company my wife and I set up had its beginnings in mines in Antarctica, thus our choice of name. The colonization project sprang from the company and I retained the name in memory of her."

"Oh. Is she dead?"

He glared at the boy. "Yes, she died."

"Perran, don't be insensitive. I apologize on behalf of my son. He's too young to understand these things."

Lorcan was not so sure. "This was your additional reason for inviting me to your castle? I am pleased to meet your boy, but now the introductions are over, perhaps we can move on to more urgent matters."

"I wasn't quite finished," said Kala. "Perran would love to see the project at first hand, and it would be very educational for him. I was wondering if it might be possible for him to visit your ship, the *Bres*? He would be accompanied by a guardian, of course."

"Out of the question!" blurted Lorcan. "I'm sorry," he went on in a milder tone, "but my ship is neither a tourist attraction nor an educational facility. Many areas are unsafe, and I cannot spare any staff to give guided tours."

Was the woman mad? She was regarding him calmly, as if she were making the most reasonable request in the world.

"He would be content with only visiting the finished parts, and he wouldn't bother anyone. Simply to see the ship would be enough."

Lorcan ground his teeth. Tense moments passed, and then he leapt up, knocking over his stool. "Dwyr Orr, I am a man of great patience, but you have exhausted it. Your request is preposterous! It's offensive and unconscionable. You seem to think I'm running some kind of tourist attraction or-or day care facility. No, your boy cannot visit my ship. Not today, not tomorrow, not ever! Now, we have urgent business to discuss. Are you willing to talk now, or are we to sever our partnership and go our separate ways? I can assure you, both options are equally attractive to me at the moment."

Kala also rose to her feet, calmly and deliberately. She walked up to Lorcan, drawing so close he could see fine threads of red in the whites of her eyes. He thought she might try to strike him, but she only said, "Please calm down. It was only a question."

"I am perfectly calm!" he yelled. "And if I'm not, whose fault is that? You drag me down here to your barbaric wilderness, populated by drooling fools, bewitched by cultish rituals and fantasies, and expect me to indulge your child's whims and fancies. Who do you think you are? Who do you think *I* am?"

The Dwyr's lips thinned and her eyes blazed. "Ua Talman, you are in *my* domain. Watch your speech. I do not take insults lightly."

"What are you going to do? Throw me from the castle battlements? Chain me up in a dungeon? Send me to your chief torturer? Your culture is a blight on the planet, an anachronism, an affront to human civilization, and I shall be glad to leave you and your kind far behind."

He was beyond caring about diplomacy with the deluded woman. She was a throwback to a brutal age, eschewing the very technology that lifted humanity from the swamps of its brutal, animal past.

He fully expected her to send for thugs to seize him. If she did, he would comm the leader of his military forces. His military would rescue him, and then retribution would rain down on the EAC.

But the Dwyr didn't call for guards—she laughed. She chuckled, holding a delicate hand over her mouth. The boy, Perran, watched his mother, sharing in her amusement.

When she had her mirth under control, she said, "Is that really how you see us? I suppose it's to be expected. At first glance, we must seem quite primitive. And I suppose our style echoes that of earlier ages. But how can you forget about our military aircraft, ships, and starships, our infantry? Do you think we could have helped to attack the Caribbean Islands with only swords and spears? Haven't you watched the EAC's progress across the globe?"

"No, but...but..." She had taken the wind from his sails. He felt outmaneuvered. "I assumed your forces were only a stopgap measure, a necessary evil, until—"

"Please sit, Ua Talman, and I will explain."

He picked up the overturned stool and sat down.

"You are a man of science, am I correct?"

Before he could answer, she continued, "Why am I even asking? Of course you are. How else would you be able to travel to the stars? Scientific discoveries are what have made the Project possible. Science has brought you everything you desire. It wouldn't be an exaggeration to say you worship it like a god."

"Actually, that would be a great exaggeration," said Lorcan tersely.

Ignoring him, the Dwyr went on, "What if I were to tell you there is another layer to the universe, and that science has not even brushed its surface? A dimension that lies beyond the parameters of everyday experience and rational thought."

"What are you talking about? Multiple universes? Quantum mechanics?"

"Perhaps quantum mechanics is a part of the explanation for the phenomena I mean, yes. Perhaps the strange behavior of quantum particles has something to do with it. But the things I have observed and experienced are on a macro scale: Forces that don't exist in any physics textbook, impossible connections, events that are beyond reason.

"The EAC is not moving backward, Lorcan, it is moving *forward*. What you see around you isn't a rejection of technology, it is the acceptance of a new truth, a better way. For example, you look at my home and see a relic of the past, don't you? But ideas of the past, the present, and the future are observational fallacies. Time is not a ribbon we travel along.

"If you were to read ancient history, you would see that. at one point, humans were moving toward this deeper under- standing of the universe, but they chose science instead. Don't mistake me, that discipline has its value, but it is far from every- thing. There is so much more to know, and the EAC is involved in the exploration of those unknown areas of our understand- ing. You may, one day, stand upon an alien planet, Ua Talman. But, you never know, I may already be there to greet you."

"But...but..." He rubbed his forehead. The woman was clearly insane. He decided it would be better to humor, not antagonize, her. The EAC was useful to him, at least until the BA were finally defeated and he could take the remainder of the resources he needed.

Two long trips to Earth in succession had exhausted him, and he had plenty to do back on the *Bres*. He needed to cut to the chase, agree their next step, and return to his ship.

"Dwyr Orr, I'll think on what you've told me. Now, how about this? Your boy can visit the *Bres* for a few days, providing he doesn't get in anyone's way."

"Thank you. He won't be any trouble, I assure you. Perran is very mature for his age."

"Now that's settled, can we please discuss our ongoing strategy?"

22

"Hans, so glad you could make it."

I bet.

The former Deputy Prime Minister, who had stepped into his deceased superior's shoes, stared coldly at Hans from the far side of the conference table. Bone-thin, sparse gray hair clinging to his scalp, and bespectacled though surgery to correct eye defects was cheap and common, the new PM was an Establishment archetype.

And he hated Hans.

The man was, naturally, careful to never express his opinion openly. Only in the late evenings, when the select few of the inner government circle would meet for nightcaps and cigars at an exclusive club, would Beaumont-Smith give vent to his true feelings about the head of SIS. *Jumped-up immigrant* and *the kind of man who buys his own furniture* were two phrases waiting staff had overheard and passed on to Hans's contact.

No matter that it was Hans's great-great-grandparents who were the immigrants. To someone like Beaumont-Smith, if you couldn't trace your family back to one of William the Conqueror's companions, you were scum.

The Cabinet ministers and military leaders sitting around the conference table had the decency to look embarrassed. Hans had a feeling most of them were unaware he hadn't been informed about the emergency meeting. If he hadn't shown up, Beaumont-Smith and his cronies would have insinuated he must have been too ill to attend, casting doubt on his fitness for his role, or even implied he must have forgotten or decided not to come.

"My pleasure, Prime Minister," he replied. "And may I take the opportunity to congratulate you on your new position, despite the sad circumstances that led to your appointment."

"Sad circumstances indeed," said Beaumont-Smith. "I would that it had been any other way."

"I'm sure you do," said Hans, noticing no empty seats at the table.

One of the PM's aides simultaneously realized the faux pas and leapt to her feet. "Please, take my seat, Mr Jonte."

Mustering as much dignity as he could, he strode around the table to the woman's chair, which sat next to the Prime Minister, while the aide left to find a replacement.

As he sat down, he tried to maintain a confident, capable facade. Lying in hospital, he'd felt reasonably healthy, but after leaving it he'd soon realized he was far from recovered. Withdrawing the treatment for his damaged lungs had made walking more than a few paces extremely fatiguing, as if he were climbing a mountain. As the men and women sitting around the table watched him, he also became painfully aware of his singed beard and hair, inflamed skin, cuts, and bruises.

He smiled easily and picked up the copy of the agenda that lay on the table. He couldn't afford to appear weak.

The meeting had only just started, and the first point to be discussed was the one that interested him the most.

"I'm sure Mr Jonte requires no introduction to anyone

present," said Beaumont-Smith, "so we'll proceed to item one without any further ado?"

The Chair nodded.

The PM cleared his throat. "As we all know, Her Majesty Queen Alice's funeral will take place this coming Sunday. All arrangements are in place. The proposal we must discuss today is the date of His Majesty King Frederick's coron—"

"Prime Minister," interjected the Chief of Defense Staff, a man called Hennessy, "I'm sure I'm not speaking only for myself when I say that time is pressing. I should be working on military strategy, not stuck here discussing matters of pomp and ceremony. I'd like to propose we reorder the agenda so we can get to the important topics first, and I and my military colleagues can depart and leave you to decide what day Freddie gets his crown."

"I see," said Beaumont-Smith, trying but failing to disguise his displeasure.

"Well, we could put it to the vote, I suppose," said the Chair.

Hennessy gave a loud, audible sigh.

"Which items would you prefer to discuss first?" asked the Prime Minister, looking at Hennessy over the rims of his glasses.

"The report on the attack on the General Council," the Chief answered, in the tone of someone explaining something to a toddler, "and the plan for dealing with the new alliance between the AP and EAC."

"Does anyone second this motion?" the Chair asked.

"Seconded," said Montague, the First Sea Lord and Chief of Naval Staff.

"Who says aye, please raise your hand."

Hans lifted his hand, along with most of those present.

"Motion carried."

A muscle twitched in the PM's jaw. "Very well," he said. "If everyone would please turn to documents fifteen and sixteen? I hope you've all had the opportunity to read your copies."

Hans located the relevant papers and began to hastily scan them. His department had helped to carry out the investigation while he'd been incapacitated, but no one had sent him the completed reports. Another of Beaumont-Smith's 'omissions'.

The reports could be embarrassing, and he knew he had to tread carefully to avoid being blamed. If anyone should have known about the plan of the attack on the General Council, it was SIS. Yet his staff had been entirely in the dark. He was relieved to see the reports somewhat exonerated his department.

He saw something interesting and read it more closely. Hundreds of man hours spent trawling satellite data had revealed a small private shuttle had departed from within EAC territory and traveled to one of the AP's colony ships, *Bres*, three days prior to the attack.

The preliminary conclusion of the main report was that the AP/EAC Alliance had been forged less than two weeks ago, and the assault on Barbados had been an operation rapidly engineered by the two organizations. The fast pace of action meant that by the time SIS double agents had learned of the plan, it was too late to warn the General Council.

SIS was already at work finding out what the allies were planning next.

"The report isn't bad as far as it goes," said Beaumont-Smith, "but there's a glaring omission. What I'd like to know is, how the hell did the AP and EAC know the time and place of the General Council meeting? I mean, don't we have *any* security to prevent the leaking of such sensitive information?"

He glared at Hans.

"Hundreds of people were invited to that meeting," Hans retorted, "against my advice, if you remember. If *certain individ-*

uals hadn't been intent on turning the whole thing into a propaganda exercise, taking advantage of the Queen's attendance to bolster flagging confidence in the government, far fewer attendees would have been present, and the chances of a leak would have been considerably reduced. I refuse to be held responsible for the wagging tongues of every media rep and business mogul."

"Those people were notified at the last minute," the PM retaliated. "They couldn't possibly have—"

"We already know the attack was mounted at lightning speed," said Hennessy. "Is there any point in trying to assign—"

"So you're saying it must have been someone who knew the details weeks before the meeting who passed them onto the EAC or AP?" asked Hans. "That would narrow the field to SIS and the people in this room. *My* staff are thoroughly vetted and completely trustworthy." He let the implication of his words hang in the air.

"Now look here," Beaumont-Smith spluttered, "if you're suggesting anyone here would knowingly put Her Majesty's life in danger..."

"For goodness sake!" exclaimed one of the cabinet ministers. "More people died than the flipping Queen, you know. Good people, with families and loved ones. Her Majesty's death was tragic, but let's not lose focus."

"Exactly," Hennessy said. "Focus is what's needed here. We suffered a catastrophe in the Caribbean, and I don't want to be pessimistic, but things aren't looking good for us going forward. I think that, regardless of where the fault lies, we have to agree: No more General Council meetings until this war is over."

"Circumventing the democratic process should be a last resort," said the PM. "It's admitting defeat before—"

"Admitting defeat for *you*, you mean," said Montague. "Perhaps a vote of no confidence is in order."

"That's *entirely* unnecessary!" Beaumont-Smith was pink with fury. "And the thin end of the wedge. Postponing Council meetings is the first step on the road to martial law. That's what you want, isn't it?!"

Hennessy leapt to his feet. "That's an outrageous accusation!"

The PM also stood. He rested his hands on the table and leaned over it, saying, "This government will *not* give in to bullying. Any more pressure to hamper the Council's due process will be viewed as a traitorous act."

"I'm not staying here to be threatened and insulted!" yelled Hennessy. "The military leaders will hold a separate meeting, where *we* will decide the Britannic Alliance's next moves. When we come to a decision, we will inform Parliament. Officers, if you would come with me...?"

He marched to the exit. Montague quickly followed, and after some dithering, so did all the military attendees.

In the silence that followed their departure, the ministers appeared shocked and dismayed, and Beaumont-Smith seemed about to explode with impotent rage.

Hans sat quietly twiddling his thumbs.

His long years of sowing mistrust and suspicion through the BA's higher echelons of power were paying off. A schism between military and government had appeared. Most importantly, King Frederick's coronation—the thing he most wanted to prevent from happening—hadn't even been discussed.

The fracturing and strife were unfortunate but only to be expected, and the final outcome would be worth it. Now all Hans had to do was to pick his moment.

"Ministers," he said, "I'd like to propose that I join our military leaders' meeting. I don't think they'll object, and it would be helpful to have a governmental presence at their discussions."

No one objected, so he left.

His painful lungs and injuries still bothered him, but his mood was high. From among the ashes of the ancient, failing monarchy, a new republic would arise: a shining light to lead humanity into the future.

23

The patient had shaken off the last effects of sedation and was fit to be discharged from the sick bay, but Wright had no idea what to do with him. Thanks to Ellis, he was no longer aggressive, and he even had civilian clothes to wear from the *Valiant's* printers. Wright thought he could probably find a small cabin for him, but then what? They were preparing for battle, and even if they weren't, the notion of the mystery man hanging out with the marines was crazy.

It was obvious he wasn't BA military or SIS. The distress signal was unexplained, but his rescue had clearly been a mistake. He could only be a local, who had somehow become trapped in the cave. It was only by a huge amount of luck he'd been saved from certain death.

The *Valiant* was no longer in her former high Earth orbit, when attempting to return him to West BI might have been an option. She was now far beyond the home planet as the navy and marines gathered forces for an assault.

Wright looked at the patient, sitting quietly on the edge of his bed. He resented the burden of responsibility for the man when he had so many more important things to do.

"Can you tell him we won't be able to return him to West BI just yet?" he asked Ellis. "That he'll have to stay aboard until after the battle?"

She looked at him like he'd asked her to levitate. "How am I supposed to do that?"

"It isn't that hard, is it? Just explain, in your language."

"Major, he doesn't speak my language."

"Huh? How did you calm him down earlier?"

"He must have liked my singing. I did ask him if he spoke Welsh, but he didn't understand me."

"But you've been talking to him all this time?"

Ellis had been keeping up a monologue, talking to the patient ever since they'd released him from the restraints. In truth, Wright had enjoyed listening to her melodic native tongue, though he couldn't understand a word of it.

"Only because it seemed to soothe him. He's been through a lot, sir. No wonder he reacted violently when he woke up. He must have thought he was dying in that cave, and then he found himself aboard a starship among strangers. Must have been a helluva shock."

"Yeah." Wright reached for an interface. "Well, we can soon solve the translation problem." He opened the relevant software and turned the mic to face the patient. "Can you get him to say something?"

Ellis touched the man's arm and spoke again in Welsh.

He answered graciously, his voice soft and deep, and inclined his head in a slight bow. Then he eyed the interface.

Wright checked the screen.

Language not identified

"Try again," he said to the corporal.

Ellis spoke once more. Her mother language contained unfamiliar sounds, which Wright thought he'd heard the patient make too, yet now he observed them more closely, it was clear neither understood the other.

When the man replied this time, he spoke for longer and the interface captured twenty or thirty seconds of speech. That should have been plenty for the software to pinpoint the language, but when Wright looked at the screen again, it repeated the same message.

"I don't get it," he said.

Ellis also peered at the interface. "It isn't that weird, is it? He must speak a rare language."

"The banks contain every human language spoken today and for the last five hundred years. It isn't possible for the software not to recognize it."

"Maybe it's got a bug."

"Maybe," Wright repeated, though he doubted it.

A medic strolled out from the staff office. "Don't forget these," she said. She was carrying a small, black plastic bag, which she handed to the patient. "We dumped his rags," she added to Wright. "I hope that was okay."

"Sure."

"Great. If you need anything, let me know."

The man was examining the plastic, rubbing it between his fingertips. After apparently satisfying his curiosity, he opened the bag and took out his arm and neck torques.

"Whoa," Ellis breathed. "Can I take a look?" she asked, holding out her hand.

The man passed her the neck torque.

"It's so heavy!" she exclaimed. Turning the thick gold band over, she looked closely at the intricate design.

"It must be pure gold," said Wright, recalling his first sight of the strange jewelry. He wondered where the man had gotten it from. Perhaps he'd found it when he'd wandered into the cave.

"Look, this is the same as one of his tattoos." Ellis showed him the animal that pranced around one curve of the torque. "I think this is a deer, but this...I'm not sure. Wait, I know what this is! It's a dragon."

Wright regarded the animal that curved around the other side of the torque, the open, fanged mouth, spurting flames, and the wings sprouting from a serpentine body. "A dragon?" he asked. "How do you know?" The creature was only vaguely familiar to him. All he knew was it was mythical, not real or even extinct

"They were in the old stories my grandda used to tell me." The corporal passed the torque back to the man, looking thoughtful.

The patient slid his armband over his shirt sleeve and put the dragon torque around his neck. Ellis watched him for several long moments, then, as if on impulse, she took one of his hands in both of hers.

The man didn't object. It was as though an unspoken exchange was going on between them.

"What is it, corporal?" asked Wright.

"I-I can't say. I wish I could talk to him."

"What can't you say? Do you know who this man is? Where he's from?"

"No—or at least, not with any certainty."

"I guess it doesn't really matter. Wherever he's from, we can't take him back right now. I wish I knew how he managed to send that distress signal, though."

Wright felt a yawn forcing its way up from his chest. He'd been on duty for thirty-six hours, preparing for the forthcoming battle, and he needed to get some sleep. "Let's find him a room. Maybe you can teach him how to use the entertainment system. I want him occupied and out of the way. Do you think you can make him understand he can't leave his cabin?"

"I can try, sir."

"Okay, let's go. C'mon, buddy." Wright stood up.

"Sir, can I stay in his room with him?" asked Ellis. "I could look after him and keep him out of trouble. Maybe teach him English."

"Absolutely not. Your orders are to support the training sessions."

"Isn't it too late for that now? How long do we have until we reach the rendezvous?"

"Probably not more than twenty-four hours," Wright conceded.

"Then there's no more training for a while. Everyone will be getting battle ready."

"They should be, but so should you."

"I will. And keep an eye on him. I can do both."

Ellis's demeanor had entirely changed over the few hours she'd been helping to deal with the mystery man. The surliness, argumentativeness, and acrimony were gone and had been replaced by the eager, alert, gutsy attitude from Wright's first encounter with her. Something about the patient had changed her. In her new frame of mind, she could be an invaluable asset.

"Sir," she said, interrupting his train of thought. "I hope you don't mind me asking, but, is everything okay with you?"

Wright frowned. "I'm fine, thank you, corporal."

"It's just that, ever since Colbourn got back, you've changed. Like, something's gnawing at you."

"Your concern is unwarranted, Ellis," he said, icily. *Who did she think she was?*

Returning to the question on his mind, he mused Colbourn would probably have something to say about giving the corporal new duties other than the ones she had assigned. On the other hand, she would be too busy to notice right now. He decided, in this case, it would be better to ask forgiveness than permission.

"All right," he said. "He's your responsibility—until you get the order to suit up."

24

W hen Taylan learned exactly what the BA had planned in retaliation for the assault on the Caribbean Territory, she was deeply troubled. She'd joined up imagining she would be fighting the EAC military, and possibly the AP's too. What she hadn't envisioned was attacking civilians. Whether or not she agreed with the aims of the Antarctic Project, she didn't think the people involved in it deserved to suffer for choosing that path in their lives. She was sure that, like her, they only wanted what they felt was best for them and their families, even if the AP's methods were questionable.

But she was on track to take part in the fight, whether she liked it or not. The only other option was to refuse, and, at that point and place in time, her objection would result in being spaced. The BA wouldn't tolerate a dissenter on one of their ships in the midst of a battle. And she needed to survive. She had more people to worry about than just herself.

At least she could occupy her time in the hours leading up to the battle looking after the mysterious patient.

She watched the strange man walk around the small cabin

Wright had found for him, examining every object closely. He looked under the bunk, pressed the mattress, ran his fingertips over the blank interface on the wall—jumping with surprise when it sprang to life—opened the drawers in the desk, and even touched the overhead, apparently intrigued by the light that emanated from it.

He stepped into the small, square box that comprised the restroom. To her amusement, what interested him most there was the head. She didn't think he understood what it was for, so she flushed it. He leaped higher than he had when he'd opened the interface. The shower similarly baffled him. She wasn't sure how to explain how to use the head, but she turned on the shower as a demonstration.

The man laughed, apparently partly in shock and partly in delight.

She laughed too, and reached into the cubicle to allow the water to run over her hand before wiping it on her face. She beckoned him to come closer, and then took his wrist and pushed his hand into the stream. The look of delight on his face was so childlike it was funny.

He rubbed the water on his beard.

"That's right. It's for washing, see?" She wet her hand again and rubbed her neck. Then she mimed taking off her clothes and stepping into the shower.

Understanding lit the man's eyes. He pretended to take off his shirt and wash his chest, smiling.

"Yeah." Taylan nodded.

He held his hand under the water, appearing to enjoy the feel of it.

She was enjoying herself too. For the first time since that bitch Colbourn had ripped Kayla's necklace from her neck, she felt normal, light-hearted, even, despite the shadow of the upcoming battle. The cloud of bitterness and anger had lifted. Assuming they survived, helping this man was going to be fun.

She decided she would find Boots and bring him to the cabin. He could be the man's companion while she was on duty.

He pretended to take off his shirt again, but this time he mimed washing it in the water.

"Haha, no. No need for that." She walked to the laundry chute and opened it. "You put your dirty clothes in here."

She returned to the shower. "Better turn this off. Mustn't waste water. Come here." She stepped back into the cabin.

"You get top rack," she said, patting the upper bunk. "I'll sleep down below. I hope you don't snore." She pointed at herself and then the lower bunk. "That's if we get a chance to sleep." How to tell him they were about to engage in a battle? It would be impossible. She guessed he would figure it out when the fighting started.

What would happen to him then? It might be best to lock him in his cabin until it was all over.

"Hey, this is crazy," she said. "I don't even know your name. Let's begin your first English lesson," She touched her chest. "My name is Taylan. Taylan," she repeated, emphasizing the syllables. "Can you say that? Taaayyylannn." She pointed at his mouth.

The man's brow wrinkled. "Taayylann."

"That's great. Taylan." She patted her chest again.

"Taylan," said the man.

Next, she gently tapped his chest. "Who are you? What are you called?"

He replied with a name that caused all the strength in her legs to evaporate and shock to radiate through her. She managed to slide onto the lower bunk.

It couldn't be.

Ever since Wright had told her about the strange person he'd rescued from the cave in West BI, someone who appeared to have survived for an impossible length of time, and ever since she'd seen the man's torques with their carvings of beasts and dragons, she'd been harboring a wild speculation about who he might be. But she wasn't the kind of person who believed in ghosts, fairy tales, or even the ancient mythologies of her homeland. To her, they were all stories for entertainment and part of the culture and heritage she was proud of, but they weren't fact. She'd never believed in any of the people or creatures of the ancient legends. She'd never thought they actually existed.

It wasn't possible.

The man was watching her with concern.

He sat down next to her and said something in his own language.

"You *can't* be," she protested.

She must have misheard. Her mind was playing tricks on her. The man was speaking a foreign language in an unfamiliar accent, and her imagination must have inserted another word in place of the one he'd actually said.

She decided to try again. "I'm Taylan." She touched her chest and felt her heart pounding against her breastbone. Fearing the worst, but not sure exactly what the worst would be —what would it mean if it really *was* him?—she pointed at the man.

He repeated the name she'd heard before.

"No, no, no!"

It had to be a mistake, or something to do with his pronunciation.

Or it was only a coincidence.

That was it.

A coincidence.

Red alert! Red alert! sounded her comm. *Enemy ships approaching. Battle stations.*

25

The *Belladonna* fired. Pulse bolts spurted from her cannon and sped across space.

Dwyr Orr sat on the flagship's bridge, thrilled by the chase. The dreadnought was leading the EAC formation, the tip of a four-sided spearhead. Spreading out behind the ship in four lines came the rest of the fleet.

The AP's battleships approached from another direction, racing to meet the enemy.

Kala recalled the *Belladonna's* launch ceremony—the blessing, the breaking of the bottle of champagne, the celebratory rituals, the post-launch party—it had been a wonderful moment and a milestone in the history of the EAC. She loved the ship's sleek lines and powerful armaments, including a particle lance and pulse and plasma cannon, but her pleasure was bitter-sweet. She also longed for the day when she wouldn't need starships or weapons, when the Crusade would unlock the secrets of the universe and harness its natural power.

When that happened, she would assert control of the solar system and habitable planets of the galaxy and return everything to its natural order.

"Direct hits," reported the weapons officer.

But the *Belladonna's* pulses evaporated on the hulls of the BA corvettes, causing no apparent damage. The distance remained too great, most of the bolts' energy dissipating into space before they reached their target.

However, the EAC was closing the gap.

Kala smirked, imagining the dismay of the BA's commanding officers now they understood their plan had been leaked and they were flying into a trap.

The *Belladonna's* captain, a small, dark-haired man, cleared his throat. "From the trajectory of their ships, it appears the BA is heading for the *Bres*, not the *Balor,* as we thought, Dwyr."

"Then we change the intercept point. I'll inform Ua Talman in case he doesn't already know."

"The navigator is already working on it." The captain looked uncomfortable for a moment, then added, "I believe your boy is aboard the *Bres?*"

"He is. And?"

"I just want to reassure you I'll do everything in my power to ensure he's unharmed."

"Thank you, but your assurances aren't required." In response to the captain's puzzled silence, Kala went on, "The fact that the BA intends to attack the *Bres* isn't bad news. It only means they never stood a hope. Perran is the future of the EAC. He's inviolable. His presence will protect the colony ship, the same as mine protects the *Belladonna.*"

The captain inclined his head. "We're fortunate to have you aboard."

Was there a tinge of irony in his response?

It didn't matter.

When she'd revealed the EAC's deepest beliefs about undiscovered physical laws to Ua Talman, she'd noted a similar attitude of disbelief and, perhaps, amusement, but she hadn't taken offense. Most of the people she met were ignorant, blind children when it came to the Truth. They could only see what lay before them and clung to simple, Newtonian ideas about how nature worked. The captain didn't need to believe her, only follow her orders.

One day, Lorcan and the other doubters would see how right she was.

She got up and strode to the captain's holoscreen, which displayed an ever-changing vista of the ships involved in the battle. "Fire again."

"But—"

"I know the range is still too long. I want to harry them."

Naturally, the captain didn't want to expend the *Belladonna's* finite power capacity unnecessarily, but there was more to a battle than trading hits.

"I want them to understand they have no hope."

On the holoscreen, the AP vessels crawled upward from the bottom left. The BA had to have noticed their second enemy by now.

The captain gave the order, and four bolts of pure energy tore from the flagship's cannon.

The BA admiral had to be assessing the ships bearing down on them, and their firepower. He had to know the battle was already lost. The BA was outgunned and, with two adversaries flying in from separate regions of space, it was soon to be outmaneuvered.

She expected some attempt at defense, and then a quick surrender. They would try to save the lives of their men and women. The Alliance was losing ground on Earth, and now it would lose its dominance in space.

"Again," she said. "Fire."

This time, as the pulses streamed toward the BA fleet, the corvettes, trailing the bigger ships, returned fire. The bolts collided with the *Belladonna's,* exploding in bursts of energy. Finally, a response. The BA was fighting back, deluded, imagining it might still win. Or did it only want to make it through to the *Bres* and destroy the ship as a last act of defiance?

"Their fighter ships are launching," the captain warned.

Kala nodded, satisfied. She would enjoy the fight. "I'll leave tactics to you from now on, captain. I'll liaise with Ua Talman as the battle progresses. You know the overall strategy."

"Thank you, Dwyr."

She returned to her seat and opened a direct comm to Lorcan.

"You were right," was the first thing he said, after a lag.

"That's gracious of you to admit," said Kala. "I told you my sources were reliable. Did you doubt it?"

"Perhaps a little. It's wise to be circumspect. I've been trying and failing for years to infiltrate the BA, and, to be frank, I couldn't quite believe they would be so bold as to attempt to attack my colony vessels."

"They want to hit you where it hurts," said Kala. "Losing one of your ships would be a huge setback and a heavy blow to your people's morale."

She heard the captain's orders to the weapons officer. The *Belladonna* was now sufficiently within range of the BA fleet for their hits to count.

"You don't need to tell me that," said Lorcan. "But now they know we're one step ahead. That's got to unsettle them."

"Do you know they're targeting the *Bres*, not the *Balor*? My source got that wrong."

"Perhaps a last minute change of mind," said Lorcan. "The substance of the intel was accurate, and without it, the BA might have succeeded. I would have been hard put to muster an adequate defense in time. I'm glad I accepted your proposal to work together."

"*The enemy of my enemy is my friend*," Kala replied. "It's an old saying, but true nonetheless."

"Now I know your capabilities, I would rather be your friend than your enemy, Dwyr."

She smiled at the flattery. *A wise sentiment, Ua Talman. Unfortunately, anyone who stands in the way of the EAC will eventually be my enemy, and one day you will be an obstacle, not a means to an end.*

A collective shout from the officers on the *Belladonna's* bridge went up, distracting Kala from her conversation. She lifted her head and saw a spray of fine sparks on the holoscreen —the traces of a BA ship disintegrating. Looking closer, she realized they'd destroyed one of the little corvettes.

"I have a battle to direct, Dwyr," said Lorcan. "Forgive me if I end our chat for now. I'll update you on developments."

The AP fleet was now coming within firing range of the BA. As Kala watched, it began its attack. The AP's battleships were closest to the leading BA vessels, their destroyers, dreadnoughts, and battlecruisers. The Alliance had certainly gone all out in this attack, throwing most of what they had at the AP.

And, despite the discovery of their plan and the combined assault by both its enemies, the BA appeared to be pushing through regardless, attempting to reach the *Bres* and destroy her no matter what damage their ships sustained in the attempt.

Murmurs of support for the AP went around the bridge, as everyone who wasn't watching a console fixed their attention on the holoscreen. The Project ships didn't appear to be holding anything back as they rained hell on the BA. The larger ships of the Alliance's fleet were better equipped to endure the onslaught than the corvettes the EAC had been targeting, and they were returning fire on a similar scale...

A second BA ship fell, victim to the EAC's pulses.

A roar of jubilation exploded on the bridge, and Kala leapt

to her feet in joy. Two ships gone! Though they were only corvettes, that had to be a massive blow to the Alliance.

The BA, forced to split its defense between two antagonists, couldn't adequately protect itself from either.

The AP ships drew closer to the intercept point, where the three fleets' trajectories crossed. It was here the fighting would be heaviest. Kala's stomach twisted in anticipation. At close quarters, the *Belladonna* could use its particle lance, and the effects would be devastating.

"Swifts launching," someone announced.

The BA was sending out its fighter ships, ready for the upcoming close-quarters action.

"Launch Scorpions," ordered the captain.

As Kala watched, the EAC's fighters flew out to counter the BA's, the tiny dots on the holoscreen moving far faster than the battleships, making them look cumbersome and unwieldy in comparison. She guessed the BA's Swifts would try to target the *Belladonna's* engines, set aft behind heavy casing. If they were damaged, the flagship would lose both velocity and power for its weapons, but she was confident the Scorpion pilots would do their job.

She returned to her seat again, her excitement ebbing. It didn't appear the BA was anywhere near the point of surrender, and the battle could go on for hours. She began to feel detached from the scene on the holo and everyone around her. Others might not feel as confident as her about victory over the BA fleet, but, as far as she was concerned, the outcome was a foregone conclusion. Now it was only a matter of watching the inevitable play out.

The BA offer to surrender would come sooner or later. Lorcan and she had already agreed they would not accept.

As Ua Talman had pointed out, utter annihilation of the BA fleet was the best way to ensure an end to the threat she had mentioned to him. She was fairly confident the man remained aboard one of the Alliance's ships. If they wiped them out entirely, and every living thing aboard them, the threat would be destroyed too. In the vacuum of space, everything died.

And the BA would never recover from such a defeat.

It would never control Sol space again.

26

E ven at top speed they were half an hour from the *Bres*, and they were already two corvettes down. Wright had watched in horror as first the *Daisy* and then the *Primrose* exploded, turned to flying dust by concentrated pulse fire from the EAC ships.

Hundreds of men and women dead, in a heartbeat.

The BA vessels were being picked off by the EAC one by one, and meanwhile the jaws of the other beast, the AP fleet, awaited them.

Ever since he'd heard the BA's objective was to destroy the AP's primary colony ship, he'd thought the scheme was madness. He could understand the thinking behind it—Ua Talman's project wasn't an intellectual or practical endeavor, it was his baby, born of grief and rage. Cutting out its heart might break him. On the other hand, it could push him over the edge, and then, who knew what he might do to get his revenge?

But now the point was moot. The BA was speeding willingly to its destruction, as Wright saw it, barring a miracle.

Colbourn paced the bridge, seething. Wright wasn't sure if it was because she held the same opinion as him, that they were on a suicide mission, or because she'd been required to give over control of the *Valiant* to a Royal Navy captain for the duration of the battle.

Probably both.

The old brigadier marched to and fro, hands clasped behind her back, casting glances at the holoscreen and wincing in displeasure and anger.

"Launch Swifts," said the captain.

Colbourn turned to Wright. "Units ready to repel boarders?"

"Yes, brigadier." It was the third time she'd asked him. The marines had been at battle stations ever since the EAC fleet had been sighted. But he guessed her sense of impotence was driving her to distraction.

The BA had committed most of its vessels to the attack, keeping only a few in reserve. Where they were, Wright didn't know. He also didn't know if he was luckier to be aboard the *Valiant* or if he would have been better off on one of the reserve ships. The idea of clinging on after the final defeat of the Alliance disturbed him. Better a quick death than a lingering one.

"Here she comes," said the captain.

The loss of two of her corvettes had attracted the EAC flagship to the *Valiant*. The massive vessel was plowing through the Swifts like a bear through a cloud of bees, intent on the honey in their hive. There wasn't anything the Swift pilots could do about it. EAC Scorpions were keeping them occupied, preventing them from getting near the dreadnought.

"What about the *Fearless*?" Colbourn asked.

But the BA's flagship was leading the charge toward the *Bres*, and had enough troubles of her own, defending herself from the AP's onslaught.

"We're on our own," the captain replied. "But don't worry. We still have our sting. Bring her round," he said to the helm.

"Aye, captain."

"What are you doing?" asked Colbourn. "Shouldn't you run this past the admiral?"

"No time. We're fighting for our lives. He can make me face a court martial when the battle's over, if either of us is still around."

Wright braced against a rail as the *Valiant* swung about.

"Railgun barrage, as soon as you have her in your sights," the captain said to Newcombe, the weapons officer.

The projectile weapon might work against their large attacker. The dreadnought would be slow to move out of the line of fire, and her forceshield would do nothing against solid titanium.

Wright gripped the rail tightly as the sharp movement threatened to throw him off his feet. Finally, the *Valiant* began to slow as she neared her new position.

"Shit! No!" someone shouted.

On the holoscreen, where one of the BA's ships had flown, now there was only a debris field.

"Which ship?" asked Wright.

"The *Resolute*," the captain answered grimly.

A painful silence descended on the bridge.

Wright had had friends aboard the *Resolute*, one of the BA's newest destroyers, friends from his training days. He felt sick and powerless.

He suddenly wondered what he was doing there, on a dubious mission and in a desperate battle. Colbourn's confession about the state of things in the upper echelons of the BA had wormed its way into his psyche, making him question everything he'd held dear all his life, making him question who he was.

"Newcombe," said the captain sternly, "when you're ready."

"Yes, sir." The woman refocused on her console. Wright

guessed she had known people aboard the vessels they'd lost, too.

Fuck! Three ships! They were three ships down already, and the battle had barely begun.

He was seized with the need to do something. He couldn't stand there and watch the destruction of everything he'd held dear for so long.

"Ma'am" he said to Colbourn. "Permission to join a unit defending the ship."

She looked at him distractedly, as if she hadn't quite heard what he was saying.

He realized that, for the first time in his years of serving under the brigadier, he was seeing her on the edge of losing it.

He repeated, "Permission to—"

"I heard you the first time," she snapped. "Permission granted."

He set off toward the exit, but before he reached it, someone yelled, "What the hell's that?!"

When he turned back, all gazes were on the holo.

He peered at the moving dots, but he couldn't see what was new. He was looking for another enemy vessel joining the battle, but he couldn't see any additional ships.

The *Valiant* shuddered. Her spinal railgun had activated and begun firing, hurling titanium slugs at the EAC dreadnought.

"What is it?" someone asked. "Is it a new weapon? Or some kind of ship?"

Then Wright saw it. *Something* was heading into the frame of the holo, and it was moving faster than any space vessel he'd ever seen. But it looked nothing like a weapon or a ship. It was an opaque, amorphous, mass, only visible due to the fact it blocked out the light of the stars as it passed in front of them.

"The scanners aren't picking up a single thing," said

Corporal Singh. "All they're reading is the light reduction. According to the other data, it doesn't exist."

"Whatever it is," Colbourn said gravely, "it isn't ours."

"No," agreed the captain. "It appears to be traveling toward—"

"I think we hit her!" exclaimed Newcombe.

"Yes," said Singh. "I'm seeing shrapnel ejected from the EAC flagship's starboard bow."

"Good shot," the captain said. "Don't let up."

But Wright could see the man remained distracted by the oncoming unknown threat. So was Colbourn. She'd stopped pacing and was stalking toward the holoscreen, mesmerized.

Wright hesitated, now uncertain about his wish to take part in repelling boarders. He had a feeling it wouldn't come to that —he had a feeling the EAC and AP would rather destroy the BA ships than try to acquire them.

The mass glided on, heading for the tip of the BA fleet. Due to her maneuver to fire upon the EAC dreadnought, the *Valiant* was hanging back, out of the imminent melee. Her remaining corvette, the *Cornflower*, flew by her side.

"What *is* that thing?" murmured Colbourn.

"The *Fearless* is about to find out," Wright said. He also couldn't remove his gaze from the holoscreen, trapped by grim fascination.

If the BA admiral aboard the flagship had noticed the approaching cloud, he hadn't taken any evasive action.

Until that moment.

The *Fearless* suddenly began to veer off course, leaving the trajectory that would have taken her to the *Bres*. She was finally trying to avoid the strange mass bearing down on her.

"Does the admiral have any information on it?" Colbourn asked the captain.

"If he has, he hasn't transmitted it to the fleet. And I wouldn't want to distract him right now."

"Uh," said Singh, "the EAC dreadnought's powering up her particle lance."

"Damn," the captain said.

"We've lost two Swifts," reported an officer.

"Divert main power to shields," said the captain.

The weapons officer slumped in her seat. The railgun couldn't operate with all the ship's spare power devoted to the shields. But without them they would be cleaved like fruit for the EAC ship's dessert.

"Dear god," whispered Colbourn.

The baffling mass was reaching out. On the holo, a finger of darkness was darting across space, moving even faster than the cloud itself.

The *Fearless* would never get away from it. The ship was like an ant trying to escape a flash flood.

Wright prayed the strange astronomical body was a harmless, directionless object that just happened to be acting like a predatory beast.

His prayer went unanswered.

The black tongue reached the *Fearless* and wrapped it in shadow.

The ship was gone, and the entire cloud had vanished too. The stars it had blanked out shone again.

The mass had disappeared as if it had never existed, and taken the BA flagship with it.

27

The whoops and hollers of her fellow marines echoing in her ears, Taylan left her position at the *Valiant's* aft hatch and went to take off her armor and stow her pulse rifle. She didn't understand what there was to celebrate. Sure, the EAC and AP had backed off—no one seemed to know why—and, sure, the Alliance had abandoned its suicide mission of destroying the colony ship, but thousands of men and women were dead. The BA had lost four ships, three falling to enemy fire, and the fourth disappearing into the ether, swallowed by some kind of cosmic cryptid. Rumor said all contact had been lost with the *Fearless*, and the scan data showed no sign of her. From what she'd heard, they'd also lost some Swifts.

Pre-fight adrenaline still ran like fire through her veins. She was alive with tension, and she didn't know how to come down. Booze was strictly forbidden aboard ship, which wasn't to say it didn't exist, only that she would be risking severe disciplinary action if she was discovered drinking. And after all the stuff she and Abacha had pulled, she couldn't risk it. Not if she wanted to remain a marine, and, now, she thought she did. For a while, anyway.

She stepped into the armory, deposited her rifle, and began to take off her suit, snapping the helmet clips open and lifting it off her head. She was the first to arrive. Everyone else was still celebrating not dying. As she pulled out the tabs on each side of her breastplate, releasing it, her rack mate arrived.

"Hey," said Abacha.

"Hey."

"That was some fight we didn't have."

She snorted a brief laugh. "Yeah."

He took off his helmet and slid it into its slot on the wall.

She caught him sneaking a glance at her.

"You doing okay?" he asked.

"Huh? What do you mean?"

"Oh, you know. You've been...distracted lately."

"Have I? Well, I'm fine." She guessed she had been feeling down, but things had changed. "How are *you* doing?"

"I'm good. Same old." Then he said softly, "Shame about the *Daisy*."

"Yeah. A real shame." Taylan hadn't been close to her former platoon, but she also felt their loss. Dying in the vacuum of space, alone and maybe wounded, was a possibility she tried not to think about. She guessed everyone aboard BA battleships felt the same. She hoped that whatever had happened to her old shipmates had been quick and painless.

"If you hadn't put in a request for my transfer to the Valiant along with you," said Abacha, "I'd be dead right now."

"Crap." She paused a beat before removing the rest of her suit. "You and me both."

"You saved my life," said Abacha.

"Aw, c'mon. It isn't like I took a bullet for you. And you've been there for me plenty of times. I'm glad you're still around."

"Glad you're still here too. After all, who else do I have to beat at xiangqi?"

Taylan grinned, walked over to Abacha, and punched his shoulder. "See you around."

"You're going? What's your hurry? I thought we could unwind over a game. You never know, I might let you win for once."

"We both know that's a lie. I'm going to see my new friend."

"You made a friend? How'd that happen?"

"I can be nice, if I try. Now I have *two* buddies."

"You mean me? I never said I was your buddy."

"And I never said you were one of the two," Taylan called out over her shoulder as she sauntered from the armory.

HER SHOCK at hearing what the stranger rescued from the mountain at Nantgarw-y-garth called himself had eased. She'd convinced herself her imagination had gone into overdrive about what the name meant.

And yet...she couldn't get rid of the niggling feeling that the impossible was true, and she knew she would never be free of doubt until she'd seen solid proof.

If this person was who she'd initially suspected he was, there was a way she could find out. The test would never stand up as a scientific experiment, but, to her, it would mean a lot.

She unlocked the cabin door. Major Wright had entrusted her with the security code just prior to the battle. When the door opened, she found the man sitting on his bed, petting Boots.

The cat miaowed, jumped down, and padded over to her. As Boots rubbed against Taylan's leg, the stranger pointed and said a word.

"Uh, she's a cat," she said. "Cat."

"Cat," he repeated, adding something unintelligible.

Boots ran off down the passageway.

The man's hair was wet. He'd obviously been trying out the shower, but he didn't know it had a drying setting.

"Can you come with me?" she asked, beckoning.

He rose and padded over to her.

She sent him back to put on his shoes, and then she took him to the gym.

The place was empty, though Taylan could hear the far-off strains of some kind of celebration going on. She turned on the lights and walked directly to the equipment store. The man waited patiently as she rummaged around in the back of the store. She was sure she'd seen what she was looking for somewhere in there. Then she saw them, lying under a pile of sparring helmets, grubby and lonely in the corner: A pair of staves.

She reached in and slid them out from under the helmets, sending up a cloud of dust. When she'd wiped them off, the staves looked new and unused. She guessed Royal Marines were rarely required to fight with big sticks, and she didn't remember any instruction in the weapons from Basic. That was a mistake in her opinion. Staff-fighting taught a lot of valuable skills different from hand-to-hand or knife combat. Her father had taught her how to use them well, both defensively and offensively. She guessed the ones in the store were there in case the trainers wanted to instruct in a modern martial art.

The man had moved to the shelves that held other practice equipment. He was examining the items, looking confused. But when he saw what Taylan was holding, his features cleared and recognition lit his face. He nodded, seeming to want to show his understanding.

Her stomach clenched.

Shit.

There was nothing for it except to go through with the test.

She found some protective gear that fitted him and put on

her own. When she walked out into the gym and stepped onto the mat, he followed her.

They faced each other.

He smiled and readied his weapon.

Shit. Shit. Shit.

He knew exactly what to do.

She lunged, aiming at his head. Her staff cracked against his as he met it easily. Then he pushed, using his greater height and weight to force her down. She slipped out from under him, making him collapse forward, and swung the end of her staff toward his stomach. He twisted out of reach, spun right round, and swiped at her.

She met the blow just in time and knocked his staff hard, trying to shock it from his grip, but he was holding it too firmly. She realized her back was exposed. She dropped to the floor and his staff whistled over her head. She swept hers upward again, this time aiming for his jaw, which was hanging over her after his move. He reared back, a fraction too late. Her staff glanced his nose.

They fought on, moving so fast her actions were pure training and muscle memory, with hardly any time to think.

She tried some feints, but he guessed her intention every time. She tried speeding up the pace even faster, but he kept up with her. And when he went on the attack, she was barely able to counter his blows.

Damn, he was good.

The split second of admiration resulted in a blow to the side of her head. Her helmet saved her from any real harm, and the man certainly didn't cut her any slack. He redoubled his attack, and she was hard put to avoid being struck again, and to stay on her feet. He loved that low swipe, intended to knock her legs from under her.

It had been years since she'd fought with a staff, and she was feeling the lack of practice. She'd never been able to persuade Abacha to give the weapons a try. If she'd been on top form, she might have been able to beat the mystery man. At her peak performance, she'd beaten her father a few times, to his great pride and admiration.

But she knew she wasn't going to see victory today.

She knew what she needed to know. How to stop the fight without suffering a concussion or a cracked rib, though? The only words the man knew were her name and 'cat'.

Sweating and panting, she jumped backward, out of his reach, and dropped her staff to her side.

The man understood the session was over. He gave a bow and spoke a short phrase.

"You fought well too," said Taylan.

It was good to spar with someone who matched her abilities. He'd really tested her limits.

But concern of a greater nature overwhelmed her satisfaction with the match. No matter how mind-blowing and difficult it was for her to accept, no matter how much she wanted to deny the truth, she couldn't do it any longer.

As well as a military veteran, her father had been a history buff specializing in ancient forms of combat. Staff-fighting was a very old sport, he'd told her, something rarely practiced any longer, at least not in the West.

Yet this man who Wright had found entombed inside a Welsh mountain could use a staff like he'd been practicing all his life.

She *couldn't* believe it, yet she had no choice.

She felt absurd. What should she do? Drop to one knee and bow her head? Was that what people did around kings?

Instead, she walked up to the man and shook his hand.

"Hello, Arthur."

28

W right closed his eyes, opened them again, and then rubbed a hand over the top of his head.

"What?"

Ellis frowned at him. "I know it's a lot to take in."

"You're telling me."

She'd asked him to come to the cabin where he'd put the man he'd rescued from West BI. After the battle with the EAC and AP, he had plenty to do, but Ellis's tone had been urgent, as if she had something extremely important to tell him, so he'd decided to spare her a few minutes.

Apparently, the critical piece of information she had to convey was that the man's name was Arthur. After that, she'd spouted a load of gobbledygook about an ancient legend, fighting off invaders to the Britannic Isles, swords, prophecies, wizards, knights, and...tables?

"Are you seriously telling me you've never heard about any of this stuff?" Ellis asked tersely.

"I don't know," he replied, exasperated. "I might have done, when I was a kid. I don't remember. But what's all this got to do with him?" He indicated toward 'Arthur' with his eyebrows.

The man was sitting passively on his bunk while Ellis faced him over a table. He was watching them talk, but he clearly didn't understand anything of what was passing between them.

Ellis slapped her forehead. "Haven't you been listening to a word I've said?!"

"Watch it, corporal."

"I'm sorry, sir, but..." She got up and jabbed a finger at the mystery man. "It's *him*. He's King Arthur. The once and future king. *In our hour of need, he will return.* Doesn't that mean anything to you?"

Wright carefully studied her. She didn't *seem* to be joking. She seemed to believe it all. Perhaps she was having a psychotic break due to the stress of the battle. All the marines in her former platoon aboard the *Daisy* had died. She would be experiencing grief and shock. Those strong emotions, coupled with her desire to return to BI, had probably made her confused and delusional. Rather than face her pain, she'd become fixated on the man under her responsibility.

Would it be better to humor her, or should he send her to sick bay?

He decided to try the former first before resorting to more drastic action. Maybe he could still reach the rational part of her mind.

"All right, Ellis. Let's say what you've told me is true. I need you to explain a few things for me."

She looked relieved. "Okay."

"If this man is King Arthur, returned from the dead—"

"No, he didn't die. He was mortally wounded and carried from the field of battle."

"Mortally means fatally, right?"

"Yes, it does...but he didn't die. That's the point. He should have died, but Merlin put him into a deep sleep, so he could—"

"Rise again. I get it." Wright sighed. He could hardly believe he was having this conversation. "So he's been in this deep sleep for...what, three and a half thousand years?"

"About that. Even historians who lived a few centuries after Arthur's time weren't exactly sure when he reigned."

"Well..." He looked expectantly at the corporal.

"Well what?"

"How could he have been 'sleeping' for millennia?! It isn't possible."

"Isn't it? Didn't you say he looked like he'd been in that cave for years? And I thought the AP had made big strides in cryonic preservation. They claim they can put people under for centuries."

"Okay, I'll give you that. But Arthur wasn't cryonically preserved. Believe me, I'd know. He looked like he'd been dead a long time."

"Only he wasn't, was he? He was still alive! Who knows what Merlin did to him so he could live so long? At that time, it might have seemed like magic, but maybe it was only highly advanced medical technology, even more advanced than we have now?"

"And how would someone living in the Dark Ages have access to highly advanced tech?"

Ellis huffed in frustration. "Look, I don't have all the answers. I can't explain everything. I'm just as amazed as you are."

"Uh, no. I really don't think you are."

"Right, so, *you* tell me who he is, how he came to be inside a sealed cave and still alive after being mummified."

"I can't explain it. I never said I could. But that doesn't mean I have to dream up a supernatural fairy tale as an answer."

The corporal glared at him, but then appeared to rein in her anger. "What if... what if we forget about the impossibility of Arthur surviving so long in those conditions? Why did we go there to rescue him?"

"We were responding to a distress call." Wright began to grow uncomfortable.

"Where did the signal come from? Did you ever find a transmitter?"

"No..."

She had a point. The absence of a transmitter, and the missing device's ability to transmit through solid rock had always bothered him, but he didn't want to encourage her in her delusion. "There was no time to look for the signal origin. EAC troops were closing in. It would have been dangerous and a waste of time to hang around trying to find it." He chose not to mention that the signal had disappeared as soon as they'd broken into the cave.

"Who do *you* think sent it?" Ellis asked.

"I don't know, but it doesn't matter. Has it occurred to you it might have been a coincidence that we happened to find him there? The signal could have been a glitch. We mounted a rescue and happened to stumble across someone in need of rescuing, but the two things might not be connected."

"He just happened to be there?! Halfway up a mountainside in a mostly uninhabited wilderness? With EAC troops nearby?"

That fact had puzzled him too. Why *had* the EAC military been so close at hand? They'd arrived so soon after the *Daisy* had touched down, they must have been in the vicinity. What had they been doing there?

"Coincidences happen," he retorted, though he knew his words had begun to sound hollow. "Just because things seem to be linked, doesn't mean they are."

"And sometimes they *are* connected, but people refuse to acknowledge the truth that's staring them in the face!"

"That's enough, corporal!" He rose to his feet. "Your story is ridiculous, and I have doubts about your mental stability. You're to report to sick bay for a psychological evaluation this afternoon."

"I don't need a psychological evaluation. Why can't you admit I could be right?"

He strode to the door.

"Can't you see how it all makes sense?" continued Ellis, following on his heels. "The EAC have taken over the Britannic Isles. We're losing our territories, and we're about to lose the space war."

The door opened, and Wright stepped out into the passageway.

"The BA is going to be wiped from existence!" yelled the corporal. "In our hour of need, he will return!"

The door slid closed, cutting off the rest of her ravings.

As he walked away, preparing to comm sick bay about Ellis's probable mental illness, he debated the wisdom of leaving her alone with the man, Arthur. But in her fantasy he was some kind of savior king, so he doubted she would hurt him.

It was time to get back to his regular duties. If Corporal Ellis had been wrong about everything else, she was right that the BA was in a bad way. If it was to survive, they would have to pull out all the stops.

29

The next step in Hans's plan had to be undertaken with utmost care. It was best if the idea didn't appear to come from him. The military leaders had to imagine they'd thought of it themselves, or they would never go through with it.

Not because his plan was bad—far from it. It was the obvious solution to the BA's troubles, in the short term, anyway. But the people he had to sway were a bunch of arrogant, bone-headed, stubborn vestiges of the days of Empire. They would automatically reject the proposal of a foreigner, someone who didn't belong to their club, who hadn't been to the right schools, and who had no friends or associates within the elite.

It was a problem Hans had faced again and again as he'd risen through the ranks of SIS. If it hadn't been for the recordings he held of prominent figures committing compromising acts, he would never have been chosen to lead the organization.

His office door opened, and his new personal assistant entered, bringing his coffee.

"Mariya, good morning. How are you today?"

"Very well, thank you, Mr Jonte. And I see you seem to be recovering well from your injuries."

"I am, thanks to that excellent home nurse you found me."

"It's my pleasure, sir. I know Josie would have wanted me to do my best to help you."

"I'm sure she would. Mariya, I was wondering, do you have a dress suitable to wear to a black tie event?"

She placed the cup and saucer on his desk. "You mean an evening dress?"

"Yes. Something expensive and flattering. If you haven't, speak up. You can get one today. I want you to accompany me to the Officers' Ball."

"I'd be honored, Mr Jonte. Thank you."

"There's no need to be grateful. You'll be working. I have a few tasks to complete tonight, and you can help me."

"In that case...I'll put a dress on the department's tab, and I'll need two hours this afternoon to go shopping."

"Ha! As you wish."

He smiled wryly as she left. Mariya was turning out to be quite different from her twin. She was equally resourceful, but much more up front. As the days had passed, she'd relaxed into her role and revealed more of her true personality. He liked her feistiness.

But he didn't have time to waste musing about his new assistant. He had people to butter up. He opened the screen in his desk and looked up the first person on his list.

The comm went through, and a face appeared.

"Hans, long time no see. Great to hear from you."

He settled into his seat and picked up his coffee. He was in his element. Today was going to be a good day.

AT EIGHT-THIRTY PM THAT EVENING, when he arrived with Mariya at the Caribbean Ambassador's Residence, the party had only just begun. He was a little early to be truly *de rigueur*. In fact, his timing could have been perceived as *gauche*, but, confident that no matter what he did he would never be accepted into Society's circles, he'd long since given up trying.

He could still cut a fine dash, however, and with Mariya on his arm he was certain of doing that tonight.

As she'd stepped from the lobby of her apartment block to join him in the limousine, her appearance had taken his breath away. He had no interest in romantic dalliances; he'd married himself to his cause many years ago, but, for a brief moment, his resolve had been shaken.

His assistant had spent her two hours of shopping and the department's budget well. Her dress was sleeveless, gossamer-thin and shimmering soft gold, and hung from her shoulders to her feet. She had dressed her hair as a perfect complement, weaving golden threads through it and studding it with white jewels. And, as she crossed the sidewalk to the car, she carried herself like a duchess.

Who would have known plain old Josephine's identical twin could have scrubbed up so well?

When she'd climbed in—most elegantly—he'd been delighted to smell a whiff of a delicious fragrance. Mariya really was a woman after his own heart. If only his heart were not already taken.

"Here we are," said Hans, turning to her as the limousine pulled up outside the ambassador's palatial residence. "You remember what you have to do?"

"Of course, Mr Jonte."

"Good. But...enjoy yourself too. That's what these events are about. Fun and shenanigans." He tapped his nose. "Let's go." He nodded to the chauffeur, who got out of the limo and opened the door on Mariya's side.

Hans waited for the chauffeur to open his door, then joined his assistant on the sidewalk. The night air was warm and humid and the sky was cloudless. On the fringes of the Islands, the battle against their enemies continued, but for now and in this place, all was calm and safe.

Together, they climbed the steps to the entrance.

A small group of ushers waited just inside the open doors, clad in red and gold uniforms. The entrance hall floor of checkerboard tiles was polished to a fine sheen, and marble columns rose to a ceiling exquisitely decorated in bas relief. Paintings of previous ambassadors hung on the walls, spaced at regular intervals. The oldest ones dated back hundreds of years.

Hans prided himself on his appreciation of taste, and he could find nothing objectionable about the scene. Everything was exactly as it should be. He breathed in deeply. Whoever was responsible for organizing the occasion had even arranged for a faint, sweet, lemon scent to imbue the air. He could also smell wine, punch, and a slight savory odor—probably hors d'oeuvres.

An usher was approaching them. Hans lifted and bent his elbow, and Mariya delicately rested her hand upon it. They walked with the usher through to the central ballroom.

As he'd predicted, the place was somewhat sparse in guests, due to the early hour, but both Hennessy, Chief of Defense Staff, and First Sea Lord Montague, had arrived. The men were too old and well-connected to concern themselves with timing etiquette. They probably wanted to get their fill of alcohol, fine food, and idle chatter before they grew too tired and needed a nap.

Both men were standing near the punch bowl, looking resplendent in their dress uniforms, chatting. Hans led Mariya over to them.

They didn't look particularly pleased to see Hans, but the sight of his assistant awakened interest in their wrinkled faces and rheumy eyes.

"Good evening, gentlemen," Hans said. "May I introduce a vital member of my staff?"

"Charmed, I'm sure," said Hennessy. "And who might you be?"

After Mariya gave them her name, Hans introduced Hennessy and Montague by their full titles, which apparently gratified them enormously.

"Any news from the fleet?" Hans asked Montague. "It was such a shame the attack failed."

Hennessy coughed and Montague's cheeks flushed a deeper-than-usual pink.

"Damned shame," the Sea Lord muttered, "but we were up against some type of new weapon. Never known anything like it. I'd appreciate your help, Jonte, with finding out what the hell it was that took the *Fearless*."

"My best officers are trying to find out what they can." said Hans. As he understood it, the attack had already been going to pieces before the flagship was destroyed. Somehow, the EAC and AP had gotten wind of the plan and were waiting for the BA ships. But it wasn't the right time to mention it. "As soon as I hear anything, I'll pass it on immediately. You have my word."

"I'd be obliged," Montague replied. "We have a strategy meeting in the morning. It's been a rough year, but I have every hope we'll meet the new challenges that face us."

"So you're working for Jonte, eh?" Hennessy asked Mariya.

"Yes, but I'm new. I've only been with SIS a short while."

"Ah, new and innocent!" Montague exclaimed. "You must tell us all his secrets."

Mariya replied, "I'm sure I don't know anything important."

"You won't pull the wool over our eyes so easily, young

lady," Hennessy retorted. "Jonte's office only deals with highly sensitive intel."

"Even so..." protested Mariya.

"Don't worry, dear, We're only pulling your leg," said Montague. "We know you won't give anything away. Jonte wouldn't have you working for him if you weren't tighter than a drum. You can leave her with us," he said to Hans. "We'll look after her."

"But we've only just arrived," Hans protested. "There are plenty more people I'd like Mariya to meet."

"We can introduce her to everyone," replied Hennessy. "Go and mingle, Jonte, mingle! We all know that's what you love doing best."

"Mariya?"

"I'll be fine, sir. I'm looking forward to hearing some military exploits."

"Ha!" said Hennessy, "if you love old soldiers' stories—"

"Old *sailors'* tales are far more interesting," interjected Montague.

Hans gave Mariya the barest of winks before turning to survey the room. While he'd been talking to Hennessy and Montague, more guests had arrived. He spotted the ambassador and his wife—a very influential woman—as well as the admiral recently appointed to replace the man who had been commanding the *Fearless*.

Where to go next?

He made a beeline for the admiral.

Mariya would do her job and do it well. She already had the old goats eating out of the palm of her hand. If only they knew. Soon, she would be flattering them, telling them how experienced, knowledgeable men of war like themselves should have more influence on how things were run; that everything would fall apart unless someone with some sense stepped in.

It was at gatherings like these where the real wheels of

power turned. Attitudes were formed, alliances were made and broken, plans were created and set in motion. He had some hard work ahead of him tonight among the glasses of fine wine and canapés, but the wounds he'd sustained in the bombing of the General Council had nearly healed and he was on top form.

As Hennessy had said, it was time to mingle.

30

T he kid had gone missing, but Lorcan wasn't worried. He hated the little shit. And Dwyr Orr had practically twisted his arm to allow the child on the *Bres*. If harm came to her son, she couldn't say he hadn't warned her. His guardian—an old man so senile he could barely string words into a sentence—was utterly useless at keeping the lad under control. He was always slinking around and turning up where you least expected him, and where he knew he wasn't supposed to be. If he'd gotten himself into trouble, it was his own fault.

The Dwyr wasn't exactly high on his list of favorite people at the moment anyway, Lorcan mused. Her abandonment of the battle at the critical moment, when everything was going their way, had been insane. Just because of some superstitious fear of whatever had taken the BA ship. He'd thought about the event for days, and his point still held: The thing had disappeared along with the ship it took. It hadn't demonstrated an intent to attack the EAC or AP fleet. They should have pressed on with their new, unexpected advantage, not abandoned the fight.

"Hey, Sparkes," he said, "play the recording from the battle."

He sensed an unspoken, collective groan from the staff in the control center. It was true that they must have seen the vid ten or fifteen times, but so what? There was always something new to learn. After all the years they'd worked with him, he thought they would have understood that by now.

In place of the scrolling scenes from the construction of the *Bres*, a new vista appeared. The BA's fleet appeared as distant points of light, little bigger than the surrounding stars. Then the screen blinked as the cameras refocused, enlarging the vessels.

He frowned. What arrogant fools the Alliance's military leaders had been to think they could have destroyed one of his beautiful colony ships! How could they not know he would never have allowed that to happen, not while there was breath in his body. Nevertheless, he couldn't deny that Dwyr Orr's warning of the impending attack and support during the battle had been very useful.

Until...

There it was. The opaque cloud had puffed into space from nowhere, off in a corner of the screen. What a strange phenomenon. In his many years of studying space and in everything he'd learned from the world's top astronomers, present and past, he'd never seen or heard of anything like it.

All around him, his staff continued working, ignoring the battle's replay, but Lorcan found himself drawn to the screen. He got up from his seat and walked closer.

There was something hyperphysical about the cloud. He was reminded of Dwyr Orr's ramblings about quantum mechanics and the 'unknown' aspects of universal laws. She might have called the mass dark matter or dark energy, though of course it was neither of those things. They were not 'dark' in the literal meaning of the word, for a start.

"The report from Deck Six is in," said Jurrah.

"What report?" asked Lorcan.

"About the boy, Perran. He isn't there. They searched the place top to bottom, but there's no sign of him."

"Yes, yes. Whatever." Lorcan resented the manpower and time wasted on the search. Every member of staff and every minute spent looking for the kid put back the completion of the Project. He had a good mind to send the Dwyr a bill.

He stared intently at the screen. The finger of cloud was reaching out. It was hard not to anthropomorphise the phenomenon. It looked like a huddled hag, swathed in rags, sending forth a bony digit, perhaps to see how fat her captive children had grown, and if they were ready to eat.

Only this finger didn't poke, it enveloped what it touched.

"It must have been terrifying," Kekoa commented. She'd begun to watch the recording too.

"What?" asked Lorcan.

"For the men and women on the ship. To see that thing coming for them, knowing they couldn't escape."

"I suppose it must have been."

Was *that* why no one else seemed keen to watch the battle again? Not because they were bored of it, but because it made them afraid?

"Do you think they might still be alive?" Kekoa asked.

"The crew of the ship? I very much doubt it, but it isn't impossible. No one has a clue what happened."

"I hope they are."

"Whether they are or not matters little, except the BA now has one less vessel with which to plague us." That was a positive outcome—the Alliance had been forced to run away with its tail between its legs. It would take time to recover from the loss of its flagship and the others destroyed in the battle, and that meant more opportunities for resource harvesting on Earth.

"Should we begin to search Deck Seven?" Jurrah asked.

"What f— Oh, that blasted kid." Lorcan returned to his seat. The battle recording now only showed the retreating ships. After a harsh, heated discussion with the Dwyr, the AP and EAC ships had also returned to their bases.

What a wasted opportunity. If only the woman...But there was no point in going over it again. What was done was done.

"No," said Lorcan. "Call off the search."

"But, what about the—"

"The kid got himself lost, he can get himself found. There are comm panels, drones, and workers all over the ship. It shouldn't be too hard for a boy his age to make contact, if he really wants to."

Lorcan harbored a suspicion that Dwyr Orr's son wasn't lost at all; that he was hiding somewhere and very much enjoying all the attention and kerfuffle from the search. He had a feeling that little whats-his-name would soon show his face when he realized no one was looking for him anymore.

"Tell his guardian he's to wait in his cabin in case the boy goes there. From now on, I don't want another second spent on that child."

"Yes, sir."

In the end, Little Perran didn't turn up for the rest of the day. But it was only when the shift was over and his department heads went to dinner, leaving him alone in the control room, that Lorcan remembered about the boy. He checked the general comms to see if he'd missed an announcement that the boy had been found, but there was nothing.

He tried comming the guardian.

"H-hello?" the old man said, his face appearing on Lorcan's interface.

"I take it Dwyr Orr's son hasn't returned to your cabin?"

"W-what's that?"

Lorcan tutted. "The kid," he said, louder. "Has the kid come back?"

"No, Perran isn't here. I was hoping he might be with you."

Why the hell would the guardian would think *he* might be looking after the child? It beggared belief.

"I think I should inform the Dwyr about the situation," the man said tremulously.

"You mean you haven't already?" Lorcan had thought it strange that Kala hadn't contacted him yet.

"N-no." The guardian paused. "She will be...rather angry."

So that was it. He didn't want to face her, knowing she would blame him. Though actually the little shit must have slipped away deliberately, easily able to outwit the old fool.

"Let's leave it till morning," said Lorcan.

"Are you sure?"

"Yes. He's bound to turn up by then, and the Dwyr will be none the wiser. If he doesn't, I'll tell her our outward comm had a fault and we weren't able to contact her."

The old man looked relieved. "If you're certain that's the right cause of action, sir."

"I am."

"T-thank you, sir."

"If you haven't eaten, go to dinner, and then get a good night's sleep."

"I will. Thank you again."

Lorcan closed the comm. He couldn't help but feel sorry for the guardian. He had a raving lunatic for a mistress and a conniving snake as his ward. His life couldn't be easy.

Rubbing his eyes as sudden fatigue hit him, Lorcan decided to go straight to his suite. He was in no mood for chatter over the evening meal—though, in truth, he rarely was—and he had snacks he could nibble on if he grew peckish. A new consignment of genetic material had arrived a few hours ago. He was looking forward to spending the evening studying it and imagining how the species might become part of the ecosystem of a new world.

He trudged the familiar passageways of the *Bres* that took him to his rooms. When he arrived, he got the shock of his life. Though later, when he looked back on it, he knew he shouldn't have been at all surprised.

The kid was there.

Bold as brass, he was perched on the edge of the sofa in the living room, surrounded by empty snack packets and idly browsing Lorcan's personal interface.

"Oh, hello," the boy said, looking up, calm as anything.

For a second, Lorcan was too overcome with rage to speak, or move, or even think. Until he finally spat out, "You little *bastard*,"

The kid's eyebrows rose. "Did I do something wrong?"

Lorcan uttered more foul expletives about the boy's parentage, related him to private areas of human anatomy, and suggested he perform a lewd act upon himself.

"You mean I wasn't I supposed to come in here?"

Lorcan didn't bother asking him how he'd circumvented the security, or how long he'd been there, or what he'd seen in his private files. As it was, he was only just holding himself back from spacing the lad.

"*You* are going home," he said. "Right now." Not taking his eyes from the Dwyr's son, he commed a shuttle pilot. The man would probably be eating, but that could wait. If the little arsehole wasn't off the *Bres* in the next five minutes, he might do something he would later regret.

"But I like it here," whined the boy. "Why don't you want me around? I saw a picture of a boy about my age in your files. Is he your son? Can I meet him? Or did he die, like your wife?"

That did it.

Lorcan marched over to the boy and slapped him so hard he spun around before he fell off the sofa and hit the floor.

Slowly, he pulled himself to a sitting position, but he didn't cry. Instead, he sat on the rug, clutching his cheek and looking up at Lorcan with malicious eyes.

"I'll tell my mother you did that."

31

T he writing was almost indecipherable. The lines were faint with the passage of time, and the pages of the book had been yellowed by the same process, so it was difficult for Kala Orr's tired eyes to separate one from the other.

And of course the script was old, too. Very old. She'd often wondered if she was the only person in the world who knew the ancient languages in which such books were written. She'd never met or heard of anyone else who had studied them, at least not these ones, written by monks and scholars who had lived and died thousands of years ago.

She sat upright, stretched her aching back, and rubbed her shoulders. How long had she been poring over the aged texts?

Seeing the sun's beams slanting through the leaded window of the library, she realized an entire night had passed while she'd been reading. That had to make fifty or more hours of study since the battle, yet she was no closer to understanding what had taken the BA ship. The books mentioned monsters of many kinds, mythical and spiritual as well as actual dangerous beasts of the time, but nothing came close to what she'd seen, not even in an allegorical sense.

Until she could hazard a guess as to what the thing was and its implication to the EAC, if it was dangerous or benign, and what it might portend, she didn't want to push on any further in the conflict with the BA.

If the astronomical phenomenon was intelligent and could be harnessed to do others' bidding, then the EAC's struggle could be over. All she had to do was to discover how to reach its mind, then she would simply direct it to swallow the rest of the BA fleet, shortly followed by Ua Talman's colony ships. But if it wasn't living, or it was living but senseless, like some kind of cosmic worm, then it was as much a danger to the EAC as it was to anyone else who crossed its path, and she'd been right to immediately withdraw her ships from the area.

She was certain of one thing: The appearance of the entity at that place and that point in time could not be a coincidence. Before turning to her library of ancient tomes, she'd searched all the information she had on bodies in space and found nothing even resembling the cloud that had arrived from nowhere in the middle of the battle. The fact that it had materialized there and then *had* to be significant.

The same synchronicity had occurred when she'd almost retrieved the man of the myths from the cave, and at the exact same time, BA had turned up. It was as if it had been predestined.

What did it all mean?

She reached out to the corner of the weighty volume open before her on the table, lifted it, and carefully closed the book. Then she stood up and returned it to its place on the shelf, sliding it between Bede's *Ecclesiastical History of England* and Nennius's *Historia Brittonum*.

Kala stretched again and crossed the library to the heavy oak door, darkened with age. After pulling it open, she passed through the quiet hallway. The castle was beginning to stir with movement as the other inhabitants rose for the new day. She began to climb the stairs wearily.

She halted.

From outside came the distant sound of an aircraft. It was not something she expected to hear in that part of the BI. If one had been chartered for a special purpose, she would know about it. As she hesitated on the stairs, the sound grew louder. The aircraft was approaching the castle. She recognized a distinctive rumble. It wasn't an aircraft, it was a shuttle arriving from space. The speed of the craft's arrival quickly turned the rumble to a roar.

She descended hastily. No shuttle was due, or, at least, no one had notified her of one.

At the castle entrance on the opposite side of the hall, she lifted the iron bar and pushed open one of the double doors. A fresh, morning sea breeze gusted in. The shuttle was already visible, a dull gray triangle swooping down from a rosy sky.

One of Ua Talman's vessels. What could it mean? Had she missed a message?

Super-heated gas burst from the shuttle's thrusters as it came in to land, turning the air beneath it hazy. Kala wrapped her arms around herself, chilled by the wind. The landing props came down, and the vessel lowered onto the pad. Finally, the ear-piercing noise of the engine faded.

Had Lorcan come to pay her a visit? Perhaps he wanted to go over what had happened at the end of the battle again, face to face. But she'd said all she had to say on the subject. He'd had the option to press on with his own fleet and finish off the BA if he'd been so certain that was the right course of action. Only he hadn't. He hadn't wanted to take the risk without the support of the EAC. That had been his decision, yet he continued to want to blame her.

She tutted and waited impatiently, her long night catching up with her.

The shuttle hatch opened and steps extended to the ground. Before the bottom step touched the flagstones, Perran clattered down them, shouting "Mummy!" and waving. He jumped the remaining gap and raced toward her.

Kala's lips hardened. Why had Lorcan brought her son back so abruptly, without any notification?

His short legs sped over the ground between them, his dark hair whipping around his head. When he'd covered about 75 meters, the steps hanging from the shuttle retracted inside and disappeared, the hatch closed, and the engine started up.

Where was Lorcan? Or Tom, her son's guardian? Had Ua Talman actually sent a young boy on the journey to Earth with only the pilot for company?

Had he risked the life of her child?!

Perran reached her and grabbed her around the waist, pressing his face into her. "I missed you!" he said, his voice muffled.

Kala took his shoulders and squatted down to look him in the eyes. "What happened? Why are you back so soon?" A sudden thought occurred to her. "Is the colony ship building site being attacked?"

"No, Lorcan told me I had to go home right away. He was so mean. He even hit me!"

"He *hit* you?!"

Her son nodded. "But I was brave. I didn't cry, Mummy."

"That was very brave. I can't believe he did that. Hitting a small child is a terrible thing to do. Did he hurt you badly?"

Perran shook his head.

"I'm glad to hear it. Maybe it's for the best that he sent you home if he was going to be so bad-tempered. Why did he do it?"

"I don't know."

"Hm..." Kala straightened up and softly touched her son's head. "Where's Tom? He didn't come with you?"

"He's still on the *Bres*. I heard Lorcan tell him he can stay there as long as he likes, and he can go with them to the new worlds if he wants."

"He did, did he?" *What a cheek.* "Come on, let's go inside. It's cold out here."

When they were in the hall, she closed the door against the wind, and let the bar fall into its slot. The rasping sound echoed from the stone walls. Taking her son's hand, she said, "I need to go to bed now, but if you go to the kitchen I'm sure Cook will be awake already and she'll make you some breakfast. But, before you go, did you get all the information I asked for?"

"Yes, and I memorized it all just how you taught me."

"Was it hard to find?"

"Not once I got inside Lorcan's private suite."

"Clever boy. Run along and have something to eat, and then I want you to put everything you learned into a file and send it to me. Can you do that?"

"Yes, Mummy. I will."

She watched him as he trotted across the hall to the doorway that led to the kitchen.

Had Ua Talman suspected Perran of snooping during his visit? Was that why he'd been so angry and sent him back without an escort?

One of the reasons she'd arranged for her son to do the job was because he was young and so unlikely to be closely watched, but it was possible that Ua Talman had figured out why he was there. That would definitely put a spoke in their relationship. After their argument at the end of the battle, however, it didn't seem so important. The accord between the EAC and AP probably wouldn't last much longer anyway.

Feeling more tired than ever, Kala climbed the stairs again, and then went directly to her bedroom. She planned on taking a three-hour nap before tackling the puzzle of the dark space phenomenon again.

But when she reached her bed, her interface light was flashing. Wondering if it was Lorcan reaching out to apologize for his ill treatment of her son, or accuse her of spying, she opened the screen.

She'd guessed wrong. The comm was from her contact within the BA. As she read the contents, a knot of excitement formed in her stomach. The intel could be her chance to put an end to the Alliance forever.

But she would need the AP's help.

That made the situation rather delicate. Since sending Perran home, Lorcan would have had time to cool off, but he was the type to hold a grudge forever. And now she had two counts against her. Yet he was also pragmatic, and he wanted to stop the BA from interfering in his operations as much as she wanted their remaining lands.

It wouldn't hurt to ask. If they were to take advantage of this new development, they would have to act quickly.

32

Taylan pressed the door button, wondering for the *nth* time if she was doing the right thing. She'd debated on whether to bring Arthur along but had decided that might work against her. Better to play on the miraculous aspects of his rescue and recovery.

"Who is it?" said Colbourn over the intercom.

She sounded annoyed, but the brigadier always sounded annoyed, so her mood was no indication of the likelihood of Taylan's success in her endeavor.

"Corporal Ellis, ma'am. I know it's highly irregular, but I'd like to speak to you in person, if I may." She cringed at the submissive tone in her voice. The old bat didn't deserve her respect, but she was going to have to fake it in order to get what she wanted.

The door opened. Colbourn sat behind her desk, already glowering. Taylan sucked in a breath at the sight of her. She hadn't seen the woman since she'd returned from Earth. She'd heard about her injuries, but she hadn't known they were quite so bad.

"Make it fast, corporal."

Taylan stepped into the office and waited for the door to close before saying, "I don't know if Major Wright has spoken to you yet, but I wondered if I could talk to you about what's going to happen to the man he rescued at West BI."

"Really, Ellis, that man is the last of my concerns right now. What do you want to know?"

Colbourn's response was about as amenable as she got. Taylan decided to go for it. She doubted she would ever find the woman in a better mood.

"It's pretty clear he's a West BI native, or at least, he used to be. I assume we're going to return him to his home at some point."

"Why would you assume that?"

Taylan faltered.

"In case it isn't obvious, corporal, we're at war. We can't go on jaunts around the solar system, taking passengers home. Do you think the *Valiant* is a taxi service?"

"No, but if you don't plan on taking him back to West BI, what's going to happen to him?"

"I imagine that if we aren't all captured, killed, or annihilated by a mysterious space octopus, I'll find the time to send him in a shuttle back to Earth eventually. Probably not to West BI as that's now enemy territory, but to another country we still hold. That would be safest for him. When that'll be, however, I simply can't say. Now, I have work to do. You're dismissed."

Taylan swallowed. *Here goes...* "When we take Arth...When we return the man to Earth, I want to resign from the Royal Marines. I want to go with him."

After Colbourn had dismissed her, her head had dipped to focus her attention on her screen. Now she jerked it up, her eyes narrowed. "I *beg* your pardon?!"

"I want to leave the marines. I don't think the patient will survive on his own back on Earth. He needs someone to look after him. If we just set him down in the middle of nowhere, with no money, not understanding the language, he'll die. It's rough down there, even in BA-held territories, unless you're rich."

The brigadier swiped her screen closed, leaned back in her seat, and folded her arms. "Why are you so concerned about this man's welfare? I know you were part of the rescue team, but I didn't think you had much to do with the actual rescue. Is he a relation or friend of yours?"

"Oh, no, nothing like that."

"Then what?" Colbourn moved forward and rested her forearms on her desk. "Are you feeling all right? Major Wright said he'd recommended you for a psychological evaluation. Is the reason for his recommendation something to do with this man?"

"He didn't explain?"

She shook her head.

That was something, at least. Wright hadn't got to the brigadier first and prejudiced her against the idea of who Arthur was. Looking back, it wasn't surprising the major had thought she was insane.

The whole thing *was* insane.

It was also true. She was convinced of it.

"I told Major Wright something he found hard to believe, so he thought maybe I was a little crazy."

"What did you tell him?"

"That..." Taylan sighed. "Okay, I'll explain it to you, but, ma'am, I need you to hear me out before you pass judgment."

"Go ahead."

So she tried again. This time, she went more slowly, telling the brigadier about the legends surrounding Arthur but not connecting him with them at first, only emphasizing the facts that coincided with the manner and timing of his discovery. To her credit, Colbourn didn't interrupt her once or roll her eyes as Wright had done. Next, Taylan went on to the rescue and the state of Arthur when he was found. She described the torques and his tattoos, particularly the dragon because it was significant to the story. His father had been Uther Pendragon, and the mythical beast had also appeared on his battle standard. She also related how the translation software hadn't been able to identify the language Arthur spoke.

Before she could get to the crucial part, however, when she would tell Colbourn she thought the ancient monarch had miraculously returned, the brigadier interrupted her.

"You think our mystery man is the same legendary King Arthur?"

Taylan let out her relief in a heavy exhalation. "I do."

It sounded less impossible when someone else said it.

Colbourn was silent.

Taylan waited for a while, and then said, "Are you from BI? Have you heard the stories?"

"I am and I have. A long time ago. All that you've told me is correct as I understand it."

"So you think he's the same Arthur?"

"No, of course not. I understand now why Major Wright thought you were mentally ill." She continued to frown, her lips pursed, not speaking.

Taylan didn't know what to make of the brigadier's reaction. It was disappointing that no one agreed with her. She'd also told Abacha about her idea, but he'd only laughed and patted her condescendingly on the shoulder.

"Leave it with me," said Colbourn suddenly.

"So you'll—"

"Dismissed."

That was it?! She wasn't going to tell her anything? Taylan didn't leave immediately, hoping if she hung around the brigadier might relent. But the woman ignored her, re-opening her interface.

Angry and frustrated, she marched to the door, but then Colbourn ordered her to wait.

So she *was* going to tell her something.

The brigadier was rummaging in a drawer. "I thought..." she murmured. Then she looked up and squinted as she focused on Taylan's neck.

She was wearing Kayla's necklace again. Major Wright had given back to her, probably without Colbourn's say so.

"I see," said the brigadier quietly, apparently understanding the jewelry that had transported back to Taylan without her permission. She snapped, "You can go."

Stepping quickly through the door before the woman changed her mind, Taylan almost walked directly into Wright.

"What were you doing in there?" he asked accusingly as the door slid closed.

"I went to see Colbourn."

"I can see that. What about?"

"Arthur."

"You aren't going to let this go, are you?"

"No. Did you tell her you gave me back my necklace?"

"No, I didn't."

"Well, she knows I have it."

Wright grimaced. "I thought she'd forget about it."

"Looks like you were wrong."

He took her arm and pulled her away from the door, muttering, "That's me up shit creek."

"I'm not so sure," said Taylan. "I think she was going to give it back to me. You only beat her to it. I don't think she'll make a big deal of it. She's...changed."

"You think?" Wright asked.

They'd begun to walk along the passageway. Taylan didn't know where he was taking her.

"I don't mean her injuries. She isn't as scary as she was."

"Hm, maybe."

Something seemed to be bothering him. Taylan realized she'd thought the same about him, that he was different now. Did they know something she didn't? What could be so bad they were keeping it to themselves?

"I thought you were on your way to see Colbourn," Taylan said.

"No, I was on my way to find you. Abacha told me where you'd gone. I was hoping to catch you before you spoke to her and save you from embarrassing yourself, but it's clear I was too late. What did she make of your fantasy?"

"It's not a..." she protested angrily, but then she gave a frustrated groan. "I know it sounds loopy, but there's no need to make fun of me."

"You're getting way too familiar, corporal. Watch yourself."

Taylan rolled her eyes but she didn't say anything.

"Another reason I wanted to find you was I have an idea for something that'll convince you you're suffering from a delusion."

"Oh right. What's that then?"

"A language acquisition program."

"Huh?"

"Learning software. It's only recently been developed. Direct computer/brain interface that fast-wires the mind into acquiring new knowledge and skills without the need for all that boring teaching and rehearsing. We plug your Arthur into it, he speed learns English, and then, after three or four days, he'll be able to tell you himself who he really is."

33

"Uh huh. Hm. Uh huh." Lorcan drummed his fingertips on the arm of the park bench.

Sometimes it made a nice to change to get away from the *Bres's* control room and his suite, and to visit in person some of the sections of the ship that were already built and finished. Here, at West Lake, he could imagine what his life might be like when the ship was finally complete and, with her sisters, she would sail into galactic space on her long journey.

He could imagine wakening from cryo for a few months of physical recuperation, and wandering down to the lake or another of the *Bres's* many natural habitats, where he could sit or walk, or even swim in the water, enjoying the pleasant warmth of the pseudo-sunlight. Then, all the strife and worry of the construction phase of the colony fleet would be far behind him. Earth itself would be light years distant, along with the ridiculously conservative BA and the insanely cultish EAC.

Once he was gone, they could continue slugging it out till kingdom come for all he cared.

He squinted up through the tree canopy, appreciating the quality of the dappled light. He hated to admit it, even to himself, but Kekoa had done a good job in creating the forest. The trees were growing healthily, plunging their roots into the rich loam, reaching up their leafy branches to the intense lighting of the overhead lamps. They might have been growing in a forest in New England for all their plant minds knew.

A breeze started up and set the foliage rustling and swaying. Through a gap in the vegetation, the surface of the lake became busy with waves. Lorcan smiled.

"Are you still there?" Dwyr Orr asked.

"Yes, yes," he replied. "Go on."

"I asked you a question." The Dwyr sounded peeved, which was unsurprising as Lorcan had in fact tuned out of their conversation minutes ago.

He'd understood the reason for her comm after the first few sentences she uttered—carefully avoiding the topic of her loathsome son. The rest was all nonsense and flattery. She clearly wanted his help and was desperately backtracking after their earlier schism. He didn't need to hear anything else she said; he only had to decide whether he was going to agree to re-form their alliance.

"I apologize. I must have been distracted. Could you say that again?"

"I asked you if you believe my interpretation is correct."

"Of what this faction within the BA has planned?"

"*Yes.*" Exasperation leaked into her tone.

"I think it's reasonable."

"Reasonable enough to act upon? This could be our best and only chance for crushing the BA so hard it never recovers."

"And for eliminating this threat that concerns you." Lorcan guessed that was her real focus. Was she regretting withdrawing from the battle and losing the opportunity to destroy the BA ships and all they contained? It would be typical of the way her mind worked. She seemed to have a weird superstition about this threat, as if it was more dangerous to her and the EAC than the entire BA.

"That might be a welcome side benefit."

Of course it would, my dear.

"My problem is," he said, then hesitated as he considered how to frame his objection, "my problem is, we had that opportunity not so long ago. Mustering the ships and crew for the battle was not easy or cheap, and things were heavily in our favor—"

"We've been over this."

"And yet I feel it's worth going over again, particularly when you're asking me to commit to a similar undertaking."

"I explained my reasoning," said the Dwyr irritably, "and may I remind you, if it weren't for *my* intel and the support of *my* ships and *my* crews, your precious colony vessel would be nothing but space flotsam by now."

Lorcan paused as a way of avoiding conceding the point. He hadn't decided what to do about her proposal and needed time to consider. Stalling, he asked, "Did your research turn up anything about the phenomenon?"

"No," she sighed, "but I haven't given up. I know it must mean something, I just don't know what."

He wasn't surprised. To someone like her, everything meant something. "Has it occurred to you that this thing, whatever it was, might return? And this time it might take one of *our* ships?"

"It's a possibility, but this time the assault will be on the surface, not out in space. Has it occurred to *you* that it might materialize out there and swallow the *Bres*?"

Frowning, he stood up and began to walk down the path to the lake. There was something about the Dwyr...he couldn't put it into words, but there was something about her that got under his skin. He had a temper and suffered no fools, but beneath it all he was generally calm and collected.

Except when it came to Dwyr Orr.

She seemed to instinctively know which of his buttons to press, needling away at him and unsettling him, forcing him to take her seriously and bending him to her schemes.

"It's important that we understand what happened," she continued, "but we shouldn't let it influence our decision on what to do here on Earth."

"I'll be frank," he said. "How am I to know that, if we go ahead with your plan, you won't back out at the last minute as you did before?"

"Those were unusual circumstances. This will be different. The BA will be at its weakest. I have no intention of backing out. This chance will never come again."

He'd reached the lake, where fresh, clear water lapped against a pebble shore. The pebbles had come from a beach on the coast of Baja California, and it had taken considerable effort to clean them of the sea salt and macro- and microorganisms before placing them around the edge of the lake. Then Kekoa had seeded them with flora and fauna appropriate to the new conditions. So much time and so much work, and the same was true of everything that made up the *Bres*, the *Balor*, and the *Banba*.

"Ua Talman," snapped Dwyr Orr, "I need a decision from you quickly. If we're going to do this, we're going to need all the time we have available to prepare."

The truth was, what she was proposing made sense. In her shoes, he would do exactly the same thing. But there was the history of his last experience of working with her, and the woman herself. His gut reaction was to say no, simply because there was something about her that set him on edge.

"I'll think about it," he said.

"But—"

"I said I would think about it."

He closed the comm.

Make her wait. Let *her* be the one to squirm in discomfort for once.

34

The waiting was unbearable. It had been four days since Taylan had seen Arthur, four days while Wright put him through the learning program that would allow him to understand and communicate in English.

She'd insisted on their separation herself. If she hadn't spent the entire time away from the ancient man, not even setting eyes on him, when he could finally tell his tale, Wright might accuse her of coaching him.

Supporting training sessions had helped to pass the time. The sergeant leading them was different from the one she'd crossed swords with previously, and she'd done her best not to go up against him, not even when she felt he was teaching something incorrectly. It was hard, but she couldn't deny that she'd stepped out of line before, when she'd been heartsick for her kids and feeling useless. Her dissatisfaction must have shown, however, because at one time the training officer had said sarcastically, "If you think you can do it better, be my guest, corporal."

So she had done it better.

To give the man his due, he'd only blinked and said, dead-pan, "Good job spotting my deliberate mistake. Everyone, copy what Ellis did."

Playing xiangqi with Abacha had also helped to keep her occupied as the days dragged by. He continued to beat her consistently. She didn't think she would ever grasp the intricacies of strategy her friend demonstrated. Every game, she would find her general blocked and defenseless and she would lose. It was as much of a foregone conclusion as the outcome of their sparring sessions.

"You know," he said when they were in an empty cabin one day, toward the end of a particularly hard-fought game, which at one point she'd actually thought she had a chance of winning, "I almost feel bad when you realize you've lost again, little chick, and your face falls."

"*Almost* feel bad?"

"Almost."

"Is that feeling strong enough to ever let me win?"

"Would you ever let me win when we spar?"

"Absolutely not."

"I didn't think so."

"But that's a life and death thing. What if I threw a fight one day out of pity and you used the same moves in a battle and died?"

"Exactly."

"But it's not the same as playing xiangqi! This is a game." Taylan wasn't seriously asking him to play badly so she could win for once. She was only kidding. Beating Abacha at xiangqi wouldn't mean squat if it wasn't a genuine victory.

"Isn't that what battles and wars are?" he asked. "Games?"

"No, people die. That's no game."

"Not to the people who die, but perhaps to those who move them around..." He lifted a chariot and moved it two squares, cutting off one of her general's avenues of escape. "Perhaps to them, it's a game. Maybe one day you'll be the person moving others around. You'll need to understand strategy then."

"Huh! I don't think so." Taylan shivered. Abacha's analogy was right on point. To the admirals, generals, and commanders, he and she were xiangqi pieces, to be deployed with a single end in mind, sacrificed as needed, important only while they remained useful.

She'd been naive. When she'd enlisted, it had been with the idea she would be able to do something about the things that mattered to her: Free West BI from the EAC, allow the refugees to return home, punish the soldiers who had killed civilians in cold blood, find her children. But to the Royal Marines she was only a unit, part of a fighting force for others to command. What she thought, felt, or wanted didn't matter. She'd signed up to try to do some good in the world and right wrongs, but in fact all she'd done was hand over the decision about *how* to do good and exactly what 'good' meant, to someone else.

"Don't let it get you down," said Abacha, studying her expression. "At least we know we're on the right side."

"Do we? I'm not so sure. If our last attack had succeeded, we would have murdered thousands of civilians on one of Ua Talman's colony ships. Have they done anything evil? If they have, I'm not aware of it. They're innocent people doing their jobs. They've just signed up to an enterprise that'll take them away from Earth one day. Are they to blame for the way the Project ravages the world's remaining resources? Are they wrong for wanting a better life?"

"No, they aren't wrong," he replied softly. "I guess that's what we all want—a better life, a safe life."

Taylan was about to make her next, futile, move, when she suddenly lost the little enthusiasm she'd had for the game. She let her hand fall to her side and said, "I concede."

"Why? There are many more moves available to you before I win." He smiled at her wickedly.

"What's the point? I know when I'm beat. Sometimes, it makes sense to give up."

"No, seriously, even now you can get out of the trap. Can't you see it?"

"If I could see it, don't you think I would have done it? Xiangqi just isn't for me."

"If you say so." Abacha shrugged and began sweeping the pieces off the board into their box.

Taylan leaned an elbow on the table and rested her chin on the heel of her upturned palm. "This whole situation's a trap." She paused, then blurted, "I told Wright I wanted to resign."

"You did?" her friend replied, surprised. "What did he say?"

"He told me it was impossible, said I had to serve out my term. I suppose even if I could resign, there's nowhere for me to go. I'd still be stuck on the *Valiant*."

"There are worse places to be. I wouldn't like to be Earth-side right now. Between the EAC-controlled countries, where technology is being phased out, the polluted, ecologically ruined areas the AP is exploiting, and the BA territories, mostly under attack, where would you go?"

"Home," she replied simply. "I'd go home."

"But what about your friend, the one who came back from the dead?"

"I'd take him with me. No one believes who he is anyway. Maybe that's what I'm meant to do," she added, musing. Her eyes widened. "Maybe I'm supposed to take him back so he can save the BI from invasion like he did before." She sucked in a breath. "I've been wrong all this time. I've been trying to make Wright and Colbourn believe me, but why? What would they do if they *did* believe he is who I say he is? It isn't like they could promote him or take orders from him. He's an Iron Age chieftain, for god's sake. He's from a time when men fought with swords in muddy fields. If he's going to save us, it isn't going to be through commanding the BA military."

"That look in your eye is worrying me, little chick. Don't tell me you're planning on doing something stupid."

She stared at him. "I have to get Arthur—"

"No."

"Off the ship."

"No."

"C'mon. I need your help."

"No, Taylan. Shaving off the cook's eyebrows, hiding a warrant officer's helmet, and sneaking a cat aboard are completely different from stealing a shuttle. We're at war. We could be executed."

"But it could be the only chance we have to save the BA."

"That's not our job. Even if this guy is the one from the legend, he's here now, right? It's up to him to do whatever it is he's supposed to do. Helping him isn't our responsibility."

"He can't be expected to do it all single-handed. He's illiterate in our language, for one thing, and he doesn't even know what a gun is, let alone how to fire one."

"There are plenty of people who can teach him that."

"But not you, huh?" Taylan frowned at him.

"No, not me. And there's no need to look at me like that. I'm only pointing out...Where are you going?"

She'd stood up. "I'm going to find out how Arthur's doing with the learning program." In fact, she mostly wanted to leave Abacha's company. He'd shown her he wasn't the person she'd thought he was. She was disappointed and angry with herself for not seeing it before.

"Let me know when you find out," he called as she left.

She didn't reply.

As she approached Arthur's cabin, the door opened and Boots walked out. The door closed, and he turned around, sat down, and miaowed, asking to be let in again. The cat's ridiculous antics made her smile and lightened her mood somewhat. She pressed the button, and when Wright let her in, Boots trotted in alongside her.

Arthur was sitting on his bed, his hair about a centimeter longer than it had been when she'd last seen him. It was now down to his shoulders, thick and shining healthily, but his eyes were bloodshot with dark circles underscoring them. The learning program had certainly taken its toll. Wires ran from the interface in the table to a net shaped to fit a human skull that lay on the bed.

"How is he?" she asked Wright, who was doing something with the interface.

"I'm fine, Taylan," Arthur replied.

She gave a gasp of joy. "You can understand me now?"

"I can. It's still hard for me, but I can understand and speak your language, at a simple level."

His voice was heavily accented, like when her grandpa spoke English, but he was perfectly intelligible.

"You should improve quickly," said Wright, "now you know the basics."

Taylan realized that, from the moment she'd entered the cabin, the major hadn't looked at her.

Her heart sank a little. Did it mean that he'd already asked Arthur about his history and discovered she was wrong about him? Was Wright feeling embarrassed for her? The thought that it wasn't King Arthur they'd rescued from a mountain in West BI made her sad, but she wasn't devastated. If it had all been a crazy dream, it didn't matter so much, knowing the man was better now, safe, and able to communicate with the people around him.

"You look tired," said Taylan. "Are you sure you're okay?"

"A medic's been in attendance throughout, Ellis," said Wright crisply. "Arthur's completed the program. There won't be any need for further treatments, so there's no need to worry." He rested his back against the bulkhead and folded his arms, finally looking her in the eyes. "Don't you want to ask him who he is and where he's from?"

Was that triumph or bitterness in his tone? She couldn't tell.

"I'll save you the trouble," said Arthur. "Please, sit down, Taylan."

When she joined him on the bunk, he took one of her hands in his. "I have much to thank you for. You have been my champion."

"Uh, no, not me. It's Major Wright you should thank. He's the one who rescued you from the mountain."

"Is that so? I didn't know that." He turned to look at the major, but Wright only waved a hand, as if his act was of no consequence.

Arthur returned his attention to her. "But since I entered this new dream, you are the one who has cared for me. You brought me the cat to be my companion, you have taught me how to use all the wondrous machinery of this world. We even practiced with staves. If it were not for you, I would have been lost and alone."

"You're welcome, but...what was that you said about entering a new dream?"

"He thinks he's dreaming," explained Wright. "I've tried telling him he isn't, several times." He gave a heavy sigh.

"No, this is reality," Taylan said. She couldn't wait any longer. "Could you tell me who you are? Your title, I mean."

She held her breath.

"I have many. Some call me Arthur the Usurper, Arthur the Interloper, or Arthur the Bastard. Others call me King of Britain."

Her hand flew to cover her mouth. "You-you really are...?"

"Yes," said Wright quietly. "That's who he says he is, anyway."

Suddenly, the major's gaze became distant and his mouth fell open. He was listening to a comm. Whatever the message was, it was serious.

35

Hans wasn't there to witness most of it. As soon as it all began to kick off, he'd removed himself from the situation, lest suspicion for engineering the coup fell on him, or, worse, he became a target.

That was the problem with leading from the shadows: Anonymity made you vulnerable.

He lived alone in his rented villa. The maid and cook went home at eight pm, and they'd already left by the time he arrived. The only other visitor he saw regularly was the private nurse who stopped by once a day, in the early morning, to administer the treatment for his injured lungs and to change his remaining wound dressing.

He'd entered the dark, quiet house on the hillside in a secluded, rural part of the country, and, after turning on the lights, he'd gone straight to the kitchen to make himself a pitcher of gin and tonic with ice and lemon. It was going to be a long night.

Settling himself in a comfortable, padded, rattan armchair on the veranda, he opened an interface and went directly to his usual vidnews channel. The reports were already coming in.

He grinned to himself, gleeful. It had all worked out so well, better than he could have hoped.

BREAKING NEWS, the headline shouted. *ARMY STORMS TEMPORARY PARLIAMENT BUILDING IN KINGSTON*

Behind the words was a frozen still of the plain, blocky edifice at night with soldiers mounting an assault on the entrance and rappelling down the walls to swing in at the windows. Pulse fire flashed in the darkness, from inside the building and outside, as government guards put up a defense.

Suddenly, the words disappeared and the picture became live. The scene had changed. The guards were gone from the entrance, except for one, who lay face down and not moving. Black scorch marks from pulse bolts covered the wall and shattered glass shards littered the sidewalk. Bursts of laser fire shone through the empty windows. Unseen ambulances were racing closer, the screams of their sirens echoing in the night.

Then the scene changed again. A news anchor was sitting behind a desk in a TV studio, talking to someone off screen. She realized she was live, and turned to the camera.

"Unbelievable news tonight, ladies and gentlemen. As I speak, the Britannic Government is under attack. MPs were holding a late debate in the new Parliament chambers when, approximately twenty minutes ago, soldiers stormed the building. According to witnesses, the fight on the steps was over quickly. At the moment we have reports of three dead, but these have yet to be confirmed. The fighting inside is still going on, and we're trying to get in contact with someone in the building who can give us an update on the situation.

"Most worryingly, it seems that, though the police were called, no officers were sent to the scene. That's right, the police service has provided *no* response and appears unwilling to protect the Members of Parliament or government workers inside the building. This may be because the troops mounting the attack appear to be our own Britannic Alliance army. It's hard to believe, but we are assured the soldiers are wearing BA uniforms. However, it's possible they may be fake and a foreign force such as the Antarctic Project or the Earth Awareness Crusade could be masquerading as our own troops in order to sow confusion.

"And it certainly is a confusing situation, ladies and gentlemen, confusing and chaotic. We will bring you updates and clarification as soon as we have them, so please..." The anchor became distracted for a beat, then said, "I'm happy to say we have a reporter on the scene. Ben Mathers is outside the Parliament building. Can you hear me, Ben?"

The screen split and in one half the street view reappeared, but this time the camera was focused on a nervous reporter. Behind him onlookers huddled, gawking at something unseen. The reporter walked a few paces and the camera followed him. Now the compromised Parliament building could be seen in the background.

"Yes, I can hear you, Sandra. I can tell our viewers that the fighting isn't over yet, and it's probably wise to stay away from the downtown Kingston area tonight. As you can see—" He cringed and ducked as an explosion rang out. The camera operator must have also bobbed down because the view abruptly shifted to the onlookers' legs and the crouching reporter.

Looking embarrassed and frightened, he straightened up and said, "As you can *hear*, it's a determined, aggressive attack on our government, and—"

"Ben" said the anchor, "we've heard the soldiers are wearing BA uniforms. Can you deny or confirm that?"

"I'm sorry, could you say that again, Sandra?"

As she'd spoken, the glass frontage of the Parliament building had collapsed and spilled out into the street.

"I said, is it our own troops who are mounting this attack?"

"I'm no expert on uniforms," the reporter replied, "but the couple that I've seen did appear to be dressed as BA military."

"That's deeply concerning. Would you say this looks like a military coup?"

"It's too early to be sure, but..."

Hans looked up, distracted by headlights approaching along the road. Only a few people lived on the hillside, and his villa occupied the highest spot. There was no reason for anyone to drive over the hill when the faster freeway went around it, especially at night when there was no view.

He put down his drink and peered into the darkness, watching the car.

The twin headlights drew closer, meandering around the bends and curves of the road, until finally they reached the bottom of his drive, where they stopped. They winked out. A car door opened and was slammed shut.

Hans closed the interface and placed it screen-downward on the table before standing up. No streetlights illuminated the road in that part of the island, so he couldn't see the car or who had been in it and was presumably now walking toward his house.

He had a sudden urge to turn off the house lights, but it was too late. Whoever was coming already knew someone was home. Should he go inside? Barricade the door? He had no guns in the house or anything else with which to defend himself. He wasn't that kind of person. His conflicts and disputes were of the mind or personality.

If the BA military had thought to include him in their...

He nearly collapsed in relief.

A woman had walked into the pools of light that spilled from the lamps on his veranda. A woman in the bright clothes of the islands, her hair wrapped in a vivid pink cloth.

Mariya.

"What brings you out here at this time of night, Mariya. If I'd known you wanted to visit, I would have sent my—"

"Mr Jonte, I'm glad to see you're safe and sound. May I come in?"

"But of course." He opened the screen door, and she climbed the few wooden steps.

"Would you share a gin and tonic with me? Or I could make you something else."

"A gin and tonic would be very welcome, thanks."

Hans went to get another glass, and by the time he returned Mariya was sitting in the second armchair on the veranda. He poured her a drink from the pitcher and handed it to her before also sitting down.

Mariya took a sip and remained silent.

A sense of calm pleasantness hit him. How nice it was to be here with an intelligent, perceptive, affable woman, sharing a cocktail, on a star-filled, warm evening, surrounded by the songs of cicadas and croaking frogs. He was tempted to forget all about the scene playing out in Kingston, despite the years of work it had taken to bring it about. He had enough money to retire. If she were willing, they could live together somewhere off the beaten track and away from worldly troubles, in as much luxury as the place afforded, spending their days having interesting conversations and enjoying simple hobbies.

Then he blinked and returned to the present. He'd worked too hard and sacrificed too much to give it up now. He also knew himself too well—he was not that old man who could content himself in mundane things. He needed intrigue and artifice, or life would not be worth living.

"Have you heard what's happening in town?" asked Mariya eventually.

"No? What..."

She'd shot him a knowing glance: *I dare you to lie to me about this.*

He laughed sheepishly. "You mean the disturbance at

Parliament? I did pick up something on the vidnews in the car as I was coming home. Has the situation developed?"

"You could say that," she replied, her gaze on her drink, where a slice of lemon floated. "The building's been taken over and the Prime Minister has been thrown in jail."

"He has?! By whom?"

Mariya's dark brown eyes focused on him again, half-lidded. Her lips curved into a lazy smile. "Mr Jonte, I've been a good employee, haven't I? You've been pleased with my work?"

"You've been exemplary. I have no complaints whatsoever."

"Would you say I've earned your trust?"

"I would. Absolutely."

"Then...I'd like to suggest we move our relationship to another level, a level where we can speak frankly and without fear of reprisal. A level of mutual respect."

"I have a lot of respect for you, Mariya. I'm not sure what you mean."

"That evening at the Ambassador's Residence, when you asked me to pump up the military men's sense of self-importance and encourage their dissatisfaction with the government, that was part of a larger plan you had, wasn't it?"

Hans was silent.

"Sir, you wouldn't have asked me to do that for no reason. Please don't insult my intelligence."

He put his hands behind his neck and laced his fingers, looking out into the darkness. "As I said, I have a lot of respect for you. That doesn't mean you should be privy to everything that goes on at SIS."

"But this isn't SIS, this is you, isn't it? Mr Jonte, Josie always used to tell me how much she admired you. She was in awe of you, and now that I know you well, I feel the same. So understand that I'm coming from the position of someone who supports you when I say I think tonight's military coup is your doing. Hennessy and Montague might believe they dreamed up the idea themselves, but it was really you, wasn't it?"

Hans took a drink, swished the bitter liquid around his mouth, and swallowed before answering. "I don't blame you for your curiosity, but do you really think someone worthy of your admiration would ever admit to such a thing?"

She'd been leaning over her chair's arm, her body turned toward him. When she heard his reply, she slumped against her seat back. "You and your clever answers. You're too smart for me. But, let's speak hypothetically. If the head of SIS *did* incite a military coup, what might be his reason? If the government is no longer in control of the Alliance, he would lose power and influence too. What could his end goal possibly be?"

Hans smiled and stood up. "All the ice in the pitcher has melted. I'll make us another batch of G and T. Then, shall we watch the vidnews and see how the night unfolds?"

36

They had killed the queen, but the bees lived on, buzzing noisily and irritatingly.

Now it was time to set the hive on fire.

Kala arrived in Jamaica aboard one of the hindmost amphibious craft, a large vessel carrying military vehicles to expedite the invasion of the final BA stronghold and temporary seat of its Parliament.

AP ships at sea beyond the immediate conflict zone in the outer Caribbean Islands had begun the attack. Missiles erupted from launchers, first targeting BA military bases and airports across the islands, and then Kingston, Fort-de-France, Bridgetown, and St. George's, devastating the capitals and sending the local populations into terror-stricken stampedes as they fought to escape to the countryside.

Then the EAC aircraft took the baton and mounted an air assault. The Royal Air Force was already in the air, but their defense was weak and poorly coordinated. The EAC planes avoided or shot down the defenders and commenced bombing the areas the AP ships had missed. The Royal Navy also responded, racing out to strike at the AP ships, but they were too few and too late. Their resources had been stretched beyond their limit for years as they'd fought to defend numerous BA territories and protectorates.

Finally, when the combined forces had pulled the sting from the BA's tail, amphibious assault vessels smashed onto the beaches, enemy soldiers pouring from them like ants from a drowning nest. They ran up the dunes and rocky headlands, mowing down the thin opposing forces and taking no prisoners.

"Could you please stay below, ma'am," said the commander on Kala's amphibious craft, a woman named Novak, "just until I give the all clear? For your own safety."

Kala nodded her agreement, though reluctantly. She knew she could get out and walk across the sand without being harmed, but she didn't want to distract or disturb her officer.

Distant sounds of fighting were penetrating the solid steel hull as she waited at the bottom of the companionway, and a hot, acrid smell began to permeate the air—the vessel's forceshield was heating up as it absorbed defensive pulse fire. But, again, she harbored no worries. The armaments along the shore were inadequately manned. As she'd predicted, the main force of the BA army had been occupied in Kingston and elsewhere in the Caribbean Islands, taking over banks and government offices and suppressing civilian protests, when the initial air assault had begun.

Taking advantage of the military coup and launching the offensive from neutral Cuba had been a piece of cake. Ua Talman had guaranteed one thousand places aboard the *Banba* for the country's elite in exchange for its government's cooperation. When it came to deciding who would take the places, there would be vicious fighting and probably bloodshed, but that was none of her concern.

From the bow of her craft came the sound of vehicle

engines revving and the vibration of their motion as they drove away, heading inland.

Kala grew impatient. The moment of victory, of utter domination over the arrogant, anachronistic, misguided Britannic Alliance, was so close she could almost feel it. Only one—perhaps two—deeds were needed for her triumph to be complete.

Boom!

Even within the vessel, the sound was loud, and Kala thought she'd felt the deck shift slightly under her feet. "What was that?!" she yelled.

"A moment, please," replied Novak from up ahead. "I don't think...No..."

The wait for an answer dragged out. Meanwhile, footsteps rang from overhead as the last of the EAC troops left the vessel.

Eventually, the commander said, "It was a wind power site going up."

Kala hadn't given orders to target the island's energy generation plant. She wasn't sure how she felt about it. In the early days of invasion, until the place had converted to the EAC way of doing things, the free energy could have been useful. Perhaps the assault had been one of Lorcan's ideas, or maybe it was collateral damage. Either way, she concluded phlegmatically, the plant was no great loss, and depriving the island of electricity would be an advantage when it came to suppressing any resistance from the surviving citizens. Cutting off resources from the remaining Britannic Isles natives had helped to crush them after that invasion.

She heard nothing for a couple of minutes, no shouts, no vehicle engines, no booted feet running.

"The area must be secure now, Commander," she called to Novak.

The officer came out to join her. "It should be fairly safe, ma'am, though I'd feel better if you would suit up. We have plenty of..." Reacting to Kala's stare, she swallowed the rest of her sentence. "I'll accompany you."

She climbed the ladder to the hatch and opened it. Kala followed.

The sun was coming up as they emerged into fresh air. Novak stepped out onto the deck, and Kala quickly did the same, eager to move on to her next tasks.

In the distance, beyond the dunes, the sky remained dark. But it was an artificial darkness, created by billowing clouds of dark gray smoke. Closer to hand were the destroyed armaments of the BA land force, twisted and wrecked. Among grassy tussocks and salt scrub lay bodies deformed into ugly angles, their blood soaking into the sand. EAC advance amphibious assault craft ranged down the beach at the shoreline. The tide was coming in, and waves were splashing up and over their hulls.

All was surprisingly quiet. Aside from the noises of the sea, little could be heard. Novak really had waited until the fighting was completely over before allowing her Dwyr out into the area. Kala was mildly annoyed, knowing the commander had delayed her gratification, but she grudgingly allowed the officer's caution had come from a good place.

"Is my vehicle ready?"

"Yes, ma'am. It's over there. I have a company awaiting us at the road." She led Kala to a ramp that ran down to the beach. At its head sat an all-terrain vehicle with two soldiers in the back seats. Novak opened a door for Kala, then climbed in the other side. Reaching out to the dashboard, Kala set the map coordinates she'd memorized. The island's net was out, but EAC vehicles could link to the AP's satellites.

They drove over the dunes, swaying and bumping, as the car took them by the shortest route to the nearest road. The tough seaside plants grew thicker and taller the further inland they drove and the ground flattened out. The way before them had already been broken through by the advancing EAC troops. It looked like they hadn't met much resistance once they'd left the shoreline.

It had all gone to plan. The military coup on top of the fighting at the outer islands had drained the already thinly spread BA defenses in the Caribbean to a shadow. Their military leaders had been astoundingly foolish. Kala didn't think of herself as a particularly clever strategist—she'd always relied on the fervent religious zeal of her followers to win many of her battles—but she would never have been so dumb as the Britannic Alliance.

It really didn't deserve to survive.

They drove out onto the road, and the waiting convoy of armored vehicles fell into line behind them.

"May I ask where we're going?" said Novak.

"We're on our way to the last known location of King Frederick."

"No kidding. I didn't know he was hiding out here in Jamaica. I guess it makes sense."

"There were several possibilities. I suspected he might have been moved to Oceania, probably Australia. It's easy to hide someone in the wilderness there. But my sources couldn't turn up anything. Next I looked in India, where the BA has historical ties. I thought he might be in a mountain refuge. But that was a blank, too. The Caribbean was the last place I looked. I couldn't believe the BA Government would be stupid enough to keep their monarch in the same location as their new Parliament, but I overestimated them, in this and many other things."

Looking somewhat embarrassed, Novak half-turned in her seat toward Kala and quietly asked, "When it's all over, will we be holding a victory celebration?"

"If you mean will we be blessing the Caribbean Islands and returning them to Earth's embrace? Naturally we will! In a month or so, when we've cleansed them of their former inhabitants."

"Hm," was all the commander responded, but she seemed satisfied.

Kala could appreciate why. She also enjoyed the celebrations.

The car crested a rise, and the road wound out through the hilly ground in front of them. The light was growing stronger, and now it was easy to see to the horizon.

She thought she could see King Frederick's hiding place. To the right a gray slate roof was visible among the trees, an unusual construction for a tropical island. Sure enough, after another minute's travel, the car turned into a driveway and came to a halt. Heavy gates barred the way. On the other side of them, an avenue of trees ran into the distance.

"Ah," said Novak. "Don't worry, Dwyr. We'll make quick work of that."

She wasn't lying.

Ten minutes later, after she'd given the order, the gates lay in a hot, twisted mess. Kala waited as soldiers dragged them off the road, hooking them with their rifle butts, the metal scraping channels in the gravel. Then her journey to find King Freddie recommenced.

They encountered some armed resistance farther down the long driveway that led to the stately home, but it was quickly dispersed. The fight had clearly gone out of the BA forces. She didn't send soldiers after the departing BA guards. They would meet their end in the mop up operation.

Inside the mansion, all was silent. Whatever servants had worked there had apparently fled hours ago. Had they taken the young king with them? That would be inconvenient. Kala ordered a thorough search of the place, from the basement to the attic. In these old houses, hiding places and nooks and crannies abounded.

She waited while the search went on, sitting on one of the antique chairs in the hall. The invasion had gone smoothly so far. She hoped there wouldn't be too much of a delay in finding the brat. From all around came the sound of her troops opening doors and running up and down stairs and along passageways. She tapped the floor with the toe of her shoe.

Finally, the shout went up. The king had been found.

Novak's head appeared over the banister railing. "He's on the second floor, ma'am."

"Good. Bring him down."

"Er, a woman's with him. She's putting up quite a fight. What would you like us to do?"

"Is it his mother?"

"I don't think so. She's too old. Probably a servant. Maybe his former nurse?"

"It doesn't matter. Kill her."

"Yes, Dwyr." Novak's head disappeared.

A few beats later, a long, agonized, child's scream echoed out from somewhere in the building.

Kala stood up, preparing to leave. She had another stop to make that day before her work was over.

YOUNG KING FREDDIE was about Perran's age, she estimated. He was squeezed in between two soldiers on the back seat of the car as they left the house that had been his home since the Britannic Isles had fallen.

The kid was blubbing like a boy half his age, his eyes and face red and wet, strings of snot hanging from his nose as he huffed and sobbed.

Kala curled her upper lip and turned to face forward.

How undignified.

Perran would never have behaved so pathetically, not even

if she herself had had her throat cut in front of him. For all his
expensive tutoring, apparently no one had taught the boy to
have a fucking backbone.

"Where are we going now?" asked Novak.

"Our next port of call is Kingston Prison."

When the commander cocked her eyebrow at her question-
ingly, Kala explained, "The BA Prime Minister is there, Beaumont-Smith."

"They put their leader in jail?!"

"I don't know why you're so surprised, Commander. I would
have thought you'd seen enough of how the BA work by now.
There's very little intelligence to their actions."

"I knew about the coup, but…"

"I imagine their military invented some crimes he suppos-
edly committed, in order to justify taking over the government
and locking him up. That's often how these things work."

"Yeah, that makes sense."

Kala frowned. The noises from the backseat were getting
annoying. "Could you put a gag on him or something?" she
asked the soldiers.

After a brief scuffle and some shouting, the kid's crying
quietened down, though it was still loud enough to be irritat-
ing. Luckily, at that moment, the square, brick building of
Kingston Prison appeared.

The prison was about three kilometers outside the capital,
and it hadn't been touched by the bombing. As with the king's
estate, the place was relatively quiet. A few guards had stayed at
their posts, but they were quickly dispatched.

The prison security system proved a more worthy adversary.
The outer double doors were locked and required bio-ID to
open them.

"Shit," said Novak, her nose nearly touching the panel. She
took a step backward and sized up the doors, her hands on her hips.

"Can you get through?" Kala asked.

"With enough time, we can get through anything. The problem is, we might take out the whole building."

"Unless you have another suggestion, go for it. I'd like to look Beaumont-Smith in the eye, but if I can't, I'll deal with the disappointment."

One corner of Novak's lips lifted. "It'll be safest if you wait in the car, ma'am."

Watching the destruction of the entrance to Kingston Prison would have been more entertaining if the head of the BA's royal family had let up his wailing, but it was not to be. Kala grimly listened to the kid in between the blasts of mortar fire.

When Novak approached the car to tell her the route into the prison was now clear, she ordered that the boy be brought with them.

"The building probably isn't stable," said the commander as they walked back to the rubble remains of the entrance, "but I guess you're set on going inside."

"Of course I am. Are the prisoners still in their cells?"

"Yes, the guards left them there when they ran off. Do you have a plan for them?"

"Not particularly. I'll think about it."

Dust and smoke hung heavy in the atmosphere around the front of the building, and the heat from the blasts radiated from the debris. Kala coughed and her eyes smarted. She lifted the collar of her shirt over her mouth and nose and gingerly stepped through the shattered concrete and bent iron spread over the ground.

Within the prison, the inmates were hollering and screaming and creating quite a cacophony, even at their distance from the entrance. At least the noise drowned out the muffled sniffles of King Fred. The lights were out, but the helmet lights of Novak and the accompanying soldiers cut into the darkness.

"We should have the Prime Minister located soon," said Novak. "If he's in here, we'll find him."

"He's here," replied Kala simply.

Some things she just *knew*. It was hard to describe, but it was an ability she'd had as long as she could remember. It was one of the things that had started her on the path to founding the EAC. Every so often an extra sense that other people didn't seem to have, a nameless certainty, would strike her. Now was one of those times. She could *feel* Beaumont-Smith somewhere nearby, feel his fear and dread, his rage toward his adversaries, his longing for the perfect, comfortable, powerful life he'd led and that was now gone forever. He stood out to her, a bright bundle of emotions in the darkness, shining out stronger than all the lost souls surrounding him.

"This way," Kala suddenly said as they came to a branch of the main corridor.

"Dammit," said Novak. A closed, reinforced door stood in their way a few meters down.

Kala carried on walking until she reached it. She grasped the handle and turned it. Satisfaction surging, she pulled the door open. The departing guards hadn't locked it.

They found the BA Prime Minister cowering in the corner of his cell, ineffectively hiding behind his bunk like a three-year-old playing hide and seek.

"Y-Your Majesty!" he breathed when, peeking out, he realized they could all see him. One of the soldiers was holding the king by the scruff of his neck. The boy appeared intent on beating the record for a fit of crying, Kala mused, her brows creased.

The PM crawled from his hiding place and got uncertainly to his feet. Addressing the kid, he said, "I hope they haven't hurt you. If you've hurt one hair on this child's head," he said to Kala, "I'll—"

"What?" She snorted derisively. "Do you want the honor?" she asked Novak.

"Me?" the commander replied. "I'd love to." She took her beamer from its holster.

This movement sent Beaumont-Smith into a frenzy of terror. He fled to the wall of his cell and tried frantically—and rather nonsensically, in Kala's opinion—to climb the walls. He looked rather like an old spider trapped in his own web.

Which, she reflected, he was, kind of.

"It'll hurt less if you don't move," Novak called out.

But the old man was beyond any kind of self control. Abject fear had seized him, and he continued to try to make an impossible escape from his doom.

It took three shots to finish him off, and Kala felt a bit sick by the end. That barbecue smell of cooked human flesh was something she'd never grown accustomed to.

The kid was now shrieking calamitously, hurting her ears despite his gag. She held out her hand to Novak, who passed over her weapon.

She fired, and the noise stopped.

"That's better."

37

Wright was like a plushy with all the stuffing taken out. He sagged as he leaned against the bulkhead, and then collapsed onto a chair. He put his head in his hands and slowly shook it.

"I can't believe it," he murmured.

Then he straightened up. Ignoring Taylan and Arthur, he said, aghast, "Brigadier, is this true?" He was comming Colbourn.

Taylan was beside herself with curiosity. She'd never seen Wright react so strongly before. He'd always been the model of self-control and professionalism, whether faced by a dumb marine who had got her foot trapped between rocks or a raging, violent sick bay patient. No matter what life threw at him, the major always kept his cool.

This was different.

He was listening to Colbourn's reply.

Arthur was also watching Wright, clearly curious, but he stayed silent.

The major suddenly leapt up and strode to the door.

"Hey," Taylan said, "what's happened?"

As if only just remembering there were other people in the cabin, he replied, "Military business. Wait here."

The door opened and he marched out.

Taylan turned to Arthur. "Stay here. I'll be back soon."

"But, didn't he say…"

She was already out in the passageway. Wright was a few meters away, moving fast. She ran to catch up to him.

He glanced at her with a look of annoyance. "I told you to—"

"You said it was military business. I'd like to remind you, I *am* military."

"Huh, you didn't want to be for a while there. Go back to your mythical friend. He needs someone to look after him. He's obviously mentally ill."

Wright was setting such a quick pace, and she had to trot to keep up.

"Arthur isn't mentally ill, he's who I said he was. He told you so without any suggestions from me. I never went near him all the time he was learning English, and before then he couldn't understand me, so I couldn't have influenced him."

"I don't really know he couldn't understand you, do I? You were both speaking foreign languages. I only have your word it wasn't the same one."

Taylan couldn't think of a suitable response, so she said, "This is all beside the point. What's going on? Why are you in such a hurry?"

His reply was edged with anger. "You seem to be forgetting your position, *corporal*."

"Aw, come on. We've been through too much together for that." Though she tried to maintain a casual tone, her heart was in her mouth. She was really pushing it, begging for a charge of insubordination. But she sensed a crack in this marine's armor. Something had deeply unsettled him, disturbed him to his core. She felt sorry for him.

As he had moments earlier in the cabin, he suddenly physically sagged again. "There's been a coup," he muttered. "On Jamaica. The Chief of Defense is leading it."

Taylan halted, surprise stopping her in her tracks. Wright strode on ahead, oblivious. She ran to his side.

"A military coup?! We've taken over from the BA Government?"

"If they're successful, I expect they'll soon be declaring martial law," he said bitterly.

"Don't you mean 'we'? You were saying—"

"That's the *point*, isn't it?" the major spat. "None of us were consulted on whether we want to take part in this. They've dragged us in, and now we're expected to just support them. It's *treason*. It's going against..." He expelled air heavily, unable to complete his sentence. His chest heaved as he seemed to fight to control his emotions.

"I'm going to talk to Colbourn," he said at last. "We have to decide where the *Valiant* sits in all of this."

"Good. I'm coming too."

Wright opened his mouth to respond, but then sighed and clamped his lips.

He'd probably decided he had enough to contend with without also trying to put her off. Taylan was relieved. She didn't like arguing with him, and she was determined to have her input into the decision making.

The fact that Arthur had reappeared at this crisis in the history of the Britannic Isles couldn't be a coincidence. She felt sure he had a role to play, though she didn't know what yet. But he'd only just learned to speak English, he knew nothing about life in modern times—he probably didn't even know he was aboard a starship in space—and he didn't even seem to believe he was finally awake after his long centuries of sleep. He needed an advocate, someone to speak for him in a way that people would understand, as well as to explain to him what was happening. So far, she was the only person who truly believed who he was. She had to be his spokesperson.

They'd arrived at Colbourn's office.

When the door slid open, Taylan boldly walked in behind Wright, acting as if she'd been invited.

The brigadier looked at her like she was the first example of non-terrestrial intelligent life.

"We have some other news to tell you," Taylan said. "It's about the man we picked up in West BI."

"Can't it wait?!"

The major paused before replying in a defeated tone, "It's probably best she stays."

"I'll take your word for it," said the brigadier tersely, glowering at Taylan.

She reached for a chair that sat next to the bulkhead and carried it over to Colbourn's desk, where she put it down next to Wright's, grateful for his support.

"I don't know much more than I told you in the comm yet," the brigadier said, addressing Wright. "I received this from the Sea Lord." She played a recording on her interface.

"*General communication to the Space Fleet from Sea Lord Montague. Along with the Chief of Defense Staff, our forces have moved to seize control of the BA Government and to take the Prime Minister, Mr Beaumont-Smith, into custody, pending an investigation into allegations of corruption, accepting bribes, compromising national security, and betraying his oath of office.*

I'm happy to report that our actions at the New Parliament in Jamaica have been successful and as I speak myself and Lord Hennessy, Chief of Defense Staff, have set up a temporary government to manage domestic, international, and space affairs. We have stepped into the breach and will remain in position until such time as we are able to re-establish the safety, security, and fair government of all members of the Britannic Alliance.

Please stand by to receive further information and instructions."

"But what about the rest of the MPs?" asked Wright, incredulous. "If they really believed that about the Prime Minister, that doesn't mean they're *all* corrupt. They could have demanded a vote of no confidence. Why'd they have to take over the whole government?"

"They didn't, of course," Colbourn retorted. "It's all nonsense. Beaumont-Smith is a waste of space, an awful, bigoted, arrogant, malevolent arsehole, but he isn't corrupt. He doesn't need money, and he can't be blackmailed. His family is fabulously rich and it's all stashed in tax havens, and his web of influence spreads so widely, he could easily quash any news reports that show him in a bad light."

"Then what's this about?"

"Buggered if I know," replied Colbourn. She gave a groan of frustration. "The Space Navy commanders have been comming each other since we received the news. I haven't said anything to anyone yet. The *Valiant* is the only marine starship. Strictly speaking, I should be liaising with the admiral, but I haven't heard from her, and I don't know if she's a part of this. If she is, I'm not sure what to do."

"What else *can* we do except fall in line?" Wright asked. "We have to follow the chain of command."

"Yes, we do," the brigadier conceded, though appeared uncomfortable about her reply. Her gaze flicked to Taylan.

"What's this news about the patient in the sick bay?" she asked.

"He isn't there anymore," Wright replied. "There didn't seem any point, as he's probably the healthiest person on board. I put him in a cabin."

"*And*? Or is that it?!"

The major hesitated.

"The news is," Taylan said, "he's—"

"Wait," Colbourn said. She was looking at her interface.

"Something's arrived from the admiral." She pressed the screen. "I suppose it won't hurt for you two to hear it."

"General communication to the Space Fleet from Admiral Kim. You all heard the news from Sea Lord Montague. I want to state for the record that I was not informed of this coup prior to its staging and had no idea what the Chief of Defense Staff and Sea Lord had planned. As you know, I'm new to this post and so this comes at a challenging time. I, and from what I understand, you also, neither concur with nor support the actions of the military heads on Earth. I will draft an official response condemning their behavior and send it to Jamaica today.

"Furthermore, after considerable deliberation and consultation with my commanders and captains, I've come to a very difficult and heartfelt decision. From this moment onward, the Space Fleet will secede from the Britannic Alliance and form its own, independent, self-governing entity.

"We have a long road ahead of us, officers. Your first step is to inform your men and women of my decision. After that, we have many puzzles to solve coming up, but I've already heard some great suggestions, and I'm convinced we will meet all future difficulties with our usual determination and vigor.

That is all for now."

Colbourn's face was a picture.

38

The flashes of light in the night sky over Kingston and the accompanying booms were like a grotesque firework display. Hans's drink had grown warm in his hand as he'd watched and listened, unable to believe what was happening.

His long years of work, the huge effort he'd put into making his plans, weighing position against position, personality against personality, event against event, his *dreams...*

It had all come to nothing.

The news anchor at the station had managed to blurt a few sentences about reports of an attack on St. George's before the station blacked out, and a split second later, like thunder following lightning, came an ear-splitting whine.

Hans knew that sound too well. Reflexively, he'd thrown himself on the floor, a sweat breaking out over his body as he flashed back to the bombing of the General Council. For a moment, he was there again, cowering on the floor as flames roared around him, devouring the wooden building. He tasted the burning smoke, choked on the ashes, was held prostrated by the fallen metal strut.

Then he returned to his hillside villa.

There was a crack, and the sky winked into daylight before night instantly fell again.

But the view had changed. In far-off Kingston, something was on fire. The capital had been hit by a bomb or missile.

Jamaica was under attack.

The enemy had targeted the media station first, cutting off an information source from the local population, and then the next target had been the capital.

Hans desperately searched for other news sites, but the net was dead. It hadn't been one news production company the attackers had hit, they had taken out the internet itself.

It made sense. Cutting off communication within target territory was like severing an animal's spinal cord, leaving in unable to move it limbs and defend itself.

The interface slipped from his hands and clattered to the floor.

Another terrible whine came, and another missile turned night to day as it hit Kingston.

He couldn't speak. He could only watch in horror. He'd reached for his glass and gulped down half the contents, accidentally breathing in some of it. He coughed and choked until he thought he would see his own lungs appearing from his mouth. Eyes watering, gasping for breath, he felt like crying, screaming, running outside and leaping off a precipice.

And still the attack went on.

All the while, Mariya had sat next to him, silent in the darkness.

Then, in a pause between missiles, she said, "Mr Jonte, we have to leave. It isn't safe here. They might widen the attack site, and you're an important official in the BA Government. They might come looking for you. We must go into hiding."

He finally got control of himself. "You're right. You're just like your sister, quick-thinking and resourceful in a crisis. I must leave, but where can I go? How can I leave the island while it's under attack?"

"I know a place, a safe place where they'll never find you. Pack a bag quickly, and I'll take you there."

He moved to put down his glass and in his nervousness knocked over the half-full pitcher, sending a cascade of gin and tonic over the rattan table. The pitcher rolled onto the tile floor and splintered.

"Leave it," Mariya urged. "Hurry."

As he ran into his house, she followed him, saying, "We should travel in my car. It's less noticeable and it can handle rough terrain. We'll have to go off road."

Hans halted in his living room, trying to marshal his thoughts. What should he take? He had some expensive jewelry that might be useful for bartering. The invaders would take over the banking system immediately. What else?

"Bring as much food as you can," said Mariya. "No, it's okay, I'll pack it. Which way is your kitchen?"

"Through there." He pointed.

"You'll need loose clothing, tough shoes, a hat and gloves. And empty your medicine cabinet into a bag and bring that too. Medication will be hard to come by."

Within five minutes, he'd thrown all she suggested into a duffle bag. He'd also opened his safe and taken out his jewelry and important documents, stuffing them into the recesses of his bag.

Mariya had also been busy. She was waiting for him in the living room with a box overflowing with packets of food.

"What about water?" he asked.

"There's plenty of water where we're going."

She stepped toward the door, her arms wrapped tightly around the box.

They quickly crossed the veranda and descended the steps to the driveway. The night sky had gone and been replaced by a false sunrise, the brilliant red and orange glow coming from the direction of Kingston.

"Quickly, Mr Jonte," Mariya implored.

Hans had paused at the bottom of the steps, overwhelmed once more by the destruction of everything he'd longed for. He stared at the remains of Kingston. What had happened to his agents, the MPs, Hennessy, Montague, Beaumont-Smith? Had the PM escaped the worst of it, locked in prison? What might become of him?

Hans scowled. The Prime Minister would no doubt slither his way out of his predicament somehow. From his birth with a silver spoon in his mouth, he'd always led a charmed life.

Mariya was tugging on his shirt sleeve.

He allowed her to pull him along the driveway until they reached her car. After they'd stowed their bags in the trunk, they climbed into the front seats.

"Ugh," said Mariya, glaring at the black dashboard. "I forgot the net is out. Never mind. Put on your seat belt, Mr Jonte."

"You can drive?"

"We're about to find out."

She started the engine. The headlights came on, and, after a few tries, she managed to move the car a few meters along the road.

"Watch out for the edge," Hans warned, feeling churlish. He wouldn't have done as well as her, but he also didn't want to plunge over the drop.

She guided the vehicle closer to the slope on the other side of the road. Slowly, the car's motion grew smoother and faster. They drove higher, and Mariya steered them carefully around the curves.

"I wish I had a straighter road to learn on," she joked.

But Hans couldn't join in the banter.

"Mariya, who do you think is doing this? The EAC? AP?"

"Isn't it both? They were working together to attack the

Outer Islands, and they prevented the Space Fleet from destroying one of Ua Talman's ships together, didn't they?"

"They did," Hans agreed, "but I thought they would scale back their operations. We were on the way to repelling them from Barbados, I thought, and they retreated from the space battle after the loss of the *Fearless*. I advised against that attack, you know. I told Hennessy and Montague it was a bad idea. Ua Talman would rather die than see his project fail, and he would make sure to take the world with him. I told them to concentrate on defending our territories here. But they wouldn't listen."

"They were a pair of silly men," said Mariya. "Oh...er..." She glanced at Hans.

"Don't worry. For what it's worth, I agree with your evaluation. I've worked with enough of the fools to know their type. Privileged upbringings, their families members of the elite, everything handed to them on a silver platter all their lives. They didn't earn their positions, they were given them, probably as a favor to someone with a lot of influence. I'd hoped to put an end to all that, hoped Hennessy, Montague, and Beaumont-Smith would be the last of their type with any kind of power."

He sighed heavily, lost for words.

"I guessed you were working toward something," said Mariya. "I just didn't know what. Don't feel too bad. You did your best. But some things are too hard for one person. There's too much history, too much inertia to fight against all by yourself."

"You're kind, Mariya. I'm so sorry about what happened to Josie." This time, he actually meant it. In the burning General Council chamber, Josephine had saved his life, and now here was her sister doing the same. He owed the two women so much.

"Where are we going?" he asked after a few minutes' silence.

"A cave, about half an hour away. It's somewhere we can shelter while things calm down. It's quite remote and should be safe. I can't think of a reason enemy troops would search all the way out there."

"How did you think of it so quickly? You seemed to know immediately where we should go."

She only shrugged in reply.

They were heading away from the coast, deep into Jamaica's heart, leaving behind the garish glow from the conflagration in Kingston. The night sky began to look more normal. Hans could make out stars in the blackness. Soon, all he could see was the starry sky and the road, illuminated by the car's headlights.

"This is where we turn, I think," said Mariya. She was already slowing the car down. When she turned, Hans thought she'd driven into trackless wilderness, but soon he could make out two worn trails in the vegetation.

"How do you know of this place?" he asked.

"I've lived in Jamaica all my life. I've been everywhere on the island and many of the other islands."

Her answer didn't ring entirely true. Hans had also grown up in one place, but he didn't know every inch of it.

The track dipped, and the car's nose followed suit. They seemed to be descending into a low valley. Mariya eased the vehicle around a sharp curve and immediately braked.

It was only just in time. They'd stopped at the edge of a lip that overhung a round hollow. The car's lights lit up the space only faintly, he could make a wide, low cave mouth on the farther side. A glow came from within.

"This is it?" asked Hans.

"Yes." She killed the engine and the headlights went out.

The light from the cave shone brighter. "We'll have to walk from here, follow the path around the edge."

"But I thought you said we would be alone."

"Did I say that? I don't think so."

"There are obviously people living there." As Hans spoke, the inhabitants he'd suspected appeared, black silhouettes moving in the cave mouth, perhaps coming to see who'd arrived.

"There are, Mr Jonte, but don't worry, they're friends. Come on, this way."

39

By the time Taylan returned to Arthur's cabin, she was feeling crestfallen, but the sight of the man, released from thousands of years spent in limbo, looking hale and hearty and very much alive and stroking Boots on his lap, lifted her spirits a little.

She figured the smile she gave when he saw her must have been half-hearted, for he reacted by asking her if something was wrong.

"Not something, some *things*. Many things are very wrong, and I don't know what I can do about any of them."

"I'm sorry, Taylan."

"Thanks." She slumped into a chair sideways and hung her arm over the back. "How are things with you? I didn't get a chance to ask you how your feeling. That fast-learning program seems intense, and have you recovered from all that time you spent in the cave? Though, honestly, apart from looking a bit tired, you look amazing."

"*All that time I spent in the cave,*" he repeated. "How long is that, in your estimation?"

"Um, about three thousand five hundred, give or take a

hundred or so years. Didn't Wright tell you, or what we know about you? I suppose not. I told him who I thought you were—who you are—but he doesn't believe me."

"Three and a half thousand years?" Arthur gave a short laugh. "This dream is extraordinary. I hope I remember the details when I wake."

"Er, Your Majesty, you aren't dreaming. This is real life. It's just that a long time passed before we needed you again."

Not that it mattered that King Arthur was back. Everything had gone to hell, and she didn't think there was anything he or anyone else could do to put it all right again.

"Of course this place is real to you, dream creature. How could it be otherwise? This is your world I have created in my mind. And it is a wonderful world. All I've seen has been astounding, and I know there is much more for me to explore. I only hope I don't wake soon. I am astonished I could invent such marvelous ideas."

Taylan sighed. "Is there anything I could do, anything that could happen, that would convince you that you aren't dreaming?"

"I don't know. It's interesting that you want to persuade me of it."

She wondered if it was important that he didn't understand he'd been revived in a future far distant from his own time, or if not understanding was better. Perhaps his mind was protecting itself because acknowledging the truth would make him insane.

"Arthur...Can I call you that? It feels weird to address you by your proper title."

"In this imaginary realm, it is acceptable. In my waking days, I don't enjoy the formalities of my position, so your familiar attitude is welcome."

She liked him more and more. "Arthur, what was it like living in your world? I've heard so many stories about it and about you, but I don't know how true they are. No written accounts survive from your time; the earliest mention we have of you was recorded hundreds of years after your death—or, rather, your entombment in the mountain. And then later writers rewrote the stories, changing them and embellishing them, injecting their own ideas and values. No one really knows who you are or what you represent anymore, and plenty of people believe you never existed." She thought of Wright, who, even though he'd heard the words from the horse's mouth, so to speak, refused to accept it.

"Hm, what's it like living in my world?" Arthur looked down at the cat on his lap. Boots was sound asleep, totally unimpressed by the fact he was lying on an ancient monarch. "I'm not sure how to answer. Your world is very different, in many ways. For one thing, if we want to bathe, we must draw the water from a well, spring, or stream. Here, it appears miraculously, and it's hot without any need for a fire, unless perhaps the fire is somewhere else? The clothes you wear are very soft and comfortable, and so is this bed. I don't think I've slept anywhere so comfortable in my entire life. I could sleep on this bed forever." He smiled and stroked his beard as he thought. "It is a...it's a peaceful world. I like it. But I would like to go outside. I'm curious to see the country around this castle."

"A peaceful world?" Taylan asked. "What makes you say that?" She couldn't imagine anywhere less peaceful than a military starship, but, on the other hand, he hadn't seen her or anyone else suited up, and he might not have understood what was going on when the *Valiant* had taken part in the recent battle.

"No one carries a sword or dagger. Even for your weapons training, you only use staves. You *can* kill with them. I've seen it done. But it's hard. It makes me think you don't really want to hurt each other."

"Oh..." She put a hand over her mouth and chuckled. It was

ridiculous, but it made complete sense. Arthur didn't have a clue about any of the pulse weapons he'd seen in the equipment store. He'd also missed the blunt knives, though she doubted that would have altered his misunderstanding.

He had so much to learn about his new environment. She felt sad, realizing the many ugly surprises he had in store.

Where to start? He'd asked about going outside, so it was as she'd suspected—he didn't know he was in space. But showing him that could be a huge shock to his system, despite his belief he was dreaming. She could introduce him to the idea of modern military warfare, however. It would be something he could relate to. "I have something to show you, if you can wait a minute."

She left him and jogged to the nearest armory, where she 'borrowed' a suit of armor and a pulse rifle. She would get into trouble if anyone found out, but in the current state of anarchy, she didn't think punishing her would be a high priority.

When she returned to Arthur's cabin, she made sure to carry her helmet and not wear it so he could know it was her.

The light of recognition came on in his eyes the minute she entered the room. He understood instantly what she was wearing, and he was interested in examining both the suit and her helmet. She activated the HUD and put the helmet on his head. The look of amazement on his face was entertaining, though he couldn't possibly understand what any of the display meant.

Next, she showed him the pulse rifle and explained as best she could how it worked, but she didn't think he grasped even the basics of its operation. That was only to be expected: In his time, the only energy source was fire. In the end, she guessed he might think of it as a kind of flamethrower.

"I knew you were a knight the moment we began to fight," Arthur said. "Your skills are excellent. I had no idea women could fight so well. I wish you were real. I would include you in my company in a heartbeat. I would make a new company, in fact, of elite female knights. You could train them."

"I *am*..." She didn't bother completing her sentence.

She was getting hot in her suit without the aircon activated, and she didn't have much more to tell him about it that he would understand. "I'm going to take these back," she said.

When she returned to the cabin, Arthur was sitting down, poring over the interface set into the tabletop, sweeping it with his fingertips. She peered over his shoulder. He was looking at pictures of Earth. Maybe Wright had been trying to find out where he came from. "Are we in one of these places?" he asked. "Would you show me which one?"

"No, sorry, but I'll explain where we are later." She sat on his bunk. It actually *was* really comfortable, more so than any other rack she'd slept on in her time in the Royal Marines. Wright must have arranged for a soft mattress to be placed on it. The major was far nicer than he liked to pretend.

"Do you mind if I lie down?"

"I don't mind at all, Taylan."

She turned over his pillow to be polite, and then rested her head on it. "Tell me more about your time, Arthur. I mean, your knights and what you did. My dad used to tell me stories about you."

"My knights? They are a group of virtuous and valiant men. It is very difficult to be admitted to my table. As well as being skilled in the military arts, you must be loyal, just, honorable, and faithful at all times. You must swear to protect the weak, poor, and vulnerable, and be prepared to give your life to uphold these values. Why do you ask? Isn't this what is expected of you and your fellow knights?"

Taylan considered for a while before replying, "I used to think so, but now I'm not so sure."

"That's a great pity."

"Yes, it is." A familiar, deep sadness and longing came over her, and she felt very far from home. "Do you know any stories, Arthur?"

"I know many, but I'm no storyteller."

"Could you tell me one anyway?"

He smiled indulgently. "You are a strange dream creature. Very well." He cleared his throat. "There was once a very noble and perfect knight..."

Taylan didn't think she'd ever heard the tale he began to tell her. It must have been one that hadn't survived to reach the ears of the first person to record the history of King Arthur. Nevertheless, she found she couldn't stay awake to listen to it. Her eyes prickled with tiredness, and her eyelids grew heavy. Soon, with the soft voice of King Arthur droning in her ears, she drifted off to sleep.

40

Kala was in full regalia, from her headdress down to her embroidered deerskin slippers. Others might have found the Dwyr's costume uncomfortable and unwieldy, and so did she, but the downsides were outweighed by the thrill she experienced whenever she wore it. Power seemed to course through her, power and another feeling she had no single word to describe—she felt as though she could do mysterious, impossible things, as if she could tap into a second layer of reality and perform feats that the ignorant would call magic.

There had been times when she'd believed she might have really succeeded in reaching that dark layer beneath the surface that others perceived as reality. The night of Perran's conception was one such time. That dark evening in the oak grove, more than mere seed had been deposited inside her. Something else had entered her, and later it had entered the embryo that would become her son. There was something otherworldly about him, something perhaps not quite human.

She had also felt herself touching the other side of the abyss when she had reached out to Ua Talman when she'd needed him as an ally, seducing him with her mind, bending him to her persuasion. She couldn't prove it, and he would never admit it to her, but something told her she'd achieved her goal.

Now, though she thought she'd been successful at manipulating Lorcan, she would not be attempting the same task again. She had no more need for him. The BA had finally fallen, and all their remaining lands would soon be hers. The main opposition to the EAC was vanquished.

It was time to celebrate.

Novak had suggested the site for the festival. Like all Earth Awareness rituals, it would be held outdoors and far from artificial constructions. The commander had found a suitable place on the outskirts of a forest, and a conveyance was awaiting to take Kala there.

She walked out of the bedroom where she'd dressed and descended the carpeted stairs to the first floor. The posthumous King Frederick's mansion had proven a convenient and luxurious abode since the invasion of Jamaica, even though the place sometimes reminded her of the sniveling brat. She'd sent for Perran to join her there, hoping his presence would help dispel the unpleasant memory of the deceased BA monarch.

Outside, a limousine was waiting that would take her the paved distance to the site before she would transfer to an off road vehicle to complete the journey.

Her stomach churned with excitement.

SHE ARRIVED at the victory celebration site three hours after sunset. Novak had chosen well. The ground was wooded, but the trees were not so thick that they obscured the view badly. By moving around, everyone would see the main spectacle. In the darkness, many figures moved. The area was thronged with attendees.

Kala wasn't so interested in the opening event. It was what came after that would make the evening fun for her. However, everyone would expect tradition to be followed, so she couldn't skip it.

A cheer went up as the EAC troops and auxiliaries noticed she'd arrived. Kala couldn't deny she *did* like the general adulation. What leader of a spiritual organization did not? But she knew it didn't drive her. She was no fake. She believed in what she did with every fiber of her being, probably more so than anyone else present, more than anyone on the planet.

The sea of men and women parted in two waves, moving to her left and right and creating a path for her to follow across the trampled grass.

She set off, slowly and gracefully, careful not to move unevenly and make her headdress wobble. At the end of the path, a structure could be seen in the torchlight. It stood about five meters tall and two meters across at its widest point. Four legs supported a central, egg-shaped chamber. All was constructed from interlaced, slim branches and twigs, like a wicker basket but more open.

As she got closer, she could see the figures of two men inside. Their forms were black against the general darkness, and they were sitting down together, perhaps clutching each other. Kala couldn't tell in the gloom.

She knew their names: Hennessy and Montague. According to her source, they were the engineers of the military coup, the final distraction and additional weakness that had spurred her to launch her attack. If the BA had anyone to blame for their defeat, it was probably these two. Consequently, despite the few local inhabitants who had so far resisted her attempts at extermination, she doubted anyone would be along to save them.

Just in case she was wrong, she'd stationed guards around the perimeter of the site.

"Dwyr Orr!" shouted a voice from the natural cage.

One of the prisoners had spotted her.

"Please," he called. "Please let us out of here. We haven't drunk or eaten a thing for two days. This is inhumane treatment, contravening the rules of legitimate warfare. We are your captives, but you must treat us fairly and attend to our basic needs."

"This is outrageous behavior," said a second voice from the cage. "We demand to be released and taken to a normal prison. Then, you must contact our families, who will pay a large ransom for our return. You may name your price, Dwyr. It will be yours."

She halted near the base of the structure, smirking. What a pair of idiots. As if she had any desire or need for money. They didn't remotely understand her or the EAC and had clearly never tried. Safely ensconced in bubbles all their lives, they'd never had any interest for anything except what would bring them more fame and riches.

With these two in control, it was no wonder the Alliance had fallen. It had never stood a chance.

She faced her people. A hush fell upon them.

"I am the wind on the sea
I am the wave on the shore
I am the oak in the forest
I am the eagle on the mountain
I am the lightning in the storm
I am the blossom on the tree
I am a wolf in the winter
I am a salmon in the river
I am a spring on the plain
I am the word of power
I am the spear in battle

I am the bringer of fire
Who spreads light in the gloaming?
Who can tell the ages of the stars?
Who can tell where the dead live again?"

A soft sigh as if a collective breath had been held and let out came from the audience.

She turned to face the captives. Staring up at them, she blindly held out a hand.

The handle of a torch was placed in it.

"Dwyr," called the first man who had spoken, "what are you doing? Didn't you hear what my friend said? We demand to be released. We insist upon it, in fact."

She strode the final few steps to one of the four legs.

"What are you doing?" the second voice echoed the first, fear raising his intonation to a squeak. "Look, if you're trying to scare us, you've succeeded. We'll tell you anything you want to know. Anything. We would have anyway. There's no need for... Oh my god!"

Kala had bent down and held the torch to the woven branches that made up the leg. After two days in the Jamaican sun, the wood had dried out fairly well. The flames quickly took hold and licked up the strut toward the central cage.

"Christ, no!" one of the men screamed. "You can't, you can't...Help! Let me out!" The speaker began to scale the inside of the egg and quickly reached the top, but he could go no farther. He continued to shout and plead, madly reaching through the gaps and trying to pull them apart.

The other man also hollered and cried, and then began to cough.

Fire was spreading across the bottom of the cage. The noise of it entwined with the men's cries of agony.

Kala turned and lifted her hands high in the air.

The crowd roared.

Now it was time for the real celebration to begin.

Over the last two days, the city and country had been scoured for wine, spirits, beer, and luxury foods, and the festival organizers had brought all that had been found out to the woods. There would be far too much than those chosen to attend could possibly consume, but that was the entire point. It was a celebration of excess, a festival of mutual thanks from the participants to the Earth, and the Earth to them for her glorification.

And it wasn't only food and drink that were to be indulged in to excess.

A while after the drinking had begun, Kala felt an arm slide around her waist, and a hand took her chin to turn it toward questing lips. She kissed the person back. Was it Novak, or someone else? She couldn't tell, and she really didn't care. Another hand slid up her back and then around her front, feeling for her breasts.

Her headdress slipped from her head and fell to the ground. She felt more hands. They grabbed her. They were lifting her up and carrying her away, away from the bright torches and into the dark spaces between the trees. More hands were already tugging at her clothes.

At her first celebration as the new Dwyr, she'd been scared of this part, frightened that someone would hurt her. She hadn't understood then what she understood now: She was theirs, sacred, precious, to be cherished and revered. She could never come to any harm, not from her devotees nor any other living being.

Except one.

The disagreeable thought intruded into her state of bliss. She still hadn't found and destroyed the single real threat to the EAC.

But she could think about it tomorrow, not tonight.

Tomorrow she would also embark on the next logical step of her plan. Now that the AP had served its purpose as an ally, it was time to turn on it. Ua Talman's project had outstayed its welcome on Earth. It had to go.

Kala was laid gently down on a prepared bed of grass and flowers, and her mind returned to the present and the joyous celebration.

The night was young.

41

The *Cornflower's* nose dipped, which meant they'd entered Earth's stratosphere. Taylan tightened her grip on her pulse rifle and looked up at Wright, who sat on the bench opposite her. She could just about make out his eyes through the tint of his visor. He had his gaze on the corvette's aft hatch, from where they would emerge onto Jamaican soil.

The last time she'd gone on a mission, she'd nearly been left for dead and ended up with a broken back.

Would this time turn out any better?

It wasn't likely.

Wright's attention had turned to her. They held eye contact for several seconds before he looked away.

What was he thinking? Was he blaming her for Colbourn's decisions since hearing about the attack on Jamaica? Or was he grateful for the forthcoming battle, the chance to go out fighting for something he believed in? The only alternative for the marines on the *Valiant* was to secede from the BA with the rest of the fleet and eke out an existence spent drifting in space, scrounging for food, water, and energy.

It would be like how things had been after she made it to Ireland. Unable to find her children, crammed into an overcrowded refugee camp, barely able to find enough food to survive, life had no longer seemed worth living. Enlisting had seemed the only escape. She'd figured at least that way she might do some good and put right the terrible wrongs the EAC had done to her people.

Had she done any good in her time in the Royal Marines? She wasn't sure.

Turbulence hit them and lifted the *Cornflower* high, then just as rapidly dumped her low. Again, the corvette rode the roller coaster, and then again, each time sending her stomach up into her throat and down into her intestines.

A nudge from an elbow.

Abacha.

She'd forgotten her friend was sitting by her side. Her nerves must really be getting to her.

He pushed his helmet against hers so they could speak without using comm, which others could listen in on.

"No puking, little chick."

"I'll be okay. You look after yourself, big man. I just thought of a xiangqi strategy that'll blow your mind. You'll never outmaneuver me now."

"Ha! I'll believe it when I see it."

A pause stretched out, but Taylan didn't move her helmet away from her friend's.

Before the thought had formed properly in her mind, she blurted, "Do you think we'll get back to the *Valiant*?" As she spoke, she realized her nervousness wasn't for herself as much as it was for Arthur. With all that was going on in the world, there was little chance she would ever find her children. They were already orphans in spirit if not in fact, and she had to trust that someone, somewhere had taken pity on them and was bringing them up as best they could. So whether she lived or died no longer really mattered.

But what about Arthur? What would he do if she were killed? He would never survive alone in her world. If the shock of reality hitting didn't kill him, his utter unpreparedness would. Skill at fighting with staves didn't count for much in the twenty-third century.

"Who knows?" Abacha replied. "The bigger question is, if we do survive, will the *Valiant* be there for us to return to?"

He had a point.

Colbourn was acting alone without the support of the rest of the fleet. The *Valiant* was well equipped, but she was no match for the entire combined AP and EAC space forces.

It was true that the brigadier had had the lucky break of her life when they'd arrived. For some unknown reason, the majority of the EAC fleet was absent, and the handful of AP ships in Earth's vicinity had ignored the BA ship's arrival. Yet the *Valiant* would still be hard put to fight off the EAC space attack. Her odds were now better than impossible, but only just.

"Taylan," said Abacha, not using the nickname he'd given her, not even calling her 'Ellis', so she knew he was in earnest."Have you thought about what you'll do if things don't go our way?"

"If it looks like we're going to lose? What else can we do? We carry on fighting."

He moved away from her and straightened up, looking ahead, but his eyes were unfocused. Then he leaned over until their helmets touched again.

"My family is from the Caribbean," he said. "Not Jamaica, St. Kitts. But I know the islands. I know how to get around, the backwoods places where it's easy to hide. In the warm climate, you don't need a lot to survive, and you and I, we've been trained to rough it."

She stared at him. "What are you suggesting?!"

"I don't think I need to put it into words. Just something to think about."

Rocked to her core, she jerked her helmet away, breaking contact.

Desertion?

The man sitting beside her had suddenly become a stranger. She'd thought she knew him, she'd thought her friend was brave, loyal, and trustworthy. She'd been wrong.

Hadn't what Arthur had said meant anything to him?

She could remember the king's speech like he'd given it five minutes ago.

It had been her idea to get him to talk to Colbourn's marines and crew. She wasn't sure why she'd suggested it, except for the fact it seemed the BA had lost its way, and that Arthur's beliefs and values were what was missing. Trying to restore them might do some good.

Colbourn had probably only agreed because she was desperate and didn't know what else to do. She'd ordered everyone aboard the *Valiant* and *Cornflower* to gather in the *Valiant's* largest gym, leaving a skeleton crew aboard the corvette. Even that wasn't big enough to accommodate everyone. They'd stood shoulder to shoulder, crowded the gallery, and leaned in at the doors.

Then Arthur had arrived.

He edged through the crowd so unassumingly Taylan didn't think anyone knew he was the speaker until he stepped onto the platform. His red gold hair made him stand out, but his expression was modest.

He began to speak, but softly, so that they all had to be quiet to hear him. He'd spoken about honor, integrity, and goodness, and what they meant to him. The terms and examples he used were hard to understand at first, but if you really thought about them, his points became clear.

He told them of the things his knights had done, acts that were selfless and virtuous, and how much they had sacrificed to stay true to their cause. He'd described their benevolence and kindness, their courage and valor. As he spoke, his esteem and love for these men long dead shone through his words, and Taylan was reminded of the awe with which her father had recounted their tales.

As the king neared the end of his speech, she found herself weeping.

Finally, Arthur had said:

I do not know who you all are or what place I am in. This dream continues so long, I begin to fear it is no dream at all, and that I am somehow in a strange, new world. But one thing I do know: You are men and women, the same as my people. Though a chasm separates us, inside you are the same as me and my folk. You share their needs and wants, their desires and fears. If you have listened and understood what I have told you, and if you hold these ideas in your minds and hearts in everything you do and say, you may one day be as honorable and valiant as my knights.

Had the speech had any effect on the listeners? Taylan thought it was more than likely most of them thought he was mad and talking nonsense. But Colbourn had been affected, and so had Wright. She saw a new resolve and conviction in their faces, and the uncertainty and doubt they'd shown for weeks had gone.

The brigadier had waited two hours before broadcasting a comm to all personnel, saying that she'd proposed to the new admiral that the Space Fleet go to the rescue of the BA citizens trapped in the Caribbean, but her proposal had been shot down.

The admiral reportedly replied it was everyone for themselves now, as Hennessy and Montague had demonstrated when they enacted their military coup without consulting anyone except their cronies. The subsequent invasion of the

Caribbean was their own fault, in the admiral's opinion, and though the devastation to the local population was regrettable, she wouldn't risk any of her personnel to correct others' mistakes.

"So you see," said Colbourn, "if we try to help our people in the Caribbean, who are probably being hunted down and murdered as I speak, we're going to be on our own. I want to do it and so does Major Wright, but neither of us is willing to order you to undertake a suicide mission. I'll give you an hour to think about it, then we'll take a vote. If the majority votes in favor, anyone who doesn't want to participate will be ferried to the Moon Station on our way to Earth."

Taylan voted immediately, hoping but not certain that anyone would vote the same way. When the results came in, it was clear that Arthur had reached them.

Now they were on their way to Earth, and she didn't know why Abacha hadn't elected to take the Moon option if he was so convinced they would fail. Perhaps he'd been worried he'd be stranded there with no way to get home.

For the rest of the ride, she didn't speak to her friend again. Just before they touched ground, he spoke to her a final time. "Don't discount what I told you, Tay. If the situation becomes hopeless, remember what I said. I'll wait to hear from you, but only for a little while."

A SHARP BANK to the left sent her sliding sideways, and then soft judders vibrated down the *Cornflower*. The corvette was under fire, no doubt from EAC anti-aircraft batteries in Jamaica, and she was firing back. Taylan clung to her harness, preparing to be slung around as the pilot jinked the ship to avoid being hit. The plan had been to come in low and fast, which would make her harder to hit, but she had to get down low first.

The vessel plummeted like a stone, so fast for a second Taylan wondered if the engines had been taken out. The fall seemed to take forever, then they powered forward. All the marines crushed into each other, in spite of their restraints. The ship had swerved sharply several times during the descent, but she seemed to have dodged the worst the EAC could throw at her.

Her thrusters roared, and Taylan was thrown in the opposite direction. The thump of landing would have jolted Taylan right out of her seat if it hadn't been for her harness. At Wright's order, she unclipped her harness and leapt up to join the line preparing to disembark.

Outside, the midday sun glared down, and her visor instantly dimmed, turning the world darker and highly defined. Data flashed up on her HUD: Conditions, a map of the terrain, and who within her field of view was friend and who was foe.

She running up a wide, sandy beach. A ridge overlooked the shoreline, and from several spots along it smoke was rising. She guessed they were the sites of armaments the corvette had destroyed. She could also spy the shell of a building peeking out above the ridge line. It had to be the place they were aiming for and so the corvette should have spared it, but it had been reduced to walls, blown-out windows, and ragged reminders of the people had once lived there. Well, that was one place the Dwyr wasn't at.

Dammit!

"Hostiles on the ridge, twelve o'clock," Wright barked, exactly as the pulses began to rain down. The *Cornflower* hadn't managed to wipe out all the opposition.

At the major's signal, Taylan headed for the area where the ridge flattened out to meet the beach. Several paths cut into the slope among the long grass. She ran up one of them, peering ahead, trying to find the source of the pulse fire. On another trail, someone got hit, fell, and tumbled down onto the sand. He was squirming, still alive, his suit breastplate blackened and smoking.

Whispers of pulse bolts unleashed on the EAC defenders.

She saw one: A helmet had bobbed into and out of view and a single shot had fired. Keeping her rifle aimed on the spot, she carried on running. Randomly, she squeezed the trigger. The soldier bobbed up again into the bolt's path. He didn't reappear.

Marines were cresting the ridge, picking off the EAC troops. There didn't seem to be many, and they were falling back.

As she reached the top, she saw Wright run up to one of the injured, a man lying on his back, writhing in pain from a wound that had almost severed his leg. The major knelt down beside him and unclipped and pulled off the wounded soldier's helmet.

"Where's the Dwyr?" he asked. "Is she on the island?"

The man's face was deathly white and slick with sweat. He closed his eyes and jammed his lips together, shaking his head. His blood pooled around him.

"Tell me," Wright insisted. "You're going to die anyway."

Still, the soldier refused to answer.

"Medic!" yelled the major. Then, to the wounded man, "If I give you something for the pain, will you tell me the Dwyr's location?"

Finally, he spoke. "Yes," he gasped. "Yes, I'll tell you."

Wright nodded at the medic who had arrived at his side. After hastily scrabbling in her supplies, she pulled out a pressure hypodermic and touched it to the soldier's bloody, exposed thigh.

He screamed.

She fired the syringe, and the man's rigid body relaxed. His eyes opened.

Before the major could even repeat his question, the EAC

soldier spat at him. The gob of spittle hit his visor and ran down.

If Wright said something in reaction, he kept to himself, turning off his external comm. He stood up. At his feet, the wounded man's body shuddered and was still. The major took out his canteen and squirted water over his visor. "We're going to search all the sites on our list until we find her," he said.

Taylan groaned. They'd been given eight places the Dwyr might be using as her base. Going to all of them would take so long, the EAC would be bound to catch up to them and capture or kill them before they could escape on the *Cornflower*.

Unless they gave up on the mission, they were truly screwed. She thought again of Abacha's suggestion, but firmly pushed the idea aside. After what Arthur had said, she knew she could never take him up on his offer.

A tall marine was walking up the line. It was her friend, as if her thoughts had called him. He approached the major, and for a minute the two stood in private conference.

By a small motion of his helmet, she saw Wright agree to something, then his order came: "Get ready to get back to the ship. We're going to the royal estate outside Kingston."

They got aboard the *Cornflower* just in time. As the corvette took to the air, the beach beside her exploded and the shock-wave knocked her sideways. But the pilot had put sufficient space between them and the ground to avoid crashing into it.

A few tens of kilometers was no distance to the vessel, and before Taylan had a chance to ask Abacha what made him think the Dwyr would be at the royal estate, they'd landed. The plan was the same simple steps: Run out, kill the hostiles, search for the EAC leader.

This time, however, they encountered a strong defense. They'd landed within the estate grounds, so they were surrounded by enemy troops. Soldiers approached from behind. moving in from the gates and perimeter fence, and they were pouring out from the mansion. The firing began as the first marines left the ship. They fought their way forward, taking out the foremost of their attackers, but it was hard going. They were forced to leave injured comrades on the ground in their battle to reach the building, hoping medics remaining on the *Cornflower* could drag them aboard before the ship left.

The strength of the resistance was both a good and a bad sign. The place the Dwyr had taken for herself on Jamaica would be well-defended, so it looked like Abacha could be right. On the other hand, the place the Dwyr had taken for herself on Jamaica would be well-defended.

Despite the danger, Taylan was struck by the appearance of the house. It was similar to the old stately homes of the BI: Huge, many-windowed, and solid.

She was sure Abacha had guessed right.

42

"**B**itch!" spat Lorcan.

He'd known Dwyr Orr was trouble right from the start. Why oh why had he entered into an alliance with her? He could have predicted this would happen.

Hell, he'd *known* it would happen, deep down, right from the beginning. How could he have been so stupid? She'd caught him off guard, and it had been entirely preventable.

He watched the pinpricks of light that represented the approaching EAC fleet on the display in the *Bres's* control room.

"Sir," said Jurrah hesitantly, "perhaps you should—"

The juggling ball Lorcan had launched with a flick of his wrist hit the man between the eyes.

"*Don't* tell me what to do!"

It was obvious what he had to do. It was only that he was furious at himself for ever countenancing the Dwyr's proposal, and about the time, money, and resources that defeating the EAC ships would entail.

Why couldn't the evil witch leave him alone for another few years? Then the Project would be finished, and she would never see him or a colony ship ever again. That had been their agreement. He'd been a fool for imagining she would stick to it.

Mustering his considerable willpower, he put a lid on his anger and returned to his seat. He opened a comm to the admiral of his fleet. "Bujold."

"Yes, sir."

"Thank you for your message. We also see the EAC ships."

"Only awaiting your orders, sir."

"You have free rein, Admiral. Have at them. Don't hold anything back. I want those vessels wiped from space."

"Understood, sir. Sir...?"

"Yes?"

"Are you aware a BA starship has entered Earth orbit?"

"No, I was not." He'd thought they'd all pissed off into interplanetary space.

"It's just one. The *Valiant*. She's, er, she's under fire from the few EAC ships there."

"Right. So?"

"So...we have two battleships stationed at Earth. I was wondering..."

"I see what you mean."

What was it the Dwyr had said? *The enemy of my enemy is my friend.*

Two could play at that game.

"I understand your proposal. Stand by for my answer. Meanwhile, you know what to do."

He asked his comm officer to hail the *Valiant's* commander.

A few moments later, she provided him with a vidlink and told him the *Valiant's* commander was Brigadier Colbourn. A harassed-looking older woman with a thin fuzz of white hair coating her scalp appeared on the screen.

"Ua Talman," she said, "I'm rather busy here. I'd appreciate it if you would be brief."

Beyond her the bridge of her ship could be seen along with

her officers at their consoles. It was clear from their expressions they were facing the fight of their lives.

"I won't take up much of your time," he replied. "But I'm curious as to why you've placed yourself in such a dangerous position. My question isn't frivolous."

Colbourn's face was blank as the time lag passed before his reply reached her, then she scowled. But as she heard his final sentence, her brow cleared into something like hopefulness.

"We're attempting to free Jamaica from EAC control. You know what they do to the civilians of countries they invade."

"And you're attempting this alone?"

Again, the lag passed. Now she looked irritated.

"I'm sure your data tells you that. If you have nothing more to say, I must go now."

Lorcan did have more to ask her, such as why the hell the rest of the BA space fleet wasn't taking part in the assault, and, considering the circumstances, if Colbourn had some kind of death wish and she wanted to take everyone in her command with her.

He forbore.

"Before you go," he said, "I have a proposal. Despite my previous alliance with the EAC, now there is little love lost between us. I'd like to offer you the services of the two ships I have in your vicinity. In exchange, if your venture is successful, I want the BA to allow the continued operations of the Barracuda Sea Mine without harassment."

He awaited her reply, expecting immediate agreement. The woman was in no position to quibble. However, what she said was:

"I'm not able to agree to those terms."

"What?! But you're about to..." As he watched, a shudder ran through the *Valiant*. Had the ship taken a hit, or was she firing? Behind the brigadier, the officers looked terrified.

"Oh, very well," said Lorcan after a moment's consideration. "My ships will lend you their support."

He hated the thought of committing his vessels and crews to helping the *Valiant* without the prospect of getting anything in return, but he hated the Dwyr more. And it was obvious that if he didn't do something soon, the BA ship would be lost. Also, much as he begrudged the feeling, he couldn't deny his conscience was pricked. Colbourn and her men and women were only trying to save their compatriots from slaughter, at the dire risk of their own lives.

His reply had reached its target. Relief swept over her haggard features. "Thank you, Ua Talman. Now, I really must—"

"Yes, I understand," he replied, closing the vidlink and cutting off her response. Nothing more was needed to be said.

Contenting himself with the knowledge that even if Colbourn hadn't agreed to any kind of recompense for the services she was about to receive, he could nevertheless use them as leverage in later negotiations, he asked for a link to his admiral.

"Please inform all your commanders stationed at Earth that they are to defend the BA ship from the EAC attack."

"I was hoping you would say that, sir," she replied, "I'll relay your message immediately. And if I might say so, I think you're choosing the right side. I never trusted that woman, the Dwyr."

"Thanks for your opinion," Lorcan replied icily before closing the comm.

43

I t was hopeless. They were hemmed in from all sides. Even if the *Cornflower* managed to land in the mansions' grounds again without being blown to pieces, they would never reach her. As soon as they left the house, they would be mowed down by the EAC troops outside. More EAC soldiers were arriving, too.

It was going to be a massacre.

Still, with marines stationed at the windows keeping back the attackers for now, Wright had insisted they continue searching the house. Taylan guessed he had a point: If the Dwyr was here, they could use her as a hostage and get her army to back off.

But the woman was nowhere to be found. Taylan had searched the attic with Abacha, stepping between the thick, old wooden beams that held up the roof, peering through clouds of dust their movements puffed into the air. There had been plenty of interesting things to see in that dark place— boxes filled with the relics of hundreds of years of occupation, heirlooms of generations of inhabitants, paintings moldering in their frames, books infested with insects, trunks that had once contained clothes but were now mostly mouse nests.

But no Dwyr.

"You know," Abacha said as they descended the ladder after their fruitless search, "there's still a chance we could get away."

"What chance?" asked Taylan. "The place is surrounded."

"I don't mean all of us. I saw—"

"Not *this* again!"

"Hear me out." He'd reached the bottom of the ladder and talked to Taylan as she climbed down after him. "There's some cover near the back of the house, a shrubbery, outside the kitchen. It leads to an overgrown orchard, and that reaches all the way to the fence. If the whole platoon were to try to leave that way, they would soon be spotted, but a couple of us, keeping low? We might make it."

"I don't get it. If you want to desert, why did you suggest to the major that we came here?"

"I thought catching the Dwyr was the only chance we had, but she isn't here. It's the end of the road for us if we don't do something, and I'm not ready to die, not for the BA, not for anyone."

Taylan felt a twinge of pity, though she was disappointed in her friend. She didn't want to die either, and certainly not for the BA. She'd seen its ugly side and she didn't view it in the same way anymore, but there was more to life than simply staying alive.

"I'm *not* running away because the odds look bad," she said. "If Wright had thought that in West BI, I wouldn't be here. He knew what was right then, and he does now."

"I'm not talking about right and wrong. I'm talking about survival."

They'd crossed the landing on the uppermost floor. The major had given the order to assemble in the ballroom on the first floor after they'd finished their search. The room was in the center of the house and had no windows, so it offered protection from the attack.

"If you want to make a run for it, be my guest," said Taylan bitterly. "I won't tell anyone. But leave me out of it."

Abacha didn't reply.

They descended the stairs without speaking a word to each other and walked across the wide hall, heading for the ballroom. Hisses of pulse fire were coming from all around as the EAC forces pressed in on the house. The marines at the windows were doing a good job of keeping them back, but eventually the power packs in their rifles would fail, while the EAC could resupply.

The ballroom was getting busy as others also returned from unsuccessful searches.

Wright was there, his hands on his hips, his visor up, looking defeated.

Taylan put distance between herself and Abacha, thinking if he was going to try to make his escape, she was too disgusted with him to say goodbye. She decided to speak to the major.

He looked better with his helmet covering that tuft of hair that always stood up on the crown of his head. She wondered if he knew about it. He was a good guy, even though he was too in love with the military for his own good and never seemed to believe anything she said.

"Hey," she said as she reached him.

He replied sternly, "Corporal—"

"C'mon. Can't we talk to each other as friends for once? How much longer do we have?"

His rigid bearing softened. "It might not be as bad as it looks. I just heard from Colbourn the *Valiant* found an unexpected ally. The AP has come to her defense, and they're currently going at it with the EAC ships."

"That's great news—for them, not so great for us. Unless the *Valiant* can beam us aboard like in the sims."

"I don't know whether to ask the *Cornflower's* pilot to attempt a landing." His brow furrowed. "It would be madness, but it's the only chance we've got. If even a few of us could make it out to her—"

"He'd probably do it, but..." She didn't bother stating the obvious.

"I know. It's never going to work. No one would make it ten meters from the door before they were shot down, and it must already be too late anyway. We're due an airstrike any minute. I keep expecting the EAC troops to withdraw."

Taylan sucked in a breath as a true understanding of the situation hit her.

"What?" Wright asked.

"She's here!"

"She...?"

"Dwyr Orr is still here! We've been searching for ages, but her soldiers have only kept up a pulse fire attack when they could have launched grenades or mortars, or just bombed us. She didn't manage to get out when we arrived."

"Shit, I think you're right." He began sending a comm, telling everyone to keep on looking, to go back to the places they'd searched and search again, to tear the place apart.

A marine near one of the ballroom walls turned too fast and clumsily knocked over a Grecian-style statue. The white marble figure tumbled heavily onto the polished tiles. A crack echoed from the walls, and the statue broke into several pieces.

But that wasn't what everyone was looking at. Behind the space where the statue had stood crouched a woman in a long, black dress. For a breathless second, everyone froze.

Then she bolted.

Taylan didn't think she'd ever seen anyone move so fast. The Dwyr flew across the room like she had wings on her heels. She ran diagonally across a corner, confusingly not heading for the door. The unexpectedness of her direction caused the marines to freeze for another second in surprise.

It was enough time for her to reach the wall. As she touched the spot she was aiming for, Taylan saw a very faint outline in the wallpaper and two cuts in the decorative rail.

There was a secret door.

She shouted a warning, but the Dwyr had pushed it open and was disappearing inside.

Meanwhile, hisses came from the direction of the main entrance to the ballroom. No one had noticed that the EAC soldiers had finally managed to get inside the house. Pulse bolts were streaming in from the doorway, cutting through the marines like scythes. They turned and began to fire back.

Taylan ran for the secret door.

THE PASSAGEWAY WAS PITCH BLACK. She lowered her visor, and her night vision activated. Rough, pitted brick walls rose on each side of a space only a meter wide. The floor was brick, too, though uneven. Thick, ragged cobwebs hung down, recently broken where the Dwyr had passed through them. They flapped lazily in a mild breeze. The passageway led to an exit somewhere outside.

Her helmet was picking up the sound of soft footsteps ahead, though they were hard to hear over the noise she was making herself. She guessed Dwyr Orr had tried to leave via the secret passage when the marines had arrived and hadn't quite made it. She'd been waiting, trapped behind the statue, while Wright stood just a short distance away, unable to make it the final few meters.

Well, she was still not going to escape.

Taylan sped up. Her target couldn't be very far ahead. She lifted her pulse rifle and fired, speculatively. The flare wiped out her vision for a moment, but that was the only result. The Dwyr had to be farther away than she thought, or the passage curved.

She noticed it had begun to slope downward. Did it go underground, to travel beneath the gardens and perhaps emerge outside the fence? She didn't know a lot about these old homes of the aristocracy.

Whatever. The Dwyr was not getting away. Taylan fired again, and lost her vision again for a quarter second. She strained her ears, listening to her helmet's audio. The faint foot-steps had stopped. Now all she could hear was her own heavy tread.

Her chest tightened. Had she lost her?

Something heavy smashed into her back and she was flung forward and down. Before she could rise, the thing hit her again, but this time she heard the crack of her armor splitting and agony burst in her kidneys.

She shrieked.

The Dwyr must have been hiding in an alcove, waiting for her approach.

Whatever was embedded in her back was ripped out again, jerking her body and flooding her with new pain. Summoning all the energy she could, Taylan shifted to one side, cramming herself against the wall. A metallic thunk hit her ears. The Dwyr had missed with her third blow.

Her nerves screaming, Taylan twisted around. Throughout her ordeal, her hand had remained fastened on her rifle. The Dwyr's robed figure loomed over her, holding something long and pointed. One of the things that hold torches on walls?

Taylan was already firing, aiming vaguely in the direction of the woman. Pulses flew out, filling the passage with light. The Dwyr looked monstrous, and the expression on her face as flashes threw it into relief was terrible.

Taylan was in too much pain. She could barely cling onto her rifle, let alone aim it. Her shots were going wide.

The long, sharp object lifted once more, her blood dripping from its tip.

If the Dwyr hit pierced the front of her armor, she'd kill her.

With a cry of effort, Taylan wrenched her arm over her body and fired again.

She heard a screech. She'd hit the Dwyr. Fire erupted from the woman's robes, and her makeshift weapon clattered to the floor beside Taylan's head. Issuing an awful scream, the Dwyr ran off down the passage, her arms thrust over her head, trailing flames.

Then she was gone, only the smoke of her burning clothes and flesh remaining.

Taylan couldn't move. Hot liquid was seeping out beneath her, soaking her skin. Her body was a ball of agony, worse even than the time Wright had blown her free from the boulders. She couldn't breathe. A great weight seemed to be pressing on her lungs.

She seemed to be looking down a tunnel. All she could see was the brick ceiling above her, where spiders crawled. Her vision was darkening, and she didn't think it had anything to do with her visor.

Fuck.

She didn't want to die. Not yet. She wanted to see her kids again. Somehow. Just one more time. She couldn't give up on them. They would never know what had become of her.

Blackness encroached, and she felt the thread of life slipping from her grasp.

Footsteps.

Her gasps halted. The Dwyr was coming back. She'd doused the flames, and she was returning to finish her off. Taylan tried to lift her rifle, but it her arm was useless and wouldn't obey her.

Only, she realized, the footsteps were not soft. They were not the soft tread of a woman, but heavy, running, booted feet. It was the sound of soldiers. The EAC must have fought their way into the ballroom and now they were coming down the secret passage to find their Dwyr. They might stop to kill the BA marine dying in the passage, or they might not bother and let nature take its course.

But the footsteps were those of just one soldier. Or was it a marine? Wright must have seen her run into the opening in the wall. Had he come after her?

The footsteps stopped.

Her vision fading, she couldn't make out the shadowy form leaning over her.

Someone removed her helmet.

"Little chick, you look bad."

"A-Abacha?"

"I'll carry you." He knelt down and eased his arms under her.

As he lifted her, she cried out. She couldn't help it.

He took care to avoid jolting her body or bumping her against the walls, but the pain was still so bad she could barely speak.

"You came to find me," she whispered.

"I wasn't going to leave without you."

"But wh-what about surviving?"

"I thought about it, but some things are more important."

So he had understood Arthur, after all.

entle hands peeled Kala's charred robes from her body, lifting off with them great strips of blackened skin. The pain was beyond anything she'd ever experienced, beyond any agony she'd ever imagined, yet it paled in comparison to her wrath.

Someone had hurt her. Hurt *her*, who could not be hurt! They had done the impossible. How could it have happened?

When she'd tried to kill the soldier pursuing her, she'd known she might not succeed—she had, after all, a weak body; her strength lay in her mind and spirit—but it had never entered her head that she might be harmed in return. The fact defied her comprehension.

"This salve will ease the pain, Dwyr," said one of those attending her.

A cool sensation arose from her thighs.

"I have something that will allow you to sleep while we complete your treatment," said another.

"No," Kala murmured. Her voice sounded strange, like the scrape of sandpaper on wood. "No. I want to see."

She tried to rise onto her elbows, but her arms were too stiff and gave an agonized protest to her efforts.

"Dwyr, please lie still."

She grimaced. Her face felt strangely tight. "I must see," she croaked.

"See what?"

She'd emerged from the secret passage on the other side of the perimeter wall. The rest was hazy, but she thought someone had grabbed her and thrown her onto the damp ground, covering her with their own body and putting out the fire engulfing her. As far as she could tell, only a short time had passed. The fighting was still going on within the mansion.

She needed to see what was happening. She needed to know that the person who had shot her would not survive. After the outrage that had been inflicted on the body of the Dwyr, her assailant could not be permitted to live.

"See...the battle."

A flurry of whispers ran between her helpers.

"I...am...your...Dwyr," she gasped.

"Yes, yes, Dwyr. Of course."

She was lying on a stretcher, and she felt it being lifted up. The view overhead changed from the low canopy of trees to open sky and scudding clouds. A light rain sprinkled her face. Strains of fighting arrived on the wind: The fizz of pulse rifles firing, running, groans of injured soldiers, and then an explosion roared out.

"Now you aren't inside, our soldiers are storming the mansion," said the person attending her.

"Lift me up," Kala said.

Murmurs came from those around her. She heard someone say, "I don't know where to touch her."

"Touch me anywhere, dammit! I must *see*."

A hand slid under each of her shoulders and grasped her under her arms. The person's touch was gentle, nevertheless she bit back a scream. As she was levered up, the fence bordering the estate grounds appeared in her view and in the distance stood the stone facade of the mansion. Smoke poured from the windows and flames flickered between the roof tiles.

A heavy firefight was taking place in the grounds. The figures were difficult to make out in the smoke, but the BA troops who had invaded her home seemed to be forcing their way out. The flash of pulse bolts was strongest around the open double doors of the front entrance.

A deep rumble sounded overhead like thunder heralding a storm.

No!

The person who had hurt her could not be allowed to get away. No one could defile her body and live.

The rumble grew louder until she seemed to feel its vibration pass through her. A shape darted above, casting her momentarily into shadow, and heated air blasted down.

The BA soldiers' ship was returning to take them to safety.

She struggled to move, despite the pain.

"Please, Dwyr, you must remain still."

Frustration and rage gnawing at her, she had no choice except to watch as her soldiers fell to the bolts spurting from the ship's guns. Then the vessel landed, and the BA troops' firing intensified, compelling her own to remain behind cover. As the ship's ramp extended, some of the enemy ran from the house and created two straggly lines. Between them, their wounded were helped or carried to the vessel, followed by others who had waited inside. Her soldiers attacked and hit some of the troops in the lines, but if one fell another took his place. Finally, the defenders broke and ran for the ship.

In less than a couple of minutes, they were all aboard. The ramp retracted, and the vessel leapt into the sky with a deafening roar. Soon, all that was left was scorched earth, a burning mansion, and her own defeated troops.

The hands holding her upper body upright carefully lowered her to the stretcher. Kala let out a cry, but it was not due to the agony of her burns—fury and a dreadful sense of impotence battled within her. Never had she been so outraged or felt so powerless.

"We'll take you to the treatment center now, Dwyr. They can give you something to help you sleep while we tend to your injuries."

Kala didn't reply. As her stretcher was lifted and she was borne from the scene, her mind was already elsewhere. Before, the BA had merely been an annoyance that stood in the way of her plans and that had happened to harbor the individual who posed a threat to the EAC. Now, it harbored someone else, someone who had actively harmed her person, violating the sanctity of her being.

The Britannic Alliance had become an object of her deepest hatred. She would not rest until every last member of it was crushed and the one who had hurt her was made to pay for the crime. The deaths of Hennessy and Montague would be sweet bliss in comparison.

45

In a strange twist of circumstances, it had been the AP who had come to their rescue, Taylan discovered when she woke up later, in the sick bay once again.

Their battleships had successfully held off the EAC attack on the *Valiant*, allowing the *Cornflower* to return to her safely and both vessels to escape. And though the mission had failed in that they hadn't captured or killed Dwyr Orr or taken back Jamaica, the rumor was BA Space Fleet was reconsidering its decision to secede. There was a chance it would try to oust the EAC from the Caribbean and re-establish a strong foothold for the Alliance on Earth.

It was as if the effect of Arthur's speech was spreading.

She didn't remember any of the retreat from the Dwyr's mansion. As soon as the medic had seen her wounds, he'd dosed her to her eyeballs. After that, the first thing she remembered was the sick bay doc complaining at her for screwing up all the great surgery she'd done on her back. She learned the spike Dwyr Orr had thrust into her had pierced her vertebrae and nearly severed her spinal cord.

Abacha came to see her every day for a game of xiangqi.

They spoke of many things, but neither of them mentioned the conversations they'd had while stuck in the desperate situation on Jamaica. Taylan didn't think they would ever speak of it again. Her friend seemed back to his normal self. She thought it was only that he'd become infected with the general malaise of selfishness and apathy that had generally affected the Britannic Alliance.

It was good to see him so regularly, and she was grateful for his visits, but there was someone she'd also expected who didn't arrive for so long, she thought he'd forgotten all about her. Then, one night, after visiting hours were over, he snuck in. The medic was in the office and the other patients ignored him, part of the subterfuge.

"Hey," said Wright, "how are you doing? I would have come before, but I've been busy."

"Hey." Taylan tried to sit up.

"Do you want some help?" He adjusted her pillows and helped to lift her to a more upright position. When she was comfortable and he'd sat down he said, "How are you feeling? Not too doped up on painkillers, I hope. I don't want you turning insubordinate again."

"Will I be excused if I am?"

"Of course not, I just like to prepare myself."

"As it happens, I'm not. The doc is weaning me off them."

"Then you are in pain?"

"It isn't too bad, honestly."

"Good." He rubbed the top of his head.

"What's been happening?" she asked. "Abacha won't tell me much. He says he doesn't want me to worry about anything. Is there something I should worry about?"

"I wouldn't say so. It's mostly positive news. We seem to have set a good example to the rest of the Space Fleet. And Colbourn says they've realized that becoming an independent entity wasn't very practical. Unless they plan on joining the AP and leaving the solar system, they're always going to rely on Earth for food and energy. Rations won't last them forever. So it's either make nice with the crazy witch queen, or take back our lands."

Taylan sighed. "Starting with Jamaica I suppose?"

"I think so, but I don't know for sure yet." His gaze dropped to her necklace. "Or it might be the BI. It *is* the original homeland. I think Arthur would like that too."

"Yeah, what's been happening with him? I haven't seen him. Is he okay?"

"He's another one who's been busy. He's a popular guy. Word got out to the other ships about our unusual passenger, and now everyone wants to meet him. There's something about him, some sort of...uh..."

"I think it's called charisma."

"Yeah, that's it. He's got it in bucket loads."

"Does he still think he's dreaming?"

"He hasn't mentioned it for a while. He might be trying not to think about it."

"It's going to be hard for him," said Taylan, "when he finally realizes, I mean. His entire world is nothing but ruins and dust, all his family and friends dead and mostly forgotten. His language, his culture, all of it, just...gone."

"Yes, but he's already learned a new language and made friends. In time, he should be okay."

"So do you believe me now, about who he is?"

"I'm still reserving judgment."

Taylan rolled her eyes.

"Does it really matter?" Wright went on. "Whether he is an ancient king or not, he's changed things around here. That's what counts."

She decided she would have to give up on him ever agreeing with her about Arthur. "Who are his friends?"

"Well, you, for one. He talks about you all the time, telling everyone he meets about an excellent female fighter he knows. I wouldn't be surprised if he offered to make you a knight. And he loves the cat. He takes it everywhere with him." Wright frowned. "I didn't know we had a cat aboard. I wonder where it came from."

"No idea," she replied, and then she yawned.

"I'm keeping you up," he said. "I should go."

"No, I'm not tired. Don't leave. It's nice to talk."

"Yeah. Beats yelling at each other, anyway. But I do need to go. I have reports to write."

"Okay, if you have to."

A look passed between them, and Taylan was reminded of that moment on the *Cornflower*, just before they landed in Jamaica. As before, she couldn't guess what he was thinking.

"Goodnight, then," she said.

But the major was no longer looking at her. He'd become distracted, listening to a comm. He rose halfway to his feet, and as he continued to listen, he sat down again. Then his mouth fell open.

"What is it?" asked Taylan.

Still he didn't reply, paying attention to the message. Suddenly, he leapt up and strode quickly away.

"Major," she called out, "what's wrong? Where are you going?"

Were they about to be attacked by the EAC? Or had the AP switched sides again? She hadn't gotten around to asking him what was happening with them.

"It's the *Fearless*," he replied as he left the sick bay.

The *Fearless*? What did he mean? Hadn't that been the ship that was swallowed by the mysterious black cloud?

He reappeared in the doorway, heading in the opposite direction. "She's been found, out in the Asteroid Belt."

Then he was gone.

Taylan and Wright's story continues in...
THE FEARLESS

Author's Note

KING ARTHUR IN OUTER SPACE? A weird combination of ideas, right?

I can't remember how old I was when I first heard about King Arthur and the Knights of the Round Table. I think I must have been so young I wasn't forming proper memories. Arthur and his knights have been embedded in my mind all my life, strongly entwined with my sense of 'Britishness' and even a little, I suppose, to my identity.

What I do remember from my childhood is watching Bing Crosby in *A Connecticut Yankee in King Arthur's Court*. Later, I read T.S. White's *The Once and Future King* and Marion Bradley's *The Mists of Avalon* several times. These are the versions of Arthur's story that stick out in my memory, but I'm sure I had many more encounters with the myths as I was growing up.

Later still, as my interest grew, I studied versions that were closer to the original tales, such as Malory's *Le Morte d'Arthur* and *Sir Gawain and the Green Knight*, author unknown. Tolkien fans might be interested to hear he wrote a translation of Sir Gawain's story. The Victorian revival of the myth produced more works I've studied, like *The Lady of Shallot*. Even now I can vividly see the moment "The mirror crack'd from side to side". And, of course, it's impossible to discuss renditions of Arthur's story without mentioning *Monty Python and the Holy Grail*.

As a young woman, I visited Tintagel in Cornwall, long-rumoured to be the site of Camelot, though, assuming Arthur existed, it's doubtful he lived there. Having said that, recent archaeological investigation has found that Tintagel was probably the site of a thriving community, trading goods from far afield in the ancient world. So, who knows? It's easy to see why Tintagel inspired the imaginations of King Arthur enthusiasts. The coast there is rocky and wild, and the sea has carved caves in the cliffs that are perfect for Merlin to hide in.

Did Arthur exist? We will probably never know for sure, but as Wright states towards the end of *The Valiant*, it doesn't really matter. It isn't the truth of his existence that's important, but what he represents.

I admit that, at first glance, combining Arthurian mythology and science fiction might seem a strange endeavour. It certainly seemed strange to me when the idea popped into my head two or three years ago, but the more I thought about it the more sense it made. Science fiction explores concepts about the future of humanity, what challenges we'll meet and how we'll overcome them; it shows us at our worst and our best. The characters often win through in these situations because they hold onto the values that Arthur embodies: Courage honour, loyalty, integrity, and determination.

When we do finally make it to other stars—I firmly believe one day we will—it's going to be the behaviour the Arthurian tales illustrate that helps to get us there. I wanted to write a series that celebrated those values. As to whether I've succeeded, I'll leave that to you to judge.

A few words about the origin of some of the names in the Star Legend series: Nantgarw-y-garth isn't a real place, it's an amalgamation of two Welsh place names, and neither of them are purported to be the site of Arthur's entombment. Welsh village names that appear later in the book are actual places, but, I'm sad to say, I've never been to them. I planned a trip to the Welsh Marches before the dreaded virus struck, but that's been postponed. Perhaps I'll make it there before I finish the series.

'Dwyr' is inspired by the Druid traditions, and the 'Ua' of Ua Talman is based on the old Irish meaning, 'descendant of'. His ships, the *Bres*, *Banba* and *Balor* are named after characters in Irish mythology. Though Taylan is Welsh, I gave her this unisex Turkish name because it means tall, skinny person as well as elegant and gracious.

If you're familiar with Arthurian legend, you may be able to spot some characters from those stories that appear in *The Valiant* under other names. I'm not going to state them here for obvious reasons. As the series progresses, more of the old favourites will make their appearances, again under other names.

I hope you enjoyed *The Valiant* and will go on to enjoy the rest of the Star Legend series. If you have time, please leave an honest review, and if you would like to say hi or meet other readers who like my work, pop over to Starship JJ Green Shipmates.

If you're interested in reading more about Arthurian myths, I recommend all the sources I mentioned above and *The Holy Kingdom*, by Adrian Gilbert, Alan Wilson and Baram Blackett. The authors make some plausible arguments that there were two Arthurs, one related by marriage to the Romans, and the second a genuine king of what is now Wales. And if you're interested in Britain during the Dark Ages (which were not really dark), I recommend Simon Roper's Youtube channel, though he focuses mainly on the Anglo-Saxons, who were the people Arthur probably fought.

JENNY GREEN
    Cambridge, U.K.
    November 2020

. . .

Sᴵɢɴ up to my reader group for exclusive free books, discounts on new releases, review crew invitations and other interesting stuff:

https://jjgreenauthor.com/free-books/

DOWNLOAD YOUR FREE READERS' GUIDE TO THE SCIENCE FICTION NOVELS OF J.J. GREEN

Printed in Great Britain
by Amazon

12120064R00172